THE SANITY WARD

JOHN A. RUSSO

WOLFPACK
PUBLISHING
— EST 2013 —

Thanks to our marvelous discovery, we have the means to facilitate awareness, enhance memory and, in general, produce a sensational increase in the efficiency with which the mind works. We are like modern alchemists who have found the true philosopher's stone, and we will now use it to conjure up amazing perceptions and great leaps of creative imagination that will make yesterday's flights of genius seem dull and ordinary by comparison.

—*Dr. Melvin Lieberman, Director of Blue Ridge Hospital*

———

In the madhouse
wring your hands,
press your pale forehead against the wall
like a face into a snowdrift.

—*Natalya Gorbanevskaya*

THE SANITY WARD

1

There was something greedy, something selfish about Aaron's lovemaking that Jenny had never noticed before. She tried hard to pretend it wasn't there. But it spoiled her pleasure. It scared her. She needed to feel cherished and secure.

She was snuggled against him, her body sideways against his, the way they always rested after making love. For a long time he didn't speak. Neither did she. Finally, when she almost thought the bomb wasn't going to drop, it did. He told her this would be their last time. He had decided they should stop seeing each other. "You're looking for a father, not a lover," he said.

She held her breath, frozen with dread, stunned by the harshness of his pronouncement, his unilateral decision about their lives. Her face was pressed against the wiry, tickly hairs on his chest. Some of the hairs were already turning gray. Tears welled in her eyes despite her effort not to cry like a little girl. His gray hairs hadn't bothered her before. But now they were threatening proof of the age gap that was driving him away. She was nineteen, and he was eighteen years older.

"I don't love you like a father, I love you like a man," she managed to say. It sounded terribly lame, inarticulate. Aaron could twist it around the way he had twisted some of the points in her articles last year when he was teaching her freshman journalism class. Why was she becoming better at formal writing and lousier at simply talking to people, especially the ones who were most important to her? Even though she tried to say exactly what she felt, somehow the right words never came out of her mouth.

"I'm thirty-seven," Aaron said, springing evidence on her. "The same age your father was when he disappeared."

"Coincidence!" she snapped. "Don't hold *that* against me, Aaron, please!" She pushed herself away from him and sat up, and tears fell on her naked breasts.

"Is that all it is? Just a coincidence? Are you sure, Jenny?"

"Yes!" But all of a sudden she wasn't so sure. He always had the ability to tie her in knots, making her doubt the inner workings of her own mind. "You're being unfair," she accused. "You know what I've been going through lately. I couldn't help reliving it even if I didn't want to."

She was only twelve years old when her father kissed her good-bye and never came back. That was seven years ago, but he had been famous enough that his name could still make news. Even if she would've succeeded in burying all her memories, they would have been dredged up last month on the seventh anniversary of his disappearance, when it became legally feasible to have him declared dead. Jenny's mother wanted to marry again, so she had gone to court to obtain a death certificate. Jenny hadn't argued, but the finality of the procedure had almost made her ill.

"You'll never be able to totally give yourself to any man till you get over your thing about your father," Aaron said.

He spoke with absolute conviction, perfectly sure, as always, that he understood her better than she understood herself. The maddening part was that she half believed he might be right. The major event of her childhood may have affected her subconsciously in the way he thought. How could she know without a shred of doubt that it wasn't so? Angry and confused, she said, "You know it's not something I can simply erase. It happened to me, so I have to deal with it. I'll always wonder what happened to my father. I may never get over the pain till the mystery is solved, but it doesn't mean I don't love you, Aaron!"

"That's exactly right, Jenny. You'll never get over it because you're never going to know the answer. The intrigue is so much a part of you that it gives you a certain allure, but it also stunts you emotionally. You're never going to grow up. You'll always be looking backwards, into your past, instead of building a solid future. Anyone who falls for you, the way I did, will eventually be disillusioned when he finds out he's in love with a woman who's part child."

2

They said he wasn't Norman Teague, but he knew that he was. His name tag said: HASKELL. In the seven years since he had been here, he had learned to respond to the name Haskell when he was addressed by the doctors or the guards. But he would never forget who he really was. He was Dr. Norman Teague, the NASA scientist who had disappeared seven years ago and had been declared dead. He had almost given up all his dreams of ever being free. But now he had hope. Now, apparently, someone was coming to help him. If his chance materialized, if it didn't turn out to be only a cruel ruse, he would soon tell the world his story and take his revenge. In the exercise yard, he stayed apart from the other inmates of Blue Ridge Hospital, which was not actually a hospital but a sanitarium and a prison. It was situated in a remote, mountainous part of West Virginia. Hardly anybody lived within a fifty-mile radius. The place had a spooky, forbidding look that encouraged people to stay clear. There were bars on the windows of the three square, gray-stone, two-story buildings. Anybody looking at them saw an outer barrier of barbed wire, then an electrified fence, and guards with machine guns posted in look-out towers at the corners of the fence. Although Blue Ridge was a small institution, holding about a hundred patients, it was located in the middle of a vast, practically inaccessible tract of hills and forests heavily posted with No Trespassing signs.

WARNING.
HAZARDOUS AREA.
PERSONS DISCHARGING FIREARMS MAY DRAW
FIRE.

Hunters seldom wandered onto the land, and the few who did were scared to shoot at anything. Deer were as safe here as if they were on a game refuge.

Teague peered through the electrified fence, past the chest-high tangle of barbed wire, at a doe and a fawn who were staring back at him. They were about twenty-five yards away, almost camouflaged completely among some tall cedars. He envied them their perfect freedom. They had lucked onto a place where they could not be slaughtered unless a guard went berserk and machine-gunned them.

The obstacles made Teague severely doubt that he was going to be rescued. It seemed an impossible feat for anyone to pull off, even with help supposedly provided by an "inside man." Maybe the doctors were toying with his mind again, experimenting with the effect that false hope might have on his intellect, his emotions. Maybe they figured that if hope were offered then snatched away enough times, he'd more easily succumb to their brainwashing. He'd start to believe he wasn't himself but someone else named Haskell.

In an old issue of *Newsweek,* Teague had read about how Soviet dissidents were sometimes injected with drugs that produced arthritis, blindness or schizophrenia. Then they were tossed into hospitals or asylums so they couldn't any longer be a danger to communist society. On the wall of his cell, Teague had taped up a short poem written by one of the Soviet political prisoners:

> *In the madhouse*
> *wring your hands,*
> *press your pale forehead against the wall*
> *like a face into a snowdrift.*

Because he was allowed to read certain magazines and newspapers, he had a rough idea of what was going on in the outside world. The periodicals usually came to him with whole articles removed or sections excised. He was denied access to radio and television, since those media could not easily be censored. His captors didn't want him to glean information about key people and events of his past life. They didn't want to help him keep alive his memories of who he really was. He had no idea what might have become of his wife and his two daughters. But if all went well perhaps he'd be seeing them soon. He wondered how they'd react. Would they be glad to see him, after they got over the initial shock? Or would they prefer to keep him out of their new lives? Well, they wouldn't be able to. Not after he broke his story. Not after he came back from the dead.

Staring through the lethal chain-link fence, he began to do a set of fifty jumping jacks. All through the seven years he had been here, he had kept himself mentally and physically disciplined, despite the extreme difficulty of doing so. Most of the other inmates were smoking and loitering, letting their minds and bodies slowly turn to flab. But Teague's muscles were still wiry and hard and his perceptions were sharply focused. He believed that, unlike himself, most of his fellow inmates deserved to be here. Some were alcoholics or heroin addicts; some were perverts or potential traitors; some were truly criminally insane. Once upon a time they had all been engaged in work vital to the nation's interests, but now they couldn't be entrusted with defense secrets or diplomatic secrets anymore. So they had to be kept where they couldn't do any harm.

Teague finished his jumping jacks and without a breather did a hundred pushups. Then he began to jog around the perimeter of the compound, staying within ten feet of the electrified fence. If he got any closer, there was always the chance he might stumble and fall against it. On the other hand, he needed to stay close enough to it not to have his jogging impeded by clusters of inmates in the shade of the lookout towers. Some of them stared at him, shrugging their slumped shoulders as he jogged by, as if he were obviously madder than they. To him, it was a cruel irony that he was lumped in with these misfits. All his life he had been a staunch patriot, a dedicated scientist, and he believed that he could yet render his greatest service to his country. Those who had him locked up were mistaken and misguided. What he knew absolutely must be told. Time was running out. The nations of the world must unite, and *would* unite for the first time in history, if Teague could make them aware of the common threat that they all faced.

Recently he had read an article in *USA Today* about a new defensive weapons system nicknamed "Star Wars."

A great political debate was raging over whether or not the United States, in developing such a system, would instigate a destabilizing effect on the balance of nuclear terror. But Teague knew that Star Wars had nothing to do with protecting the U.S. against the Soviets. And if he could escape from Blue Ridge, he'd tell the world the real reason for the international arms race. Teague wasn't against Star Wars. He knew full well that the system *had* to be built. But he also believed that the American people and the Russian people should be told exactly *why*. Unfortunately, his heretical beliefs had landed him in this godawful asylum. It was like being in limbo. Sometimes he had to struggle hard against the feeling that he really had passed away.

With a grimace of determination, he jogged past a trio of inmates who were conversing animatedly, and one of them—Abraham Vickers—motioned for him to come over, but he pretended that he hadn't seen Vickers wave his hand. Nothing was going to prevent him from finishing his laps before the whistle blew ending the outdoor recreation period. He knew what Vickers must want anyway. And it didn't amount to a hill of beans.

Abraham Vickers shook his big high-domed head and scratched his huge belly, watching Teague jog along the fence. Then he turned back to the conversation he and his friend, Kevin Thompson, were having with an inmate whose name tag said: CHUDKO. It might be his right name or it might not. Vickers's name tag said BLAKE and Thompson's said PERRY. The only reason Vickers knew Thompson was really Thompson was that they had known each other in the outside world.

Vickers had always been bald, sunken-chested and flabby; but Thompson, a former Air Force test pilot, had once been in excellent physical condition. Now he was balding and fat, his complexion almost as gray as the strands of hair combed across the top of his scalp. He was speaking with far more fervor than he appeared physically or emotionally capable of, as if he hoped the sheer intensity of his diatribe might help make it convincing, even though the substance seemed so incredible. "I *am* who I *say* I am," he insisted to the amused, skeptical Chudko. "I was test flying an A-11 spy plane— you probably never heard of such a creature, but I assure you it exists. The prototype alone cost the government 57 million dollars, and that was back then—God knows what it'd cost now, with inflation. It was designed to replace the U-2. You've heard of that, haven't you, Chudko?"

"Of course," said Chudko, grinning contemptuously. Recently incarcerated at Blue Ridge, he had an aloof attitude that did not sit well with most of the other inmates, but few of them had an itch to tangle with him, because he seemed too young, too fresh and too strong. He was a big man with wiry black hair and thick lips curled into a perpetual leer. He claimed to be an astrophysicist. Abraham Vickers, whose specialty in the outside world had been space-age laser weaponry, had sounded Chudko out and told Thompson that the man seemed to know what he was talking about. So now Thompson wanted to impress him. And, since Chudko found Thompson amusing, albeit in a rather pathetic way, he didn't want to end the entertainment prematurely, by indulging in too much outright mockery of Thompson's tall tales.

"I'm talking about a plane capable of a top speed of 2500 miles per hour," Thompson elucidated. "That's damn near Mach four. And the A-11 can *cruise* at an altitude of eighteen miles. So I was pushing her to her limits, when suddenly I spotted three dots of light approaching, so fast that they seemed to almost *material-ize*. They hovered on three sides of my cockpit—front, back and to my right—and at first I just stared at them. I couldn't believe it. They were *saucers*. Each one was at least three times as big in diameter as the length of the A-11's fuselage. I blinked my eyes. They didn't go away. They just kept gleaming in the bright sunlight above the clouds, effortlessly keeping up with me, and I was going at 2500 miles per hour: When I finally stopped trying to convince myself these three saucers couldn't be real, I started trying to elude them. But no dice. They could do everything I could do—and twice as easily, too. They had me hemmed in. I radioed the control tower, told them what was happening—but of course they already knew *something* weird was going on, because they could see the strange blips on the radar. I requested permission to open fire—but I didn't even wait for confirmation. I fired three air-to-air missiles at the craft hovering directly in front. But the projectiles vaporized in midair: Then a blue light enveloped my cockpit, and all the instrument dials were spinning senselessly. My controls were utterly useless. And I felt my plane being *sucked* toward the saucer I had shot at, and then I was suctioned directly beneath it, and up into its hull, just as if me and my plane were on an invisible freight elevator."

"So, if you got sucked into a saucer, what're you doing in *this* place?" Chudko asked sarcastically.

"Just listen," said Vickers in a soft, imploring voice. "The story makes sense, if you'll only listen to all of it."

"Sure, sure," Chudko scoffed.

Oblivious to the comments of his companions, Thompson went on, even more fervently than before, and with an edge of fear in his voice, as if he were reliving a terrifying experience, instead of merely describing it. "I felt a tingling, all over my body, and all I could see was blue...a cocoon of blue light. Then I started to feel like I was *moving*. A strange force was pulling me, tugging at my skin, making me tingle all over, and the best I can describe it...it was like a *shadow* of myself was being sucked out of me, going right up into the air! And I could see the plane down below, with me still in it, like I was asleep—or dead—in the cockpit. How could it be? I couldn't figure it out, and I didn't have time to.

I felt myself turning, turning, flat on my back now, on a bed of air. I mean, there was absolutely nothing I could feel beneath me, yet I was supported by magic or...or by *levitation*. Up till now, I had managed to keep myself relatively calm, but now I panicked, in spite of the steely nerves a test pilot is supposed to have and I could have sworn I always *did* have. All around me, as I kept revolving in a state of seeming weightlessness, I could see ten or twelve creatures who at first reminded me of *insects*. They had large white heads and small chins, and their mouths were little ovals. Their eyes were pale green, like their mouths, but the eyes were large, with a metallic gleam, wrapping partway towards the backs of their heads, as if they could see more than just straight ahead. And they were communicating with each other, making a steady, buzzing sound, like a low rasp or mumble—but their lips weren't moving, they weren't *talking* in any human sense. I wanted to get up...but I couldn't. Something was holding me down on my bed of air..."

Thompson paused, panting for breath. His eyes were glazed, focused on some far-away world.

"You're one hell of a bullshitter, I admit that," Chudko said, chuckling dryly.

"Shhhh," cautioned Vickers, whispering hoarsely as if he didn't want to disturb somebody in a trance.

Thompson went on, talking mostly to himself now, trying to cope with what he believed had happened to him. "Everything was fluorescent...extremely bright and white. Two of them were staring down at me, as if they were the leaders, the head surgeons, and the others were there to observe the operation. They were doing something to me—I could feel them doing something without having to actually touch me. They kept humming to themselves, or to each other. I realized they were picking my brain...my thoughts...it felt *so* strange...and every time they did it, I got tireder...and tireder...like all my energy was being sapped. Everything was getting blurry...the insect faces blurring...and finally I fell asleep, even though I was scared to. I simply passed out. I knew they intended to keep my airplane—somehow that idea was communicated to me, through the same kind of telepathy the creatures used with each other. The next thing I knew I was down on the hot sand, the desert, and the saucer was lifting into the sky. But all of a sudden something went wrong—either an equipment failure or a miscalculation. The saucer veered, then hovered sideways, and crashed into the side of a mountain. And the other two just zipped away and disappeared."

For about ten seconds there was silence after Thompson finished his tale, and his eyes started to unglaze as he slowly brought himself back to the present.

Then Chudko said harshly, "You're full of shit, you know that? You say your name's Thompson, not Perry? Well, you *can't* be the Thompson you're babbling about. I read about him when he was killed, seven or eight years ago. He's the one who crashed into the mountain, not any aliens from another planet."

Thompson blinked rapidly, his mouth gaping open. "You don't *believe* me?" he blurted. "Well, I can prove it to you. How about it, Vickers?"

"Here comes Teague," Vickers interjected, scratching his pot belly. "He's done jogging."

"He'll back me up," Thompson pounced. "Teague! Hey, Teague! Come here!"

Wiping sweat from his brow onto the sleeve of his blue sanitarium uniform, Teague grimaced, not wishing to become involved in any sort of argument. Walking over to join the group, he wondered why Kevin Thompson had to be such a garrulous fool, always running at the mouth to anyone who'd listen. Always trying to convert skeptics. Always pleading for respect and understanding, only to be taken for an idiot.

Suddenly Teague whirled, startled by a loud, hysterical laugh. Behind him, a short, pudgy inmate had approached the electrified chain-link fence.

"No!" Vickers cried out.

But, smiling like a simpleton, the inmate touched the fence delicately with his right index finger. There was a sizzling and crackling sound as the finger started burning —but the inmate merely chuckled as he watched it turn to a charred nub.

"The blasted imbecile," Chudko yelled.

Teague, Vickers and Thompson backed away, horrified.

The masochistic inmate seemed beyond pain. He stared at the nub of his finger, and emitted a gleeful laugh. He touched another finger to the steel fence and watched it go up in flames. Then another. And another.

A score of inmates gathered around in a tight, protective circle, placidly watching, obscuring the view of the guard in the nearest tower.

Finally, the deranged inmate threw his body against the fence and electrocuted himself, laughing euphorically until he died.

3

Blair Chaney already had good close-up footage of Teague, Thompson and Vickers. On pure whim, he filmed the smoldering body of the inmate who had committed suicide, then zoomed back to a wide shot of the guards beating and shoving the inmates in the yard, herding them toward the main building where they had their cells. Even from a hundred yards away, the *oogah-ooging* of the alarm grated on Chaney's nerves. When it had first sounded he had been scared that he must have been spotted somehow. But it had turned out to be only an inmate electrocuting himself.

Chaney hadn't figured this for a truly dangerous gig, even though the place was run by the CIA. The security measures at Blue Ridge Hospital were primarily designed to keep the inmates from breaking out, rather than to stop anybody from breaking in. As far as the outside world was concerned, the inmates didn't even exist. So why would anyone be thinking of coming in after them? The guards in the lookout towers habitually kept their eyes trained on the blue-uniformed prisoners directly below, with an occasional glance out toward the surrounding field and forest on the half-hearted chance of spotting maybe a lost backpacker, or one who was pretending to be lost in the hopes of satisfying a streak of foolhardy curiosity.

They weren't especially looking for a sly professional, skilled in espionage and covert action, like Blair Chaney. So he had been able to work himself in close enough to get exactly what he needed. Flat on his stomach in an earthen hollow beneath the trunk of a fat cedar, he was wearing camouflage fatigues and had the exposed portions of his face and arms mottled with green-and-brown camouflage paint. He was armed with a 9 millimeter Ruger pistol and a 16 millimeter Bolex camera with a 250 millimeter lens. Next time he came here he expected to be armed quite differently because he would be coming to get three of the prisoners out.

To him, the inmate electrocuting himself was a fortuitous circumstance, a good omen. The noise and confusion surrounding the incident made his retreat from his place of concealment even easier than it would have been otherwise. Once he had stashed his disassembled camera in his backpack, he faded back into the forest. It took him an hour to hike out to his car, over the rugged, heavily wooded terrain. Locking his gear in his trunk, he chuckled to himself, thinking of how much the footage would excite the man he was working for, a writer named Rolf Kollar. But he made up his mind to edit out the scenes of the inmate who had electrocuted himself. He wanted Kollar to believe that all of the inmates of Blue Ridge Hospital were strictly political prisoners and that none of them were truly insane.

As far as Chaney was concerned, he was working for a nut, one even nuttier than the inmates behind Blue

Ridge's electrified fence. But he stood to get rich on this mission. Unless Kollar stopped believing that Colonel Kevin Thompson was alive and was telling the stark naked truth about what had happened to him seven years ago.

Kollar was obsessed with flying saucers and such nonsense. He promoted himself as a "ufologist" and a "lay scientist." Apparently he had had very little formal education, either in America or in his native Germany. But he certainly had a sharp nose for commerciality. Twenty years ago, he had come here after escaping over the Berlin Wall, and now he was a big self-made man. His books—weird ones like *Astronauts from Outer Space* and *Our Extraterrestrial Ancestors*—were all bestsellers, capitalizing on people's need to believe that "something else is out there."

Strangely enough, after foisting this garbage off on the public, Kollar didn't seem to be satisfied with mere fame and fortune. He couldn't quite understand why credibility and respect still eluded him. In his wacky little mind, he lusted after some kind of scoop that would vindicate his outlandish theories.

Well, Blair Chaney was going to hand it to him on a silver platter—in return for half a million bucks. Seven years ago, as a covert operator for the CIA, Chaney had participated in the "roll-up" of Teague, Thompson and Vickers. Now he was going to help blow their cover. Then he was going to live like a king somewhere in South America, like all the filthy rich stock-market pirates he was reading about lately, who fattened their Swiss bank accounts, then took off and told everybody to go to hell, while they installed themselves in fortified palaces, beyond the reach of the law.

Up until now, outwardly, Chaney had been a patriot.

He had always worked for the United States—first as a military officer and later as a CIA agent. But inwardly his patriotism had given way to cynicism, in Vietnam, where he began doing the kind of dirty work that no decent American was supposed to condone. He was a Black Beret, the leader of a SEAL team, which stood for Sea, Air and Land guerrilla warfare. Under CIA guidance, his mission was to disrupt the infrastructure of Viet Cong villages. This meant working in the jungles at night, infiltrating areas where no American troops were supposed to be, for the purpose of assassinating village chiefs, kidnapping respected religious or political figures, and killing and robbing merchants or tax collectors—making it look like the Viet Cong did it, so the people would turn against them. If anyone stumbled upon a SEAL team in action—man, woman or child—the intruder had to be blown away or the mission would be compromised. Chaney remembered the first time he "got wet." They called it "getting wet"—making your first kill by slicing someone's throat, so the blood would gush all over you. He had to do it to a slim little teenage girl who woke up and couldn't be quiet while two guys were garroting her father. Chaney had nightmares about it afterwards. He started to wonder who he was killing and why. He didn't really *know*. He never spoke to them, he couldn't speak Vietnamese anyway. For all he knew, the Viet Cong could have been fucking with the CIA, feeding them phony intelligence, making the SEALS hit people that the Viet Cong actually *wanted* wiped out—South Vietnamese sympathizers, for example. But Chaney kept on following orders, taking a cold-blooded pride in the skills he was honing, not letting himself dwell on questions of ethics and morality. Later, he hired on with the CIA in Central America and Latin America. He came to believe that all of Vietnam must have been a sort of advanced boot camp to train operatives for terrorist activities run by the United States all over the world.

He concealed these heretical perceptions from everybody who hired him. He was always efficient, cold and thorough—at all times a professional—so that his services were very much in demand. He continued to allow himself to be employed strictly by his own government; but he knew that if and when a better opportunity came along, he would be pragmatic enough to seize it. Privately he now thought of himself as a soldier of fortune, the sole citizen of a country called "Blair Chaney" to which he owed his total commitment, allegiance and loyalty.

4

"Teague still looks the same," said Rolf Kollar. "A bit grayer...but the same. He's easily recognizable. The other two have changed considerably. Of course this happens to some people in confinement, almost as if a hidden side of them, the worst side, begins coming out and taking over. A Jekyll and Hyde phenomenon." He paused, staring at the images flashing before him on a movie-scope. "On the other hand, they may look different because they are different men."

"No way!" snapped Clarence Corrigan. "Thompson is still telling the same story he told seven years ago!"

"I'd like to hear it for myself," said Kollar.

"You will soon enough," interjected Blair Chaney. "So for now let's not argue about it."

"Nobody calls me a liar," Corrigan muttered. But he was scared of Chaney, so he let his anger subside. He was a sanitarium guard, Chaney's inside man at Blue Ridge Hospital. When Kollar had asked for a tape recording of the inmate in question, Corrigan had maintained that it would be impossible to smuggle in the necessary hardware. So this was why Chaney had had to sneak in close enough to film from outside the fence, with a telephoto lens.

The three men were viewing the result in the basement of Kollar's Long Island home. Even with being able to stop the movie-scope, freezing specific frames, the close-ups weren't conclusive. Kollar wasn't as impressed as he had expected to be. He was mainly interested in Thompson, and yet, comparing seven-year-old photos of the Air Force test pilot with today's footage of the sanitarium inmate name-tagged PERRY, he couldn't be absolutely sure they were the same person.

One issue was settled, however: the film footage was current, not old coverage of men long gone. Kollar had checked it and found no splices. The emulsion numbers were in order. It was the Kodak raw stock he had bought himself. At the head of it were the shots of his home, his car and his dog that he had taken to establish the timeliness of what he was looking at.

The dog, a huge German Shepherd trained to rip a man's throat out upon command, was sitting, ears perked, in a corner of the basement. From time to time he would get up and pace close to Chaney and Corrigan, menacing them with low-throated growls. It was the same kind of dog used by the guards in the concentration camp where Kollar had almost died forty years ago, and having such a dog on his side these days gave him a measure of comfort. He was afraid of Chaney and Corrigan both, but especially of Chaney. The man, after all, was a traitor, willing to divulge CIA secrets and to turn on his former employers like a snake. Not that he hadn't been a snake while working for them; he liked to sneer and brag about his lurid adventures—some of them possibly true—which involved poisonings, kidnappings and stranglings of businessmen, scientists and politicians, Americans as well as foreigners, who were deemed "dangerous to U.S. security."

To Kollar, Chaney was a man who had lost his principles, patriotic or otherwise. Devoid of loyalty to anyone or anything other than himself, there was no "higher purpose" he could be counted upon to uphold and therefore none that could be utilized to manipulate him.

Corrigan was less to be feared because he was only a sanitarium guard—an occupation that didn't demand much cleverness or deviousness; just watchfulness and callousness. Kollar had dealt with the worst manifestations of the guard mentality in Auschwitz and in East Berlin, so Corrigan was a pale threat by comparison. Big, beefy, and not particularly bright, he seemed motivated mainly by greed. And he didn't appear shrewd enough to spearhead a scheme of CIA entrapment. So, while Kollar knew he had to watch him carefully, from Corrigan he didn't get the same kind of chill that he got from Chaney.

Kollar flipped the room lights on and started rewinding the reel of film. Looking over his shoulder, Chaney said, "What's bugging you? This is what you wanted, right? You've got the proof you were looking for right in your hands."

"Not necessarily," Kollar said, turning from his work table to meet Chaney's cold gaze. In a yellow polo shirt and brown slacks, the soldier of fortune had a deep tan and a broad-shouldered, athletic build. He reminded Kollar of a perverse version of the All-American Boy, grown up to spew out bullets and grenades instead of footballs and baseballs. When he spoke his tone had an eerie calm about it that was more menacing than blatant anger:

"I told you I helped put Thompson away. You wouldn't even know where he is, if I hadn't told you."

"I need to more carefully examine this footage," Kollar explained levelly, his German accent emphasized under stress. "Not because I question your word, but because you haven't seen Thompson for seven years. Much could have transpired. What if this man Perry is Perry? What if somehow he's not the same man you locked up?"

"What the hell?" Corrigan snarled. "He damn sure *looks* like Thompson. If he *isn't* Thompson, why does he tell me he won't leave the sanitarium without Teague and Vickers? He insists they're the only ones who can back up his story."

"Haskell might be Teague," said Kollar. "And Blake might be Vickers. And still, Perry might be Perry."

"Surely you're not looking for an excuse to back out of our arrangement," Chaney said. Again, his tone was calm. But even the German Shepherd sensed the under-lying menace and paced closer, snarling, glistening fangs bared as if to take a chunk out of Chaney's leg. "Keep that dog away from me or I'll kill him," Chaney said.

Kollar believed the threat even though, on the surface, the carrying out of it seemed improbable. Was Chaney packing a hidden weapon? Or did he think his bare hands were enough? In any case, the dog seemed afraid of him, too. The mere sound of his voice had made the animal hesitate.

"Back, Taurus," Kollar commanded. "Sit, boy, sit!" He stared the animal back into a corner, then faced Chaney, clearing his throat, fighting his nervousness and fear. "I'm still in this all the way," he said. "I just want to be sure, before we go ahead with the break-out, that we aren't making some sort of ghastly mistake. I'd like to make some photographic enlargements of select frames and compare them more precisely with the authenticated photos. I'll be able to match head positions that way, and look at same-size images."

"All right," said Chaney. "Scrutinize all you want. But before I go, pay me for what I've done so far."

"Me, too," growled Corrigan.

Kollar unlocked the bottom drawer of his work table, slid it open, and took out two envelopes, each containing five thousand dollars in cash. He gave each man his due. He had withdrawn the money from a safety deposit box earlier in the day. It was exactly what he owed Chaney and Corrigan, and not a penny more. He wasn't foolish enough to tempt them with the presence of more money in the house—which might motivate them to bump him off here and now, instead of waiting for the big payoff they would get if they could execute everything they had talked about over the past several weeks.

"You'll be in touch?" Chaney asked.

"Certainly. By tomorrow."

As soon as he was alone, Kollar spooled Chaney's film footage slowly through the movie-scope, eyeballing the close-ups of the three men in question and looking for angles that matched the existing still photos. Then he snipped out the precise frames that he wanted and took them into his dark room to get started immediately on the blowups. He was more excited than he had let on in the presence of his accomplices. As he watched his enlargements materializing in the developer solution, he became increasingly sure that Haskell, Perry and Blake were actually Teague, Thompson and Vickers. By the time he finished taking measurements of facial features and making minute comparisons, he was absolutely certain.

Elated, he took the photos up to his den. His dog, Taurus, paced after him. He fixed himself a martini and sat at his desk, spreading out the photos and looking at them over and over, continuing to savor the results of his work. From time to time he reached down to pat the German Shepherd's head, saying, "This is it, Taurus my boy, this will validate all I have been saying for the past ten years. Hah! This will make all of my enemies eat crow."

At last he felt he was on the verge of unmasking a government conspiracy of the first magnitude. Once before he had been close, but that chance had been snatched away. Three years ago, Jerry Spivak, a radio-tower man from the New Mexico Air Force Base where Colonel Kevin Thompson had crashed testing an A-11 spy plane, came to Kollar wanting ten thousand dollars for secret information about what really had happened on the day of the crash. Spivak dropped some hints about a UFO incident. But before Kollar could pay the money and find out more, Spivak was found dead in his apartment. Over his head was a garment bag taped to a vacuum cleaner hose which in turn was taped to an open gas jet. The official version carried by the news media was that Spivak had been leaking government secrets to foreign agents and had committed suicide when the CIA began closing in on him.

Such a meticulously grisly way for a man to supposedly kill himself. Kollar had never believed Spivak's death was really suicide. And now that he had proof that Colonel Thompson was still alive, he was more determined than ever to break the story of the UFO cover-up. But unfortunately, he found himself wrestling with a major stumbling block.

Even if Teague, Thompson and Vickers could be busted

out of the sanitarium, they would have a tough time proving they were who they said they were. They were legally dead. Their identities had been changed by the CIA. They were registered as "patients" under false names—with birth certificates, fingerprint files, and all other background documentation contrived to match their new identities. According to Chaney, when the CIA did this sort of thing it was not a halfway measure. It was therefore a certainty that completely phony, but convincing, records would have been concocted for the "new" men as well as the "dead" ones.

Chaney and Corrigan weren't intending to pitch in to expose the subterfuge. Their job would be over once the break-out was accomplished. They weren't willing to take any further risk. They were going to simply disappear with the huge amount of cash Kollar was obliged to heap upon them.

So he would need help from some other source in order to break his story and verify it in a way that would convince all skeptics. Thumbing through dossiers he had compiled on Teague, Thompson and Vickers, he reviewed information about their surviving family members and former close associates. He had to decide whom he might approach, whom he might involve as a dependable ally.

His number one candidate was Jenny Teague, Dr. Norman Teague's nineteen-year-old daughter. In his file, he already had a clipping of a recent *New York Times* interview in which Jenny had stated that in her own mind she would never consider her father deceased until the day she was able to view his remains. This was the kind of predisposition Kollar was looking for. He reread the background information that led into the newspaper interview, as he formulated his plans.

Seven years ago, Dr. Norman Teague, Colonel Kevin Thompson, and Dr. Abraham Vickers all were members of a so-called "think tank" called Universal Dynamics, Inc., which was based in Washington, D.C., and was heavily involved in top-secret projects. Teague and Vickers both disappeared on their way to a meeting there, and subsequent rumors had it that they either defected to the Soviets or were kidnapped to be grilled, tortured and possibly killed by the KGB. Teague's field was advanced rocket propulsion systems, and Vickers' specialty was space-age laser weaponry, so they would have had much to give to America's enemies. Coincidentally, their friend and associate Colonel Kevin Thompson was killed while test flying a spy plane, just three days prior to their disappearance.

Teague's wife Martha, an aeronautical engineer, was now employed by the Cameron Foundation in Manhattan. She and her boss Dr. Gary Cameron, the noted astronomer, writer, and popularizer of space science, were planning to be married. Jenny Teague refused to comment on this when asked her opinion of it for the New York Times. But it was clear to Kollar that she would find the betrothal repugnant, since she was still hoping that her father would come back to her.

Twelve years old at the time of the disappearance, Jenny was now a sophomore at Georgetown University. She was a bright student, consistently on the dean's list, which would enhance her credibility when and if she helped Kollar break his sensational story. In the *Times,* she came across as intelligent and highly articulate, even through the fog of uncertainty surrounding the questions she was being asked. She had known Thompson and Vickers when they worked with her father at Universal

Dynamics. So she should be able to positively identify all three men.

Kollar had a grudge against Jenny's mother, Martha, and her fiancé, Gary Cameron, and he could certainly throw a monkey wrench into their lives by bringing Norman Teague back from the dead. When his first book, Gods from Other Galaxies, was ready to be published, he had submitted the galleys to Dr. Gary Cameron, in hopes that the famous scientist would write a glowing blurb and maybe even a foreword that would help sell the work. But in a cold, contemptuous letter, Cameron had replied that he thought the premise was preposterous and the "proofs" farfetched. In Cameron's opinion, Kollar had stretched certain facts and bent others to try to give weight to the notion that the human race was descended from astral visitors; Kollar's writing was "not scientific but mythological in nature." After the book had become wildly successful, both Gary Cameron and Martha Teague had gone out of their way to heap discredit upon it. Appearing as Kollar's adversaries on TV shows debating the UFO phenomenon and the "ancient astronaut" theories, they had showered him with smug insults in an effort to make him lose his following. His ego and his pride still smarted. If he could expose the Blue Ridge cover-up, he'd knock Gary Cameron and Martha Teague down from their high perch of "scientific respectability."

5

Watching Jenny Teague sing, Rolf Kollar was struck by the intensity of emotion emanating from such a slender, almost frail-looking young woman. With dark, curly hair and deep-set black eyes, she was merely passably pretty until she began to express herself in her songs; then she suddenly became more alive and more beautiful. Sitting on a plain wooden stool, wearing a baggy red turtleneck and faded jeans, she managed to stir her audience with elegantly simple lyrics about liberty, justice and truth.

Kollar figured that if she had such a strong, youthful passion for these ideals, he could probably use that passion to get exactly what he wanted from her.

Jenny got butterflies in her stomach as soon as she spotted Kollar at a corner table in the dimly lit saloon. She abruptly averted her eyes and tried to pretend she hadn't noticed him. But there was a thin-lipped smirk on his bony, angular face. And he kept staring at her, making her almost go off key.

She was singing a rock ballad, one of her own compositions that she had done before, many times, for basically this same crowd. She didn't need to sing for money, and she wasn't paid much, but it was fun being able to let people hear her own stuff. The short poems that she set to music were her outlet for feelings she considered too abstract or too delicate for the coolly incisive type of prose she was obliged to practice in her journalism classes.

Kollar was spoiling it for her. She knew he must be here to badger her with questions about her father. Why would he have the gall to imagine that she might open up to *him*? He wasn't even a serious journalist, as she hoped someday to become. He was a charlatan who had made a fortune churning out a string of bizarre, insipid bestsellers based on the absurd hypothesis that eons ago "gods" from remote galaxies had come to earth to "create" man by genetically altering lower life forms.

Jenny had recognized Kollar from seeing him on TV with her mother and her mother's fiancé. At the time, she had considered him amusing, if not entirely harmless. But she had become enraged when he started talking about her father, saying really crazy things, trying to connect the disappearance of Dr. Norman Teague to some godawful rumor about the crash of a flying saucer.

Dreading an encounter with him, she tried to think it could be just a coincidence that he was in Washington and happened to drop in at this particular bar. Maybe he was lecturing somewhere around here. She couldn't recall seeing any notices about Rolf Kollar appearing on the Georgetown campus, but she knew that because of the notoriety of his books he was in demand on the lecture circuit.

When she took a break, he crossed the tiny dance floor to her isolated table, introduced himself, and sat down without being invited. Nervously lighting a cigarette, she flashed him an annoyed look.

"Don't get haughty," he warned. "I'm only here because I have some new information about your father." He patted the black leather portfolio he had laid on the table.

His brazen air of intrigue—heightened by his throaty German accent—made Jenny curious in spite of herself. She had been mentally preparing herself to deny Kollar whatever information he wanted from her, but he had thrown her off balance by claiming he had some to impart. Even though common sense told her it was probably only a clever ploy, she hated to pass up the barest chance of learning something crucial. She reminded herself once again that Kollar was a crackpot. In person he radiated even more of the charisma of congealed fanaticism that had come across on TV.

She knew he had suffered under the Nazis in Auschwitz and the communists in East Berlin. She wondered whether his belief in flying saucers and benevolent aliens from outer space could have germinated in the concentration camp—fanciful delusions helping him escape mentally, if not physically, from horrors and atrocities that might otherwise have driven him completely insane. Viewed this way, she could entertain a reluctant compassion for his mental warp. Yet, if she was convinced that any "news" he thought he could bring her would exist only in his imagination, why was there something about his presence here that kept making her heart beat a little faster? She lit a second cigarette from the butt of her first one, while Kollar strained her patience by rehashing the details of an episode that had occurred three years ago. It involved the bizarre suicide of Jerry Spivak, an Air

Force man who had been working in the control tower on the day when Colonel Kevin Thompson crashed. Jenny had heard it before; it was a story that Kollar could not prove; in fact, it was convenient for him that Spivak was dead and could not dispute his wild claims. Jenny barely listened. She wished Kollar would get to the point about her father. His eyes boring into her, he said, "You recall I went public with what little advance information Spivak had given me. And I was widely ridiculed. But today I can tell you I have no doubt whatsoever that Spivak's death had something to do with UFOs."

"Why is that, Rolf?" Jenny asked, not bothering to mask the snideness in her voice, for Kollar's spiel had convinced her once again that he was indeed a wacko and a nuisance.

"I know you think I am crazy," he said, smirking. "But your opinion will soon change, young lady." He removed a manila packet from his portfolio, slid out an eight-by-ten photo, and placed it in front of Jenny. "Can you tell me who that is?" he asked smugly.

Jenny stared at the photo. Her hand trembled as she attempted to nonchalantly snuff out her cigarette. The print was not sharp, but she thought she recognized the face. And it was older and grayer than she remembered. And dead men do not age.

"What's the matter, Jenny?" Kollar whispered goadingly. "Why are your eyes so wide and your complexion so pale? One would almost think you are seeing a picture of a dead man who is not dead."

"Kevin Thompson," she murmured hoarsely. She tried to fight down the butterflies in her stomach, while her mind struggled with a deja vu feeling about the revelations that she knew were about to come.

"Surprised?" Kollar said, teasing her, enjoying his triumph.

"When was this taken?"

"Last week."

"It's grainy," said Jenny, forcing herself to be analytical. "I admit there's a resemblance, but Kevin Thompson is dead. This could be someone else—someone who looks like him. Perhaps an actor. Someone could be trying to pull a hoax on you."

Kollar swiftly slipped another photo out of his packet. "And this?" he demanded. "Is this an actor, too?"

Studying the likeness, Jenny became even more shaky. "It looks…it looks like Abraham Vickers."

"It *is* Vickers!" Kollar insisted. "And now…prepare yourself for a greater shock." He laid a third photo in front of Jenny.

Her face went white. The image in front of her was that of her father, Dr. Norman Teague, recently declared dead. "When was this taken?" she asked, her voice quavering despite her effort to remain calm and skeptical.

"Last week," Kollar answered, rhythmically tapping the photo with the nail of his index finger. "Last week, same as the others. Teague, Thompson and Vickers are all three still alive. They are being kept in a sanitarium run by the CIA. These photographs were made by blowing up some 16-millimeter film frames. I bought the film myself and recorded the emulsion numbers. No way could any of this have been faked. A man working for me took the pictures."

"Who?"

"Sorry, but I can't tell you that. I hope you realize I'm taking a tremendous risk merely by showing you these photographs. You might report *me* to the CIA, in which case they would probably dispose of me the way they did Jerry Spivak. But they couldn't let you live either. Both of us might become 'suicides' with *gas* bags taped over our heads."

Jenny shuddered inwardly. Trying to outwardly compose herself, she said, "You're telling me that if these photos are valid, my father is still alive. What do you intend to do about it? Why have you shown them to me? Has my mother seen them?"

Kollar grinned sardonically. "No, she hasn't. You know what she thinks of me—she'd probably throw me out of her office and phone the police immediately. The game would be up. At this point, I don't think you or I want her to see them. However, she will eventually learn the truth. Teague, Thompson and Vickers are going to escape from the sanitarium. I'm going to have a chance to interview them on tape."

Jenny stared at Kollar. Was he sane or not? His story seemed wilder and wilder. Yet, in a way, she longed to believe in it.

"If they manage to remain free long enough," he went on, "I may be able to get them onto live network television. Only when this story has been blown wide open will I be relatively safe—after the lid can no longer be kept on. But it's too big for me to handle alone. The CIA will impugn my credibility. They have identities forged for your father and the other two men. That's why I need you, Jenny. If you tell the media people that Teague, Thompson and Vickers really *are* who they say they are, the public will believe you—much more readily than they'll believe me."

"But I still think the photos could've been faked somehow," Jenny argued, trying to convince herself as well as Kollar. "It strikes me that good actors could impersonate men who, if they weren't dead, would have aged seven years. I mean…I guess I'm really not certain this is my father." She blinked and averted her eyes from the photo.

"You are certain," Kollar said knowingly. "You have always yearned for him to come back to you and have always dreamed that it would happen. But now it is like seeing a ghost, and it has you frightened. This is only natural, Jenny. Much as you love your father, there must be a side of you that does not wish to see your new life plunged into turmoil. But you also know that you have to see this through. You have to help the man who brought you into this world. For the past seven years, he has been in a terrible and desperate situation, and you cannot in good conscience abandon him."

"What exactly will be required of me?" Jenny asked, alarmed by the tenseness in her own voice. She could feel herself being pulled down into the depths of a lurid mystery that had the potential of branding her as a criminal or a lunatic.

"I want you to meet all three men when they come out the sanitarium," said Kollar. "I'll make you a deal. If you tell me they're impostors, I'll wash my hands of the whole affair. I won't break the story. Think it over. I'll get in touch with you again. In the meantime, remember that you have everything to lose, possibly your father's life as well as your own, if you tell anyone about the evidence I've shown you."

He put the photos back into his black leather portfolio. Then he left the saloon.

Jenny had two more sets to sing, and she forced herself to get through them. Her performance was lifeless, like an airplane on automatic pilot. Her mind was in a jumble.

Even when she was a little girl, she had refused to believe that her father could be dead, and with the passage of time she had never really grown out of it. His body had never been found, and neither had that of Abraham Vickers. The two scientists had simply disappeared on their way to that "think tank" meeting. Obsessed with the mystery, Jenny had insisted on going away to college, rather than living at home, even though there were many excellent colleges right in New York City. She had chosen Georgetown University because it was in Washington, D.C., where Universal Dynamics, Inc., was located. She wanted to be close to her father, his last known footsteps. She often fantasized that she might someday track him down. She envisioned herself delving into his disappearance, with some investigative journalism of her own.

Because of her fantasy, her ambition, she approached her assignments with a passion that was missing from most of the other journalism majors. Professor Aaron Stasney took her under his wing and she became his star student, working hard in class and even harder on the college newspaper. They put in a lot of extracurricular hours together, but they refrained from becoming lovers till her sophomore year, when he was no longer grading her. He was witty, almost handsome, recently widowed. Before starting to teach, he had worked for ten years as a reporter for a big newspaper in Minneapolis. The anecdotes that peppered his lectures were vividly entertaining, enlightening, sometimes funny, sometimes appalling. Jenny still shuddered when she thought of the story he told to illustrate the pitfalls of becoming overemotional in the presence of events that had to be reported factually. He was covering a head-on collision between a truck and a school bus, and arrived on the scene to find little kids impaled by steel rods that had been flung from the truck like spears on the moment of impact. It wouldn't have happened if the rods had been secured properly and if the truck driver hadn't been drunk.

"I couldn't hold in my feelings," Aaron confessed. "I wrote an article full of grief and rage. It belonged in a book of sermons, not in a newspaper, but I didn't understand that at the time, and I blew my stack when the editor rewrote it on his own, without consulting me, because he knew I was in too deep a state of shock to do a good job. You see, no matter how impossible it may seem, one must learn to preserve a certain degree of emotional detachment in order to report the news factually."

Poor Aaron, Jenny thought. He always tried so hard to be levelheaded, factual, analytical—it was his main strength and his main flaw. She knew she could use some of his vaunted objectivity right now, but she wouldn't go to him for advice. Not after the way he had picked her apart, saying she'd never be able to fall in love till she got over her thing about her father. The break-up had happened two months ago, but she still missed him, still thought about him constantly. But she wasn't ready to give him another shot at hurting her. Even though she had seen new evidence to support her gut feeling about her father, she didn't have it in her hands to show Aaron, so he wouldn't believe her, he'd just be more convinced than ever that she had a so-called "hang-up."

Despairingly, she realized she had no one to confide in. She had no really close friends in college, nobody she could ask to bear a burden so heavy, so dangerous. She was overwhelmed with a resurgence of the loneliness and coldness she had felt all through her childhood.

Maybe Aaron was right. Maybe she was emotionally stunted. Maybe that was why she was able to express her deepest feelings only in her songs—in other words, at a distance. If she followed Rolf Kollar on his crackpot escapade, perhaps it would help put her demons to rest.

What about in the meantime? How would she live with this new rush of uncertainty? She dreaded facing her family while harboring the facts, half facts, or lies that Kollar had thrust upon her. But final exams were only two weeks away, and after that she'd have no excuse not to go home. On her own, she couldn't have found a summer job that paid half as much as the one her mother had lined up for her at the Cameron Foundation. She was also expected to help out with the arrangements for her mother's marriage to Dr. Gary Cameron, which was scheduled to take place in July. How jolly. If she tried to tell her mother that her father might still be alive, she'd be accused of making things up, grasping at any straw to wreck the wedding. Regressing to her childhood.

As a little girl, she had cried herself to sleep night after night when she learned that her mother was dating another man, Dr. Gary Cameron, her father's supposed friend. She had acted like a brat, screaming about her mother's unfaithfulness, and telling Gary Cameron to his face that she would always hate him. But, as she passed through puberty and into her middle teens, she made some grudging adjustments. Her grandmother, Helen Dudley, had a long difficult talk with her, pointing out her selfishness, making her see that her mother deserved some happiness because, after all, just as Jenny was becoming more and more interested in men and in romance, her mother had a mature need for male companionship that could not be permanently set aside.

"Your mother already has a tough time with your sister Sally," Grandmother Dudley said. "Sally isn't responsible for her behavior because she's not well, poor child. But you, Jenny, are old enough and bright enough to know better. You have to try as hard as you can to act like a grown-up. I know you can do it if you make your mind up."

So Jenny had grown used to walking on eggshells, never daring to make any waves within her family. Any change in the "normal" rhythms might spook Sally, whose state of mind was always so precarious. Sometimes, when she was angry or jealous, Jenny thought that she had more right to be messed up than her younger sister did. Sally was only two months old when their father disappeared—too young to even remember him. But his absence seemed to have a worse effect on her. At first Sally had seemed to be developing into an unusually cute, intelligent little girl, but it didn't last. By the time she was five, her flights of childish imagination and flamboyant behavior were becoming more and more quirky, erratic and disorganized, finally reaching the point where she had to receive professional help. But instead of improving with psychological therapy and counseling, her emotional problems had worsened. She was eventually diagnosed as a borderline schizophrenic, and had to be kept on a regimen of anti-psychotic drugs to prevent further deterioration.

Sally's psychiatrists had wanted to know if there had been any history of mental illness in the family. Jenny's mother and grandmother had been able to say that there had been none on the Dudley side and, as far as they knew, none on the Teague side either.

But suddenly, with a jolt, Jenny found herself wondering: If Rolf Kollar was right and Norman Teague was in a sanitarium, what if he belonged there? Maybe it would explain why Sally had mental problems. Perhaps she had inherited a faulty gene. If the CIA had Jenny's father locked away, they might have felt they had to do it—to prevent him from going off the deep end and giving away vital defense secrets. Such a harsh measure wouldn't be morally justifiable, but at least it would be understandable from the viewpoint of those who were guarding the nation's security.

Jenny didn't know what scared her more. The thought of never seeing her father again, or the thought of having him come back to her in some kind of demented, deranged condition.

6

Norman Teague gave Rolf Kollar an excuse to press Jenny for a quick decision. By means of a note smuggled to Clarence Corrigan, Teague let it be known that he would not allow himself to be rescued unless he could be given proof that his eldest daughter was participating in the escape plans.

Kollar appreciated Teague's prudent, self-protective instincts. After everything that the imprisoned scientist had been put through, why should he easily trust anyone? Why shouldn't he try to make sure that he wouldn't be stepping out of the frying pan and into the fire? Clearly, he had enemies as well as friends who would love to get their hands on him. It wouldn't do him any good to escape from the CIA, only to fall into the hands of the KGB.

"Your father needs to know if you are for him or against him," Kollar told Jenny on the telephone. He made the call from a booth in Manhattan to the saloon where Jenny sang, for he did not wish to have any further overt contact with her that might cause him to be incriminated once the sanitarium break-out occurred.

"He...he asked about me?" Jenny stammered.

"Yes, he did. He wants proof that you are with us all the way."

"I guess I'm surprised to be hearing from you so soon."

"Well, I wanted to give you more than two days to make up your mind. But your father had other ideas. He obviously loves you very deeply, Jenny. It is extremely important to him to know that he will have you as an ally on the outside."

"All right," she said, sucking in her breath. "All right, I'm willing to help you. But how can I convince my father if I can't even speak to him?"

Kollar already had it figured out. He got Jenny to send him two photographs, one of herself as a twelve-year-old, the way her father would remember her, plus a recent one, showing the way she looked as a mature, attractive young woman. A few days later, Clarence Corrigan was able to smuggle these "soft items" past the electronic surveillance equipment at Blue Ridge. On the back of the older photo was a message in Jenny's handwriting, refer-ring to an incident that had happened when she was a little girl, an incident of the sort that presumably would be recollected only by intimate members of the Teague family. On the back of the more recent photo was a hand-written message from Jenny telling her father how much she loved him and yearned to see him as a free man. The "proofs" worked. After receiving them, Dr. Norman Teague got word to Corrigan that he would follow instructions and go along with the escape plan.

Two days later, Kollar drove down to West Virginia,

heading for a "safe house" set up by Blair Chaney on the outskirts of Wheeling, a town described by Chaney as "a dirty, ugly little dump full of unemployed steel-workers and dumb hillbillies too drunk or stupid to pay any attention to us." Making the trip with Kollar was Jason Rawlings, a young, enthusiastic ufologist who had helped him research his current work in progress, a book entitled *Rendezvous with the Gods.* The research had consisted of videotape interviews with people who claimed to have been engaged in extraterrestrial encounters. Rawlings was twenty-three years old but, to Kollar's dismay, he had the looks and personality of a somewhat sappy teenager. He still had acne. He loved comic books and video games and Steven Spielberg movies. Even though he was often helpful, he was also sometimes an embarrassment to Kollar, since he was exactly the type of UFO groupie who caused critics of Kollar's work to smirk, call his fans a "cult," and feel entirely justified for holding him in contempt. But Rawlings was an excellent technician because he loved everything contemporary and electronic. Kollar was depending upon him to put together a set-up for doing videotape interviews with Teague, Vickers and Thompson, once they were busted out of the sanitarium. "You don't want anything Mickey Mouse this time," Rawlings had explained, fingering his pimples. "None of this half-inch or eight-millimeter stuff people use for home movies. We've gotta use professional format, two-inch videotape. That way we get a crystal-clear master and top-quality dubs, so nobody can say our image is too blurry or grainy to tell for sure that these guys are who we say they are."

Driving down to Wheeling in a Volksbus loaded with camera and lighting gear worth a small fortune, while

Jason Rawlings read comic books and sipped Cokes, Rolf Kollar worried about everything he was jeopardizing—not only his career, but his life. Supposedly, Chaney was carrying out his part of the operation in such a way that, if it went sour at this stage, Kollar's involvement would not come to the attention of the authorities. But, naturally, Kollar didn't trust Chaney to fully protect him. He trusted Corrigan less. He had a hunch that if the sanitarium guard got caught, it wouldn't take much torture or "truth serum" to make him open up. One reason Kollar had survived the concentration camp years ago, was that he had learned to sniff out potential turncoats and avoid them like the plague. But this time he hadn't been able to pick and choose his collaborators; he either had to go along with them or drop the whole scheme. Once the three escapees were in his hands, to break the story he'd have to go public. He'd be in the limelight. While it was one thing for him to sit back and write books full of iconoclastic theories, it was quite another thing for him to take dangerous chances to turn those theories into facts—all in the pursuit of truth, vindication and scientific respect. If he could record evidence of the UFO cover-up and the phony deaths of the three men on tape right away, he might be able to protect himself to some extent if the FBI or the CIA started closing in.

Snapping his comic book shut, Rawlings interrupted Kollar's reverie. "What do you think of the Manuel Campos thing?"

He was referring to the last case history he had researched for *Rendezvous with the Gods*. Back in 1966, a Brazilian farmer named Manuel Campos had claimed to have been abducted aboard a spaceship and seduced by an alien woman. Wild as the story sounded, it was backed up by two highly respectable physicians and two psychiatrists from the University of Sao Paulo, who had testified to Campos's sanity and to the presence of physical evidence—unusual scars, skin discolorations, and a high radiation count in his blood—that seemed to confirm that something truly "strange" had happened to him. Twenty years after the fact, Jason Rawlings had flown to Brazil to interview the parties concerned, updating the case by taking new depositions on videotape.

"Campos is probably a liar," said Rolf Kollar. "To inseminate themselves with human chromosomes, I doubt very much that extraterrestrials would employ such a crude method."

According to his story, told on tape through an interpreter, but told pretty much the same as he had told it back in 1966 in his original deposition, Manuel Campos had been plowing a field at dusk when a cloud of blue light surrounded his tractor and it stopped moving, even though the headlights were still on, the motor was running, and the engine was in gear. Manuel panicked and started to run, but immediately his legs were immobilized and he found himself in the presence of five humanoid creatures in pale green space suits and helmets. He passed out, and awoke to find himself inside their spacecraft. Talking to each other and to Manuel in voices that sounded like a mixture of barks and quavers, they got him to relax, somehow making him understand that they did not mean to hurt him.

They removed all his clothes and coated every part of his body with a thick, clear, odorless and tasteless liquid. Then they performed various experiments on him, taking blood samples, making small incisions in his skin, and probing at him with tube-like instruments—tests that frightened him very much even though they were absolutely painless. When they were finished, they left him lying on a firm, ovular, plasticized mattress, totally alone and stark naked, fearful of what might happen to him next. All at once he noticed puffs of gray smoke coming from apertures in the silvery walls of the room where his captors were keeping him. He started to gag, and leapt up screaming, thinking he was being gassed to death. But just then a woman entered, as naked as he was, and came over to him and stroked him soothingly.

The gray smoke no longer made him nauseous, and he had the thought that it must have been injected into the environment to enable the woman to breathe freely without a space suit or helmet. She was the most beautiful female Manuel had ever seen, even though she was so different. Her hair was fair, almost white. Her eyes were pale blue, slanted outwards. She had a small, straight nose. Her cheekbones were high and wide, but the bottom part of her face was triangular, with a pointed chin. Her body was lovely, quite slender, with high breasts, thin waist and wide hips. Her skin was cream-colored, with a smattering of pale freckles on her arms. The downy hair under her arms and in her pubic area was of a faint strawberry hue.

Lying down beside Manuel, she embraced him and squirmed against him so that there was no mistaking what she wanted. Despite the bizarreness of the situation, he began to respond erotically; soon he forgot himself and went at it as passionately as the alien lady; in the throes of a powerful orgasm, it vaguely occurred to him that the cold, viscous liquid that had been rubbed all over his body might have possessed some aphrodisiacal properties. After some parting caresses, the woman simply got up and left him. But she turned toward him momentarily, pointing to her belly, then to him, then upwards as if to the sky. He took this to mean that she would have their baby after she returned to her home planet, probably in some distant galaxy.

"Manuel's a peasant living on the edge of a jungle," said Jason Rawlings. "Doesn't even have a grade-school education. Can barely read and write. How would he be able to make up stuff like that?"

"How do we really know what his reading level is? He could be pretending."

"Huh? What do you mean, Rolf?"

"We know he has a lack of formal education—that much is documented. But it doesn't mean that some educated person—a cousin, a nun, a priest, maybe—didn't take him in hand and tutor him. Illiteracy can be faked. For all anyone really *knows*, Manuel might have a pile of UFO magazines stashed in his shanty."

Rawlings smirked. "You've gotta be kidding. The man was so damned *believable*. If you had seen him in person—

"Seeing him on tape was enough, Jason. I admit he's absolutely convincing—until one begins to analyze."

"For instance?" Rawlings delved into a thermos bag, popped open another Coke, and began to guzzle it.

"Well, for *instance* Kollar lectured wryly, "you and the Brazilian investigators seem to have bought the notion that a man of Manuel Campos's limited background couldn't possibly have invented a story so wildly imaginative. But, notice how he's bright enough to lead the investigators to certain scientific assumptions that tend to enhance his story's plausibility. He says that the liquid rubbed on him could've been an aphrodisiac, conveniently furnishing an answer to anyone who might wonder how he could bring himself to make love in a situation of extreme anxiety and fear. He also says that the gray smoke probably enabled the alien woman to breathe without a helmet. This is *not* the kind of thing that occurs to a man utterly unsophisticated and unaware of the problems of interplanetary travel."

"Hmmm," said Rawlings, using the back of his hand to wipe drops of Coke from his chin. "What about the high radiation level in his blood?"

"We didn't test for that ourselves. We have only the word of the Brazilian doctors."

"But why would they lie? If they're in on a hoax, they have yet to make a profit on it, and it's been on the books for twenty years."

"People do things for all sorts of motives. There have been many weird hoaxes over the centuries. Piltdown Man, for example. There is some strong evidence that Arthur Conan Doyle may have perpetrated that one."

"Huh! The guy who wrote Sherlock Holmes?"

"Yes, I'm afraid so."

"Cripes!" said Rawlings, shaking his pimpled head. He guzzled the last of his Coke, thereby germinating more pimples. Grinning to show he was joking rather than attempting an insult, he said, "Rolf, you called it a crude method for extraterrestrials to use to inseminate themselves. You don't really think straight sex is crude, do you?"

"It's not exactly beautiful, is it? Nor is it scientific. Why wouldn't they simply take a sperm sample from Manuel, to be tested, sterilized, and used later? Why would this alien woman have been ready to conceive precisely at that moment? It'd be too much of a coincidence. Besides, if we analyze the fantasy, I think it tends to discredit itself."

"How?"

"Well, Campos is a Brazilian native, of Indian descent, short, swarthy, dark-skinned, with broad, flat facial features. But yet that part of Brazil has many Anglos, mostly of German ancestry, so Manuel would have seen many women of that type and may have lusted after them even though they were untouchable as far as he was concerned—they might as well have been living on another planet. Note how the creature in his story was tall, slender, high-breasted and fair—the exact opposite of the short, dumpy squaws who would've been more readily available to a man like Manuel."

Rawlings laughed, a silly teenage-sounding giggle. "You're saying he imagined it. It's part hoax and part wet dream."

Kollar grimaced at the distasteful crudeness of Rawlings's metaphor. "I think we can allow that he might not have consciously imagined it. He might *believe* that it actually happened—if so, it'd explain why he seems so convincing. Perhaps he could even pass a polygraph test."

"Shit!" said Rawlings. "I was fascinated by the details of the story. I really wanted to believe in it."

"Especially the erotic aspects, eh, Jason?" Kollar chuckled. He thought that his gawky, pimple-faced companion probably never got any sex except what he paid for in the brothels of the world that he could visit while he was running around doing research on Kollar's money. The idea of an intergalactic copulation would have turned him on as hard as it had turned on the Brazilian peasant.

"No, I meant the *scientific* details," Rawlings protested, his pimples blushing.

"As serious investigators, we have to guard against that sort of gullibility," warned Kollar, as he negotiated the narrow, twisting mountain road, on his way to Wheeling, West Virginia, in pursuit of definitive proof of his theories.

7

Now that she had thought about it and thought about it, Jenny Teague doubted that her father could be insane, even though she still had some fears in that regard. The thing that seemed to argue against insanity was that he had disappeared with Abraham Vickers. They couldn't have both gone insane at the same time, could they? A couple of days after the disappearance, according to the police, an anonymous telephone tip had claimed that they were captured, tortured and killed by KGB agents. The tip had made sense at the time. Since no ransom was ever demanded, military secrets instead of money seemed a logical motive. Or political suppression. Knowing her father's stubborn sense of values, Jenny could see how he might have disagreed with "higher authorities" on some issue involving professional ethics or moral accountability.

If the CIA really did have her father locked up, they might punish him, maybe even kill him, if they discovered he was planning to break out. Finding her two photos on him would probably be enough to incur their wrath. What if something went wrong and he blamed her? He might think she had told on him, sabotaging his escape attempt. How could he know this was something she'd never do? How could he be sure that her love for him had not changed? She wanted him to believe it. That was why she had sent the photos to Rolf Kollar.

She tried to push all her anxiety to the back of her mind and go on with her classes at Georgetown University. Under the strain, she was chain-smoking worse than ever, trying to convince herself that the lower, raspier sound of her voice when she was singing lent a course, authentic texture to her folk ballads. She almost hoped she wouldn't ever hear from Kollar again, but at the same time she was anxious for the next contact, hoping she wouldn't have to keep hanging on tenterhooks.

At her off-campus apartment, between classes, she got a phone call. It turned out to be her mother. After jumping for the phone, she sagged against the wall, fumbling for a cigarette. She could hear her own heart pounding. She was so relieved and disappointed that it wasn't Kollar that she almost blurted everything out. The only thing that stopped her was that her mother sounded upset, on the verge of tears. "Oh, Jenny, Sally's taken another bad one, just when I thought she was doing so well. I hate to disturb you, you have enough pressure on you. Grandmother said not to call, but I decided I shouldn't just leave you in the dark. She's your sister, after all."

"Of course, Mother." Jenny meant of course Sally was her sister, not of course she didn't want to be kept in the dark. She didn't see what good could be accomplished by clueing her in to every one of Sally's spells. But her mother seemed to feel it was her duty to share in the misery instead of escaping any part of it because she was not living at home.

Her mother said, "Every kind of medicine they give her seems to eventually wear off—then she has a relapse and no one can handle her. Had to put her in St. Francis again." She let go a sob that she had been trying to hold back. "God only knows how long they'll have to keep her this time."

"Were you there when it happened?" Jenny asked.

"No, just your grandmother. She's too old to cope with something like this. She has her own health problems. At one point she was terrified that she'd have to try to wrestle Sally down and hold her till the ambulance got there."

Jenny knew all too well how tough it could be. She had contended with three of her sister's worst fits when nobody else was around, and the first time it had happened to her she was only a freshman in high school. She felt guilty about choosing a college far from home because one of her unspoken motives had been to escape responsibility for her mentally ill sister. Her hand shaking as she puffed on her cigarette, she wished she didn't have to take part in this conversation, even though she realized she had a duty to commiserate with her mother. "It happened at the apartment then?" she said lamely.

"Yes it did, unfortunately. But better there than on the way home from school where somebody could have taken advantage of her. I'm only sorry Grandmother had to get hit with it. I wish you were here, Jenny. I can't wait till you come home for the summer so you can help us manage everything without going to pieces."

"How's Gary? Isn't he helping you?"

"Well, of course, dear, I don't know how I'd survive

without him. But he has his work at the Foundation and so on. We both do. It's so demanding, on top of everything else. That's why I wish you were going to college right here in Manhattan."

Jenny was startled by the words that came out of her own mouth. "Maybe I'll consider transferring, Mother."

"You really mean it?" Martha Teague's voice sounded a bit brighter, even through her anguish.

"I'll think about it, but I'm not promising," Jenny said. Once more she came close to breaking the news that her father might still be alive, but she caught herself. Nervously stubbing out her cigarette, she realized that the hope burning within her was already making the idea of coming home seem more palatable. She wouldn't need to stay in Georgetown, close to her father's ghost, if she would soon be able to be near to him in the flesh. With her father home, the most terrible things—like coping with Sally—would seem less staggering, less frightening. She could get away from Aaron, too —from her crazy need to see him again and make up with him in spite of the way he had psychoanalyzed her and hurt her pride.

"If you were commuting to college, it'd be so much easier on all of us," Jenny's mother pressed. "Please say that you'll transfer next semester."

"I'll promise to seriously think about it," Jenny said.

Her mother said good-bye, still sounding worried and upset, but less so than before. Lighting another cigarette, Jenny wondered if she should have tried to divulge her secret or at least lay the groundwork, but she couldn't think how she could have done it without making her mother blow up. It amazed her that the great Dr. Martha Teague couldn't calmly handle crises in her own life even though she was a model of detachment and objectivity when it came to science. She wished that Professor Aaron Stasney could have compartmentalized his own detachment in a similar way, saving it for his job instead of letting it control his love life. Then he and Jenny might've still been together. She inhaled deeply, taking in a lungful of smoke, and it set her to coughing so violently she doubled up over the sink with a sour burning in her throat almost making her vomit.

When she recovered, she wiped her tears and ran the tap, extinguishing the cigarette and tossing it in the garbage.

At that moment, she made the decision to quit smoking. She tossed the pack away—she had been down to her last three and would've had to buy more. It had dawned on her that she either had to become stronger under this strain or else become weaker and let it kill her. Quitting smoking would be good for her health, if she could pull it off, but it was even more important to her right now as a symbol of the courage and resolve she knew she'd need in order to make it.

Anyway, when she was reunited with her father, she wanted him to see her as a mature, attractive young lady, not a nail-biting chain-smoker always on the verge of losing the handle.

Two whole days without cigarettes later, she got another phone call from Rolf Kollar. Her hand went automatically to her purse, but she didn't have anything to light up. But she felt she could've stifled the urge anyway, even though it was her first real test. Kollar told her that if she wanted to see three "dead men" in the flesh, she must go to the WWVA radio station in Wheeling, West Virginia. She must stand on the sidewalk in front of the broadcast building at six o'clock on Saturday evening. He would meet her there.

It all sounded so cloak-and-dagger that she almost could picture herself dismissing the whole business once and for all as a hollow farce. But instead she agreed to go to Wheeling.

She had to get to the bottom of it all. She had to learn for sure. If a dark curtain dropped over the truth again, it would be unutterably painful. She was weary of leading a life full of unanswered questions. She was scared that even if her father could be gotten out of the sanitarium, he might be recaptured or killed before she could see him. Then she might never find out what had really happened. The cover-up firmly in place again, she might never prove to anybody, even herself, that he hadn't really died seven years ago.

8

The information that Teague had to go on to carry him into one of the most important days of his life was less than scanty, it was threadbare. Someone wanted Thompson out so he could tell his story to the world. Thompson had refused to leave the sanitarium unless Teague and Vickers could go with him. The guard named Corrigan was the go-between for whoever was masterminding the break-out. It was hazardous getting messages to one person, let alone three, in the sanitarium, because the inmates and the guards followed an institutional routine that permitted minimal intercourse between the two separate, unequal entities. So Corrigan had let Thompson know, by whisper and by smuggled note, how to conduct himself on the day of the planned escape, and Thompson had passed the word to Vickers and Teague.

Teague hated being low man on the grapevine. He believed that he had survived so far, and had kept his sanity, by jealously guarding his dignity and his prerogatives against the demeaning pressures of the institution and the numbing, fear-ridden conformity of the other prisoners. He didn't like following orders from Kevin Thompson, whose mind had gone as flabby as his body over the past seven years. But Teague had no other choice, except to pass up a rare, if enigmatic, chance at freedom, turning his back on the real (or false?) promise of seeing Jenny, resigning himself to never having any clearer picture of her than the one he now carried in his mind after making himself chew up and swallow the contraband photos of her that had been smuggled in.

He wondered—was she really in on the escape plan? Or was she up to some treachery, ready to stick a knife in his back the moment he was on the outside? It might be next to impossible to believe this of the Jenny he remembered as a little girl, but now she was grown up, changed, and possibly subverted. Teague had learned the hard way not to trust *anyone.* Even supposing that his daughter's motives were genuine, she still could be a dupe, a pawn, a lure, cleverly used by whoever did not have Teague's best interests at heart. Even so, he had decided he wanted out, no matter what the risks. He would take his chances against whatever ogres he might encounter beyond the electrified fence.

Today he might meet some of the ogres face to face—if the escape plan didn't turn out to be a figment of somebody's feverish imagination. It was now 12:45, the bright May sun high in the blue sky. Lunch had been served at noon, and the inmates were out in the exercise yard, which very few of them used for exercise, so it might as well have been called the "milling around" yard. Teague was to finish jogging, as usual, then join Thompson and Vickers in the shadow of one of the lookout towers—the one manned by Corrigan and one other guard who presumably did not know what was up, so Corrigan would have to somehow take care of him. Teague had no idea what precisely was going to happen. He was simply to do whatever Thompson told him to do, on the spot and in the exigency of the moment.

Obviously, Thompson knew more than Teague and Vickers about what was supposed to occur, but it probably wasn't *much* more, and whatever it was Thompson wasn't saying. Yesterday Teague had pressed him for details, but the ex-test pilot had replied tersely, with a shadow of the old, dashingly confident glint in his eyes: "It's better if you don't know anything more at this point." It added to Teague's anxiety, his sense of being pulled helplessly into a situation rife with alluring promises of salvation mixed with ambiguous threats of destruction and doom. Oddly enough, the fact that he was being told so little heightened his gut feeling that *something* was really going to happen, for it seemed logical to him that the masterminds, whoever they were, would not trust him anymore than he trusted them.

When he jogged over to the tower, to his astonishment Kevin Thompson was embroiled in an esoteric discussion with the inmate nametagged CHUDKO. Even in what were supposedly Thompson's last few minutes in confinement, he still apparently had the urge to convert a disbeliever and, amazingly, his efforts seemed to be bearing fruit. Teague listened to Chudko, surprised at the words coming out of Chudko's mouth, which made him wonder if Chudko was putting Thompson on:

"When I was working with NASA in Houston, my best friend and drinking buddy happened to be a biochemist. His job was to study soil and rock samples brought back by the Venus probe, the Mars probe, and so on. He was looking for organic substances indicating that primitive forms of life might've once existed on other planets. One night when he and I were out getting bombed, he began not exactly rambling, but talking *very* abstrusely. He hinted that some exceedingly *strange* specimens were being kept at Wright-Patterson Air Force Base, specimens that had been studied by our top scientists and then had been preserved in liquid helium."

"Hah! Guess who those top scientists were!" chortled Thompson, glancing meaningfully from Vickers to Teague.

Chudko went on, more intensely. "At the time, I guffawed, taking it all as a drunken put-on, but now, in light of what you've said, I wonder if my friend wasn't being deadly serious deep down, saying more than he *ought* to have said because he was under the influence of alcohol."

Teague was astounded that this kind of talk was coming from a man who had been a nasty hard-nosed skeptic as recently as two weeks ago. Was Chudko's veneer of aloofness crumbling so easily here in the institution? Was he making up stories, suddenly desperate to ingratiate himself with fellow inmates whose company he had formerly, purportedly, disdained? Or (and this possibility gave Teague a chill) might Chudko be a spy for the Blue Ridge authorities?

"I assure you," Thompson said, grinning chummily at Chudko, "that your pal in Houston was trying to tell you something profound. Right, Vickers? Right, Teague?"

Vickers nodded, his fat high-domed head going up and down ponderously, as if it were swollen with spores of secret knowledge—but Teague kept his usual poker face. He didn't see why he should care to convince Chudko of anything. Chudko was going to be left behind in the sanitarium—assuming that the escape was really going to happen. For the thousandth time, Teague wondered nervously about that. So far, today appeared to be shaping up just like any other dull, ordinary, soul-wrenching day in captivity. The bird sounds were the same. The sun was shining just like it did on any other sunny Saturday. Nothing unusual was stirring outside the compound. Not even a foolhardy deer poacher.

Teague shuddered, remembering the charred spot on the ground that he had gingerly avoided while he was doing his laps—the smudge left by the inmate who had gone up in flames. He wondered if he ought to give the faintest credibility to the idea that somebody might try to get him out of here, past the armed guards and the electrified fence.

Then he heard a faint whir that grew rapidly louder as a huge black helicopter loomed up over the treetops. *Blam!* A thunderous belch of flame, and the lookout tower at the opposite end of the compound disintegrated into smoke and rubble.

"Stay here! Don't run!" Thompson yelled.

Teague obeyed, barely controlling his wild urge to flee. The helicopter zoomed and swerved, belching flames from its front-mounted cannon. Chudko took off, but Thompson tackled Vickers before his fat little legs could start churning, then dragged him back toward the base of the tower. Dozens of inmates were running across the exercise yard, trying to find shelter behind one of the squat stone buildings. Machine guns were blasting from two of the three remaining towers. Wounded inmates were screaming, trying to crawl, their bodies ripped by shrapnel. It dawned on Teague why he and Thompson and Vickers might be safe by sticking so close to where the assault helicopter was now heading. It wasn't going to demolish Corrigan's tower. The "inside man" must have taken out the other guard who was up there with him. The chopper was using the "safe" tower as a shield, sneaking around one side and then the other, knocking out the other two towers one at a time by hitting them with demolition shells that reduced the solid structures to piles of twisted steel and smoking concrete. Then the chopper came over the fence, hovering and strafing. About a dozen more sanitarium guards darted out of the buildings, firing automatic weapons. But they were no match for the chopper's cannon and its heavy-caliber, turret-mounted machine guns. Within seconds, most of the guards were cut down. Then there was a momentary lull in the firing.

"Run! Follow me!" Thompson cried.

Charging surprisingly fast for as out of shape as he was, he led Vickers and Teague toward the hovering assault helicopter—just as it landed in the exercise yard about fifty feet from the only intact tower. A guard ran up and tried to toss a grenade, but he was riddled by a staccato burst of bullets, and then his grenade went off under him, blowing him to pieces.

Teague leapt over a severed arm a split second after it flopped in the dirt in front of him. Vickers saw it too, and started vomiting, but kept running in a half stagger.

The door to the chopper opened. No ladder. No stairs. Thompson jumped and grabbed on, but it didn't look like he was going to be able to hoist himself into the bay—he was too heavy and physically wasted. But a pair of arms hauled him in. Then Teague. Then Vickers, who flopped on the floor of the craft, huffing and puffing, stinking of puke, and looking as if he might die of a heart attack. He screamed when a yammering burst of bullets tore through the fuselage. Teague was scared out of his wits, but instead of keeping his head down he sneaked a peek at the chopper pilot; he wanted to see what his "savior" looked like. Their eyes met for barely a second. No warmth passed between them. Just a cold grin. Then the pilot went back to firing his weapons. Some of the guards must be closing in. Where was Corrigan? The pilot hit a button and the hatch closed. The chopper rose upward in a deafening roar of machine-gun fire, then whirred and pivoted so sharply that Teague was thrown against something hard—an armored bulkhead. He wanted to cry out, but he restrained himself. He rubbed his sore shoulder, thankful that he still had a thick sheathe of muscle there to prevent a broken bone. Even through his pain, he kept wondering why Corrigan hadn't been taken on board. The chopper steadied in its flight path, then was rocked by the recoil of its own cannon blast. And Teague made a guess about Corrigan's fate.

The helicopter made one more sharp turn, then accelerated into a constant trajectory. If there were any more gunbursts, they were drowned out by the whirring blades. Soon Teague began to feel relatively safe. He sat up, breathing hard, leaning against a section of armor plate that had been pierced by a couple of bullets, leaving fat, jagged holes. Thompson sat up, too. Then Vickers. The pudgy little man wiped his mouth with his sleeve, glanced down at his puke-stained shirt, then took it off and balled it up, tossing it toward the rear of the chopper. Now he didn't stink so badly, and in the tightly confined bay Teague was grateful for that. He allowed himself to feel a glimmer of hope: if his luck held, he might soon be able to ball up his own sanitarium uniform and throw it away forever. But he'd have to be careful and vigilant. He couldn't fully trust his rescuers. Otherwise, why wasn't Corrigan on board?

In a little while he felt the helicopter slowing down,

then descending, and he peered closely at Vickers and Thompson for some sign as to whether they had any idea where they would land or what was going to happen next. Thompson merely shrugged. Vickers stared straight ahead as though he were in a trance. There were several portholes in the bay, but they were all capped with khaki-colored plastic discs so that the passengers, like troops being carried into combat, could not see exactly where they were headed or what kind of gauntlet they were running. The only one who had a comprehensive field of vision was the pilot; through an aspect of his cockpit bubble, Teague caught a glimpse of blue sky and then nothing but trees. He felt the jolt of touching down, then the hatch slid open again and the engine was turned off.

"Okay!" said the pilot. "Everybody out!" Bouncing up, he unholstered a pistol, clutching it as if he might shoot anyone who didn't promptly obey. Or, was it solely for protection against whatever dangers might be outside the plane?

"Aren't there any stairs?" whined Vickers. "Do we have to jump?"

The pilot laughed, but his laugh, like his grin, was mirthless and cold. "This was a combat chopper for dropping airborne troops in Nam. Their first step out was a helluva lot longer than ours. So move!"

Teague decided he might as well be the first to comply. Ignoring the pain in his bruised left shoulder, he lowered himself to the length of his arms, hung suspended for a moment, then dropped, dipping his knees to absorb the shock. A grassy clearing with thick forest all around. For a second he entertained the notion of just running—disappearing deep in the foliage—if he could get away before a slug from the pilot's pistol thudded into his back. The masterminds behind this were apparently primarily interested in Thompson and his UFO story, so Teague figured he was more expendable to them. Instead of acting on his impulse to flee, he helped fat little Vickers jump down to the ground, taking the brunt of Vickers's weight and holding his breath against the lingering aroma of vomit. Thompson dropped down next, grunting and almost falling. Then the pilot, lithe and cat-like in his camouflage fatigues, as if he had been doing these kinds of things all his life. He looked around warily, pointing his pistol. Then he holstered it, to Teague's great relief. "I need help," he said. "We've gotta push the chopper over there."

He seemed to be pointing at a spot just a few feet away, and Teague couldn't grasp the point; the helicopter would still be near the center of the clearing, easily spottable from the air. "You mean all the way back into those trees?" He gestured toward where he had spied a half-hidden pile of dirt.

"No, down in the pit over there. It's covered by a camouflage tarp."

Following the pilot through some tall weeds, Teague finally saw what he meant. The ground sloped gradually toward the tarp, and it was further disguised by a scattering of pine branches and freshly plucked weeds. The pilot scurried around, yanking out steel pegs, then they all helped pull the tarp back and move aside some log rafters from underneath. They panted and pushed, the pilot snapping at them, till they made the helicopter tumble down into the earthen pit. They were breathing hard from their unaccustomed exertions, especially Thompson and Vickers, but they knew they had to keep moving or else they might be caught. They helped the pilot replace the tarp, peg it down and rearrange the branches and weeds over the top.

"They'll never find it now, unless they fall in," the pilot said, emitting a mirthless chuckle. "Follow me. Don't straggle. We're gonna make it. We'll soon be free as the breeze." He drew his pistol again, whirled around, and darted into the woods.

They hiked for fifteen minutes, as fast as they could go. The pilot didn't seem to make any allowances for men whose physical prowess had been blunted by years of institutional life; or else, maybe he derived sadistic pleasure out of pushing them to their limit. Having no choice but to follow him, they clambered over fallen logs, waded streams, and climbed steep, rocky places where it looked like nobody had ever climbed before. The pace exhausted Teague despite his seven-year effort to keep himself in good condition. He hated to admit that the pilot could outdo him, so he kept pushing to catch up but never really made it. The deeper wound to his ego was that big, flabby Thompson somehow managed to stick close behind him, and Vickers back only a few yards farther, so it went to show what poor physical specimens could do when they were driven by a frenzy of fear and desperation.

They finally stumbled onto a path that had been newly hacked among the trees—a path wide enough to accommodate a fairly large vehicle—and there one was, covered by a camouflage tarp. They were all pooped, especially Vickers, who was so flushed and out of breath it was a wonder he didn't collapse and die. Huffing and puffing, mopping their sweaty faces, they watched the pilot jerk the tarp away from what turned out to be a dark blue Oldsmobile. He opened the trunk to reveal stacks of civilian clothes. He didn't need to tell them to shed their sanitarium uniforms; they were already doing so, even before he started unbuttoning his fatigues. When they had all changed, they hid their discarded garments under the camouflage tarp, weighted it down with stones, and covered it with leafy branches. Then they piled into the big Olds, Vickers and Thompson slumped in back, and drove twenty or thirty yards out of the woods and onto a two-lane blacktop.

The pilot, now the driver, had kept his pistol. It was beside him on the front seat. Teague thought of making a grab for it right now. But he was scared that the man behind the wheel had better reflexes and would beat him. "What about Corrigan?" he forced himself to ask. "Will he be joining us somewhere else?"

"Perhaps in the hereafter," said the driver. "He got shot running across the exercise yard. I had to take off without him. Does that bother you?"

"No, the man was nothing to me," said Teague. He wasn't about to stick up for Corrigan, it might cause him to be the next one shot. He was pretty sure that the "inside man" had not been killed running across the exercise yard. He figured that Corrigan must have perished in the final cannon blast from the helicopter, just before they all zoomed away from the sanitarium. "Where are we headed now?" he ventured to ask. It amazed him that Vickers and Thompson didn't seem curious about anything. They were simply flopped there in the back seat like lumps of jelly while whatever was going to happen to them just went on happening, their lives still being programmed for them by other people the way it had been done for them in the institution.

"It's best that I don't tell you our destination," said the man behind the wheel, "in case we don't make it. If we're all captured and you break down under pressure, you won't be able to tell them what you don't know."

"Is there any information you *can* give us at this point, Mister…"

"Mr. Smith. No, except if we make it, you'll meet the man behind this. You'll be safe in his hands. He'll be able to answer all of your questions."

"Will I see my daughter Jenny?" Teague asked, trying not to sound as anxious as he felt.

"We're expecting her, as you know, but whether or not she actually shows up is up to her. I don't think she's going to cop out. I understand she's pretty determined to see you." Punctuating the end of the conversation, he clicked the car radio on and punched buttons till he got an all-news station.

They only stayed on the two-lane road for about ten minutes before a ramp took them onto a freeway headed northeast. The all-news station was based in Pittsburgh, and Teague thought maybe they were headed there, although he hadn't the faintest idea why this would be so. There was no mention on the radio of a sanitarium breakout in West Virginia, even though events of seemingly lesser significance got plenty of coverage, on a national and international level. How many people had been killed in the break-out? A dozen or a dozen and a half? Either there was a blackout on it, or a high body count didn't sell air time these days.

It was the first radio broadcast Teague had heard in seven years, so he was both fascinated and awed by it, like a man coming out of a partial amnesia. It felt strange to be zooming across a broad sunlit highway listening to a free airing of matters that had been practically *verboten* while he was in captivity. His ears particularly perked up over a brief report on the American Strategic Defense Initiative—"Star Wars"—and Soviet warnings against its deployment. He glanced back to see if Thompson and

Vickers were also keenly listening. They both still were slumped there half dead, oblivious to everything around them. Dressed in their new sportshirts, loafers and slacks, they looked like tired, pallid businessmen made up for a golfers' holiday but unlikely to muster enough energy to leave the clubhouse cocktail lounge.

Come to think of it, maybe a stiff belt of good scotch would revive them. Teague thought he could do with one, and he tried to remember what it used to taste and feel like. He couldn't conjure up any better memory of it than he could of his wife and two daughters. Funny how he could still long for them even though the reality of them had become so intangible over the years, as if they were no longer, for him, creatures of flesh and blood. They had disappeared from his life as much as he had disappeared from theirs.

Jerking his mind away from this disturbing thought, he glanced at "Mr. Smith," who happened to be glancing at his wrist watch. "Two o'clock," he muttered to himself. "Let's try the local news."

He punched a button and caught the tail end of a hillbilly song and a drawling disc jockey proudly proclaiming, "Yawl're listenin' to WWVA's Country Jamboree from the big little city of Wheeling, West Virginia." The music twanged to a close, then there was a used-car-lot commercial featuring a talking rabbit, followed by five minutes of news, sports and weather. Nothing about the Blue Ridge break-out. Teague almost laughed out loud at the Kafkaesque absurdity of today's daring exploits going completely unremarked. Maybe he was dreaming. Maybe he wasn't on the highway to freedom. Maybe it was all as unreal as it felt, and if he pinched himself he'd wake up, still penned behind barbed wire and an electrified fence.

9

At the safe house on a defunct eighty-five-acre farm twenty miles north of Wheeling, Rolf Kollar was also listening to the radio. Hearing nothing on the news about the break-out, he considered the possibility that nothing may have happened. Perhaps something about the setup had spooked Chaney, causing him to back off. Worse yet, disaster may have struck. Maybe Corrigan had turned stool pigeon, causing Chaney to get killed or captured. If so, CIA trigger men could be coming after Kollar at this very moment, and this might be his last day on earth. Fighting down his anxiety, he tried to believe that all must've gone well. The reason nothing was on the news could be because the CIA would have to cover up any successful escape from Blue Ridge. The sanitarium officials wouldn't dare let the public know that three "dead men" were very much alive and on the loose. They'd probably refrain from contacting civilian law enforcement agencies or else feed them a phony story. Using their own special methods, CIA "cleanup men" would work swiftly and covertly, trying to neutralize the situation and regain the upper hand.

Sitting alone in the huge kitchen of the hundred-year-old farmhouse, at a round table so large that it once must have served a family of about a dozen people, Rolf Kollar stared at the faded, flower-patterned wallpaper, sipped at his fourth cup of black coffee, and tried not to bounce up and resume pacing. His jangled nerves won the battle. He went to the stove, turned the burner up under a steam kettle, stared at the stove clock and saw that it said a quarter to three. It was a big, old-fashioned stove, and it seemed odd that the clock was still working, but it really was, for it was only a few minutes slower than his digital wrist watch. His pacing feet took him into the living room, where Jason Rawlings had set up the video equipment. It was all turned on and ready to go. Rawlings was sprawled in a threadbare blue easy chair six feet in front of the camera. He was sipping Coke and browsing through a UFO journal. Studio lights and console lights were glowing all around him. The ten-inch monitor screen was filled with a full-figure image of him and his pimples in living color. The three escapees were going to sit where he was sitting, one at a time, in order to be interviewed. If they ever got there.

"This is exciting," said Rawlings, looking up from his magazine. "Thanks for letting me be part of it."

"Aren't you scared?"

"Not too much, I guess. Chaney really seems to know what he's doing."

"We must remember always to refer to him as 'Mr. Smith' when he gets here," Kollar cautioned. "He doesn't want the escapees to learn his real name. If they do…"

"I know," said Rawlings. "He'll probably kill them."

"And us," said Kollar. "As it is, he barely trusts us."

"He might bump us off anyway, once he gets his money," said Rawlings.

Kollar nodded. He had considered arming himself against possible treachery from Chaney or Corrigan, with perhaps a small pistol tucked under his shirt or under his pant leg, but in the end he had rejected the idea. Chaney was so uncanny he' d probably have sensed that the weapon was there, and that alone might have sealed Kollar's death warrant. For five years in the concentration camp he had lived unarmed in the midst of enemies, and it was somehow a habit that he could not break. He didn't keep guns in his house. Only his dog Taurus. He preferred the protection of a warm, living animal to the protection of cold steel. Right now he missed the dog, whom he had taken to a kennel before leaving Long Island. Taurus would've enjoyed running free here in the country. But it would have been a nuisance taking care of him and keeping him from putting the escapees on edge.

The steam kettle whistled shrilly, drawing Kollar back into the kitchen. He turned the gas down and when the whistle stopped he heard tires on gravel. Leaning over the sink, he peered out the window. It was the Oldsmobile. Chaney was driving, and there were men with him. The escape must've been a success: But it seemed that somebody was missing; behind the tinted glass, Kollar could only make out four heads. He came out onto the rickety wooden porch as the men started getting out of the car, and he was almost relieved that the missing one was Clarence Corrigan. If someone had to not make it, the one he would miss least would be the sanitarium guard. Unless Corrigan had gotten himself captured, still alive and able to blab. It surprised Kollar how pragmatic he was concerning who lived and died and how it might affect his own chances, his own plans; but of course this attitude had been absolutely necessary for self-preservation in the concentration camp, and had served him well afterwards, in tight situations over the years.

The three escapees were staring at him with considerable trepidation as he came down the porch steps onto the gravel driveway. He recognized Teague, Thompson and Vickers from the films and still photographs he had studied, but Chaney introduced them to him anyway. "Rolf Kollar," Norman Teague exclaimed. "What's *your* interest in us? I might as well tell you I've always considered you a…"

"A crackpot," Kollar snapped. "Does it insult you to have been rescued by a crackpot? Or would you have preferred the KGB?"

"How do I know you're not?" Teague probed.

"Do your arguing inside," Chaney broke in sharply. "Don't piss around out here in the open where you can be spotted from the sky. I'm going to put the car in the barn."

But Rolf Kollar stopped him with a question before he could duck behind the wheel. "Mr. Smith…may I ask what has become of Mr. Corrigan?"

"Didn't make it. He was shot rappelling down from the tower. He's dead."

Kollar saw Teague give Chaney a strange look, behind Chaney's back. It was the kind of look one might give to a liar.

"Are you sure, Mr. Smith?" Kollar asked. "Perhaps he was merely wounded."

"I saw him get riddled. He fell about thirty feet. So I figured I might as well blast his tower and give him a proper burial, under a mound of steel and concrete."

Chaney slammed the door of the Oldsmobile and drove it toward the barn. Kollar motioned for the three escapees to follow him into the house. He had no way of knowing for sure that his accomplice had killed Corrigan on purpose, but he strongly suspected that was what had happened. Now Chaney wouldn't have to split the half million dollars. And neither Chaney nor Kollar would have to worry about Corrigan getting caught and ratting on them. The inside man had been the weakest link in the escape operation. So it was a relief to be rid of him, but Kollar had to hope that Chaney intended to go no further in eliminating potential threats to himself.

The deal with Chaney was that he would hang in till the taping sessions were completed and Kollar brought Jenny Teague back from Wheeling to be united with her father. That way Rawlings wouldn't have to be alone with the three escapees at any point. Excited by the presence of the "celebrities," the young ufologist was poking his head out the screen door. His pimples ablush, he held the door open while everyone entered, and blushed even more while he was being introduced. "Everything's ready in here," he said, shuffling into the living room. The eyes of the three escapees followed him, obviously wondering exactly what was "ready."

"Sit down, gentlemen," Kollar said. "Would you like coffee? Soft drinks?"

Vickers sagged into a chair at the big, round, wooden table but Teague and Thompson both remained standing, glancing all about with a nervous, high-strung attitude, as if they weren't ready to relax into a more vulnerable posture. Teague said, "I might prefer something stronger than a soft drink."

"We have it on hand," said Kollar. "Scotch, bourbon, gin, whatever you like. But it would be better if you'd hold off till after the taping session." Noticing the puzzled, suspicious looks he was getting, he quickly explained himself. "It's urgent for us to document the fact that you three men are alive. We're going to put your testimony on videotape and release your true stories to the world. Once what the CIA did to you has been exposed, we'll all be much safer. Until then, I'm sure you will agree, we're in mortal danger."

"You mentioned soft drinks," Abraham Vickers reminded, his voice mild, high-pitched, almost shy. "I feel completely dehydrated. May I have something tall and cold? Actually, I might need a couple of salt tablets."

"I'm sorry, I didn't think of that," said Kollar. "You men must've been through a lot." He gave his words a sympathetic tone even though privately he meant them as a sarcasm. What could these three softies know of suffering? Nothing that had happened to them could compare with Auschwitz.

"I didn't think we'd make it," Thompson whined. "Your man Smith ran us like dogs."

"Maybe that's why you did make it," said Kollar. "We don't have any salt tablets, but we have plenty of Coke and ginger ale." He could barely control his urge to get started taping, but he realized he had to spend some time catering to these men so they'd begin to relax and trust him. He was annoyed when he opened the refrigerator and found that most of the Coca Cola was gone, thanks to Rawlings, who was addicted to the stuff. There were only two cans left, so he got them out and put them on the table along with a six-pack of ginger ale.

While Kollar had his back turned, filling glasses with ice cubes, Teague saw Thompson edge over to the sink and snatch a steak knife from the drainboard. The ex-test pilot barely managed to slip the knife under his shirt before the man calling himself Smith came in through the screen door and scanned his cold, suspicious eyes around the kitchen.

"Everything okay?" Kollar asked, a bit jittery.

"When I set up a safe house, it stays safe," Smith told him. "I made sure nobody was following us here, so we're not gonna have any unwelcome company. There must be a couple thousand places like this scattered all over the state, and the only way anybody'd home in on this one to check us out would be if we started sending up flares."

Smith went to the table and took the glass of ginger ale Kollar had just filled and started guzzling it, not giving any consideration as to whether it might have been meant for someone else. Vickers already had his. Kollar kept pouring till everybody else got something to drink, including himself.

Teague said, "When do I get to see my daughter?"

"In about three and a half hours," Kollar answered, glancing at his wrist watch. "We're only thirty minutes from Wheeling, West Virginia, and I'm going to meet Jenny in town at six o'clock." He managed a thin, artificial-looking smile. "I'll have her here in time for dinner, Dr. Teague—the first meal you two will have shared in seven years."

"Why isn't she here now?"

"Because, as I said before, the most urgent order of business is for us to make our videotapes. Then, while I go to pick up Jenny, Jason Rawlings will be dubbing off copies for the television networks. We're also going to make copies for safekeeping in the hands of some of our close friends and associates who will make them public in case worse comes to worst and we ourselves are unable to do so."

"What about the escape?" Thompson blurted.

"You've committed a crime. You'll be blamed for the deaths…"

But Kollar cut him off, raising his voice adamantly. "I don't want to hear any more of the gory details, Colonel Thompson. As far as I'm concerned, I paid a man for delivering you to me, no questions asked. If there was a crime committed, it was when you were detained illegally in the first place. That was kidnapping, a federal offense. Since when is it criminal to rescue men from their kidnappers?"

The rhetorical question hung in the air and nobody took a stab at answering it. The issue didn't interest Teague, and he didn't see why Thompson would bring it up. It was fine with him that Kollar had been willing to stick his neck out to buy him his freedom. The important question was why. What were Kollar's true motives? How far could he really be trusted?

"I believe that if I can prove you men are who you say you are, no one will dare prosecute me," Kollar declared. "In fact I'll be widely regarded as a hero. We all will."

"But I don't think you're in this merely for that kind of glory," said Teague. "So, level with us. What's your true interest in us?"

Outrageously amused by the timbre of the discussion, the man called Smith emitted a coarse, derisive chuckle. Leaning against the sink, he chugged the last of his ginger ale, eyeing everyone, smirking, as if he believed himself to be the only sane person present. With a loud crash, he hurled his ice cubes into the basin. Kollar blinked rapidly, clearly disapproving of Smith's behavior but unwilling to challenge him. Teague sympathized with the unwillingness. Smith would have seemed menacing even without the big .45 automatic that was tucked in his belt.

Kollar made eye contact with Vickers, Teague and Thompson. "I'm not sure I'm equally interested in all three of you. It depends on what you have to tell me. I've been trying to investigate your case, Colonel Thompson, ever since your plane supposedly crashed and killed you. I know that you saw a UFO that day, and the government is trying to cover up the incident. I want you to help me bring out the truth." Kollar's voice rose, as he became more vehement. "Even though I got you out of the sanitarium, Dr. Teague, you still wish to think of me as a crack-pot, and you have the nerve to almost say so to my face. Well, I am fed up with that sort of ridicule. I deserve to be recognized as a serious researcher, a leader in the investigation of man's origins. I want to break a story that will establish my credibility once and for all, and silence my detractors."

"You're going to be amazed at how well we can help you do that," said Thompson, breaking into a broad smile that made his face look chubby and foolish. "Right, Vickers? Right, Teague?" he said, leering like a gargoyle.

"Vickers and I can corroborate Thompson's story beyond your wildest dreams," Teague said to Kollar.

"So let's get this show on the road!" Smith barked. "I'm not hanging in here any later than seven o'clock tonight. That was our deal, Rolf. After Jenny gets here, you pay me my money and I'm gone. Whatever heat comes down on you after that, I'm not responsible."

Kollar got to his feet, sliding his chair across the worn linoleum. "Colonel Thompson, will you come with me, please? I'd like you to be the first one to go before our camera."

Left in the kitchen with Vickers and Smith, Norman Teague wished he had been the one to get his hands on the steak knife, not Thompson. The ex-test pilot was so out of shape mentally and physically that he might try something he couldn't pull off. If Smith had to shoot Thompson, he'd probably keep on shooting, once his trigger finger started twitching, till dead bodies were piled all around him. Obviously the man was utterly ruthless and could kill without compunction. He had told two contradictory stories about Corrigan's death, almost as if he wanted everybody to sense the truth beneath the lies and to fear him all the more for it. First he had said that Corrigan was shot running across the exercise yard, then that he was shot rappelling down from the tower. Teague figured the second story was most nearly accurate: Corrigan had been blasted by the chopper cannon, not machine-gunned by his fellow guards. Smith had taken the opportunity to coldly eliminate one of his co-conspirators.

Even though they were into a "good guy, bad guy" act, Teague didn't trust Rolf Kollar any more than he trusted Smith. If Kollar was on the level, why wasn't Jenny there already? It would've been the easiest way for him to demonstrate good faith, instead of jibber jabbering about his precious "credibility." Teague severely doubted that his daughter was going to show up at all. If Smith and Kollar were working for the KGB, Teague and his two fellow escapees might be killed after their "benefactors" extracted all their secrets. But still, he decided not to hold back when it came his turn to be interviewed. He had waited seven years to tell his story, and in order to deal effectively with his enemies, real and suspected, it would be advantageous for him to possess a videotape of the sort that Kollar was so hot to obtain. He was sick of being controlled and manipulated and intellectually deprived in the sanitarium, and he longed to be absolutely free and on his own, free from the ambiguity of trying to distinguish friend from foe, free of all the people meddling in his life whether their intentions were good or bad. Thompson must be thinking along the same lines, experiencing the same irrefutable hunger for autonomy. That was why he had a knife hidden under his shirt. Teague felt a powerful desire to get his hands on a weapon, too. Then when the right moment came he could join Thompson in the fight for survival and freedom.

Behind the video camera, young Jason Rawlings wore a grin of unabashed excitement and triumph, but Rolf Kollar was trying to remain scrupulously calm and objective. Kollar reminded himself that thus far Colonel Kevin Thompson's story wasn't markedly different from UFO abductions described in the past by hundreds of people with no more proof than what Thompson seemed able to offer. Of course it was tempting to think that he must be telling the truth, these things must really have happened to him, and to shut him up the government had told the world that he had died in a plane crash. But unless he could back himself up with hard evidence, his own testimony would serve to convince skeptics that no matter who he claimed to be, he was quite obviously suffering from paranoid delusions and deserved to have been locked up in a sanitarium.

Thompson finished telling of how the extraterrestrials had examined him telepathically, vacuuming his naked skin with their insect-like eyes, giving him an eerie, tingling sensation, a feeling that his thoughts were being suctioned right out of his brain. Then he fell into a deep, trance-like sleep, and when next he awoke he was standing alone in the desert, the hot sand burning the soles of his bare feet, and the saucer that had dropped him off was lifting into the sky.

He slumped forward in the blue armchair and covered his face with his hands, as if it was too painful to go on remembering. Kollar hung back, patiently giving his interviewee time to pull himself together. Whether the story was true or not, it would create a sensation once it was brought before the public. Kollar wanted hard proof, if possible. But, failing that, he felt he would fulfill his mission by proving that a dead man was still alive, and by shocking the "reputable scientists" who wanted to ostracize him. He would pull their heads out of the sand and pry their eyes open to a whole universe of possibilities that they were trying wholeheartedly to deny.

"Should I keep rolling?" Rawlings blurted. "I mean if he's not gonna keep talking we're wasting tape, right?"

"*Shhh!*" Kollar hissed, angrily. "Don't you dare stop that camera!" It amazed him that his young assistant was too obtuse to realize how much Thompson's credibility would be enhanced in people's minds when they saw him so overwhelmed by an incident that had happened seven years ago. The Brazilian peasant, Manuel Campos, hadn't given any such display of emotion on tape. And, although his tale could not be called unimaginative, its sexually lurid aspects made it inherently less believable for Kollar than what he was hearing now at first hand.

"Continue at your own pace when you feel ready," he encouraged.

Thompson looked up, his eyes wide and unfocused. He began telling of the crash of the saucer, and Kollar's heart started pounding wildly as a chill of expectation shot through him. Maybe hard proof actually existed! Unless the saucer disintegrated completely upon impact, debris might have been salvaged. Remains of extraterrestrial navigators may have been recovered. Kollar made a renewed effort to remain levelheaded. He listened keenly, formulating questions he was anxious to ask in his cross-examination.

Teague knew that if push came to shove Abraham Vickers would be as useless as a fat blob of protoplasm. Obviously, he had given his all to get this far. Now he was staring complacently at the peeling wallpaper, guzzling ginger ale as if he would die without it. He probably didn't dare to even contemplate the possibility that in escaping from Blue Ridge he and Thompson and Teague might have jumped out of the frying pan and into the fire.

Smith was still leaning against the sink, his watchful eyes never still, his back never turned toward anybody. He was positioned so he could glance out the window now and then without making himself vulnerable. Even without the big .45 tucked in his belt, his presence would have been intimidating. It would probably take two people to overpower him, and Vickers didn't count. So Teague would wait. He wasn't willing to die foolishly.

When Kollar and Thompson came out of the taping room and into the kitchen, Vickers asked, "How did it go?" He sounded blandly cheerful, as if he was asking about the weather.

"Fine!" said Thompson with surprising gusto. "I'm glad it's all off my chest and preserved for others to see and hear. No matter what happens to me now, I'll know that nobody can stop me from having my say, so long as the tapes stay safe."

"They will if I have anything to do with it," said Kollar. "So which one of you wants to be next? Dr. Teague?"

"You might as well take Dr. Vickers before he falls asleep," said Teague, pretending to joke, but actually trying to stay with Thompson in case the knife could be brought into play. Smith and Kollar chuckled. Vickers jumped up, looking embarrassed, and followed Kollar into the taping room.

Teague was worrying about how he and Thompson might be able to get the jump on Smith now that they were alone with him. Their best hope would be to surprise him. Two against one, a knife against a gun. But Smith didn't seem to be the type of person to ever let his guard down. And it bothered Teague that he didn't know what additional weapons Kollar or Rawlings might have in the taping room.

He turned when he felt Thompson looking at him, and when their eyes locked for several long seconds he tried to send a silent message that they were both on the same wavelength and he was ready to follow Thompson's lead. Thompson smiled knowingly. "It won't be long now," he said. "After they put you on tape, you'll get to see your daughter."

Teague gave two short, slow nods to show Thompson he understood that they would not make their move until after Kollar left to pick up Jenny. That way the odds would be more favorable.

Kollar was allowing himself to feel a growing sense of elation. At last his great personal risks seemed on the verge of being fully justified. Not only was Dr. Vickers corroborating Colonel Thompson's story, but it was apparent that additional corroboration would be elicited from Dr. Teague when he was brought in to be taped. What an adventure the two scientists had shared! Together they had seen things that other mortals had only dreamed about. They had glimpsed the end of the rainbow that Kollar had been following all through his writing career.

Vickers and Teague were on their way to a meeting at

Universal Dynamics in Washington, D.C., when they
received a coded message that they must proceed instead
to the New Mexico Air Force Base where their friend
Colonel Kevin Thompson was stationed. No reason was
given for the change in orders. Upon arriving at the base,
they were debriefed—but painstakingly tactful as the
process was, it could not allay their doubts or diffuse the
awesome impact of what they were told they would soon
see. Even when Thompson was brought in to tell them
what had happened to him, they were unable to suspend
their disbelief. Nevertheless, after the debriefing they
were taken by helicopter to an area in the desert where
an alien spacecraft had crashed.

"We were all half in a daze," said Vickers. "Befuddled,
or maybe flabbergasted would be a better word. I don't
know how we managed to go about getting our assignments done. The scientists and the military men, supposedly hard-nosed, objective people, were every bit as
stunned as the civilian authorities on hand. The enormity
of the event dwarfed anything that had happened
throughout history—it was only a bit less intimidating
than meeting God—especially if you didn't believe in
Him any more than you believed in UFOs. When we were
being debriefed, words like "hoax" and "mass hysteria"
had tumbled through our brains, and now that we were
seeing what we were *told* we would see, we still had the
feeling that if we blinked our eyes it would all go away.
But of course it didn't, and we had to deal with it. For
one thing, now we knew for sure that mankind wasn't
alone in the universe. And for another thing, Thompson
had seen three saucers—did that mean the other two
might be coming back? And if so, would they blame us in
some way for what had happened to their comrades?"

Vickers paused and wiped his brow. Kollar glanced at the video monitor and saw that Rawlings was zooming to a close-up of the pudgy, mild-mannered scientist. His very meekness of demeanor seemed to belie the notion that he could be capable of elaborately contrived deceit. He was one of the most believable subjects that Kollar had ever interviewed.

"Sharing one of the most bizarre experiences that man has ever faced," Vickers went on, "Dr. Teague and I leaned on each other for moral support. Our job was to learn as much as possible—from the wreckage—about the design of the saucer and its propulsion system. Other scientists were there to photograph and do autopsies on the corpses of the aliens killed in the crash. To our amazement, their bodies were intact, as if they had been in a kind of suspension that had shielded them from the impact, so that they had died instead from exposure to our atmosphere once the integrity of their craft was breached. We took several days performing our on-site studies, under a complete communications black-out with the outside world. Then the wreckage was trans-ported to Wright-Patterson Air Force Base in Ohio for further analysis. Autopsies were done on the alien corpses, and then they were taken to Wright-Patterson, where I believe they are still preserved. Like the other scientists at work on this extraordinary project, Teague and I did our best to furnish military personnel and government officials with all the data we could compile. But when they got everything they wanted out of us, they drugged us unconscious, and we awoke to find ourselves caged behind barbed wire and an electrified fence.

"Blue Ridge Hospital," Kollar murmured. "You have

my sympathy. I, too, was caged like an animal...at Auschwitz."

"We were locked up as if we were lunatics who couldn't be trusted!" Vickers whined.

But at least you got clean clothes and three square meals a day, Kollar thought. *You weren 't waiting with thousands of other human skeletons to be gassed and cremated, barely managing to keep body and soul together in the smoky stench of the corpse ovens.*

"If you help us tell our story to the world," said Vickers, "we can force our government to admit the truth. I'm sure the Soviets know what's going on too, and are helping to suppress the facts. Think of it! We actually have irrefutable evidence that we aren't the only highly intelligent beings in creation. There must be an entire civilization somewhere, far more advanced than our own. But instead of seeking to befriend these extraterrestrials and learn great things from them, our government wants to pretend they don't even exist."

"Why?" Kollar probed. "Why do you think this is so?"

"Our leaders are afraid. They believe that the public won't be able to deal with the truth. Panic will upset the status quo, the delicate balance of power, or as Churchill called it, the 'balance of terror' between nations. In the resulting climate of hysteria, we earth people will destroy ourselves even if the creatures from that other world don't come back and do it for us."

"It's certainly a scenario deserving of consideration," Kollar admitted.

In close-up on the video monitor, Vickers suddenly appeared less bland. A spark of anger flashed in his pale, watery eyes. "I disagree with you completely," he said adamantly. "I am not in favor of the suppression by the state of the human need to explore and understand and deal with all knowledge, philosophical and scientific. Dr. Teague and I are of one mind on this. That is why we were both made to suffer so much during the past seven years. I expect we could've kept our freedom if we could've been depended upon to go along with the cover-up."

"But surely you must realize," Kollar said, "that the history of the human race is the history of the strong exploiting the weak. Technology has been the chief weapon of the exploiters, enabling advanced civilizations to overrun or enslave those that happened to be less advanced. And the ones who possess technological superiority seem to have no trouble convincing themselves that they are morally right—everybody else must be genetically inferior, deserving of being exploited or exterminated. It is how the Nazis explained their ruthlessness toward the Jews, and how the white race convinced itself it was not sinful to enslave the Negro and virtually wipe out the Indian tribes." He paused to let his points sink in. "What if these extraterrestrials are vastly superior to us in all the factors that to them connote a civilized, humane society? They might perceive us as an inferior life form, unworthy of any deeper consideration than we give to monkeys...or to homo sapiens whose skin color or religion happens to be unlike our own. If we are able to deal so callously toward members of our own species, how might these extraterrestrials behave toward us?"

"That is the great fear our leaders have," said Vickers, dolefully shaking his head. "It's almost as if they are suffering from a sense of their own inferiority. They think we are unworthy of coexisting with more intelligent, less barbaric denizens of other worlds, and so they can't imagine that we'll be allowed to exist. They apparently feel that we will be eliminated by our intellectual and moral superiors as a surgical, defensive measure so that our primitive warlike attitudes won't contaminate other galaxies."

"Maybe they won't destroy us," Kollar mused. "Maybe they'll simply force us to lay down our arms and stop behaving like imbecilic savages." He chuckled as an afterthought struck him. "But once we've been rendered docile, what's to prevent them from cultivating us like herds of cattle, or using us like workers in an ant colony?"

"Our leaders don't have any intention of laying down their armaments," said Vickers. "On the contrary, they've embarked on a tremendous effort to develop bigger and better weapons of destruction to be used not only against earthly nations but against any invasion that may come from some other part of the universe."

10

F ollowing Rolf Kollar's advice, Jenny Teague traveled under an assumed name. Holding airline tickets made out to "Jenny Trask" added to her sense of unreality. It seemed ironic that she should have to pretend to be someone else in order to help her father reclaim his true identity. But if all went well they both would be able to stop living the lies that had been forced upon them.

She flew Peoples Express from Washington to Pittsburgh, then had to lay over for two hours before a small shuttle plane took her from Greater Pittsburgh International to the little airport on the outskirts of Wheeling, West Virginia. All the way, she kept wondering if she was making a fool of herself. She didn't see or hear anything in the news about any escapees from a sanitarium. Maybe the whole thing really would turn out to be a figment of Rolf Kollar's imagination. Maybe Kollar himself had faked the photos, using actors as doubles for the three "dead men". Jenny didn't know what to believe at this point. She felt guilty for not leveling with her mother. She longed to see her father again, and yet she dreaded the possibility of actually meeting an older, and perhaps drastically changed, Norman Teague in the flesh. In a way, she almost wished that the whole thing would end up a wild goose chase, but at the same time she knew it was wrong of her to entertain that wish, for it would be the equivalent of wishing her father dead.

The taxi she caught at the airport had country music blaring from the radio. The cabbie was a scrawny, long-haired kid in an ersatz leather jacket. "I want to go to the WWVA radio station," she told him as he jumped out to take her overnight bag.

"That's Capitol Music Hall," he said, staring at her excitedly, as if she might be a celebrity. "Are you in the show tonight?"

"No, I just have to meet a friend there."

Disappointed, he put her bag in the trunk, next to a cheap guitar case. She'd have liked to ask him if he played guitar, but that might've opened up a conversation in which she'd have been obliged to say that she also played, and she didn't want to say anything revealing about herself. Once she got in the cab, it turned out that conversation would've been impossible anyway, because of the loudness of the radio. The cabbie sang along with every song and knew all the words by heart—a further indication of his musical aspirations—but he was seldom on key, which wasn't surprising since constant exposure to that kind of volume was probably making him tone deaf. Jenny knew and liked some of the songs too, had sung a few of them in the saloon in Georgetown, and after today's ear-beating she'd probably have to sing them again just to prove to herself she could still do it without going as off-key as the cabbie. A disc jockey roared that she was listening to "WWYA, home of the

Wheeling, West Virginia Country Jamboree," and she hoped the station wouldn't come in stronger and louder as she got closer. On both sides of the highway, billboards were advertising the Jamboree, trying to make it seem bigger and grander than Nashville's Grand Ol' Opry.

Downtown Wheeling was a fairly big place, crowded with pedestrians and motorists on a sunny Saturday. There were more tall buildings and big stores than Jenny had expected. Neither had she expected this to be much of a college town, so she was surprised at the large numbers of young people on the streets, many of them wearing jackets and sweatshirts with fraternity or sorority emblems. The older people seemed to run the gamut from business types in three-piece suits to farmers or coal miners in bibbed coveralls. Before Jenny had time to dope out the scene and get used to it, the cabbie dropped her off in front of Capitol Music Hall, a massive gray stone building with a shining white dome and a glittering marquee announcing the 60th Anniversary of the Country Music Jamboree. Shouldering her overnight bag, she glanced at her wrist watch. It was only 4:45. She had left her Georgetown apartment almost five hours ago, and she still had an hour and fifteen minutes to kill. Traveling on her own, dealing with buses, planes and taxis, always made her tired and nervous, and this time it was much worse because of her anxiety over how her escapade was going to end. But she had been able to fight down the temptation to buy cigarettes, and this made her proud. Feeling conspicuous standing in one spot on the sidewalk (as if somebody might guess just by looking at her that she was part of a "plot"), she decided to go for a walk up and down Main Street. She was wearing a maroon suit with a gray blouse, while other folks her age going in and out of stores, bars and restaurants were mostly in jeans. Normally she would've been dressed more like them, but she had wanted to look spiffier for her father.

If some other purpose had brought her here, she might've had fun exploring the local color and digging the music scene, maybe even coming up with material for a newspaper article. But she couldn't write about this trip. Not yet, and maybe not ever.

She stopped to read a poster for tonight's show at Capitol Music Hall, and was surprised at how many big stars were on the bill. It made her feel good that the cabbie had taken her for one of the entertainers, since one of her fantasies was that she could have that kind of career, instead of one in journalism, if she chose to push herself hard in that direction. The poster was in the window of a hot dog joint, and the sweet, tangy smells wafting out to the street reminded Jenny that she hadn't eaten anything since leaving home, but she was still too nervous to be hungry. Next to the hot dog joint was a Country Souvenir Shop. She spent some time admiring a display of lovely little statuettes sculpted from West Virginia coal by Appalachian artists. It hadn't occurred to her before to bring her father a present, and now she grasped at the idea as a potential ice breaker. She went in and bought him an astronaut carved in anthracite and had it gift wrapped, hoping it would please him because, after all, he had worked for NASA. But part of her feared that this reminder of his old job might not conjure up happy memories.

It was ten minutes to six by the time she walked back to Capitol Music Hall, telling herself to act nonchalant standing on the sidewalk. She almost didn't believe Rolf Kollar would show up, and when it got to be a quarter past, her doubts increased, making her very fidgety. If he didn't show, she'd be in an absolute quandary, not knowing what to make of it. Back in Georgetown she had impulsively bought one of his books and read it cover to cover, as if it might give a clue to his sanity, his veracity. She had to admit that some of his ideas were intriguing, if preposterous. His main tack was to take an "amazing fact that cannot be explained by modern science" and then extrapolate upon it by coupling it with other "strange facts." What is the mysterious power of the pyramids? Why do some primitive cave drawings resemble creatures in space helmets? Since we do not know how the pyramids were built and they seem to be beyond the technology of their time, could they have been constructed as space stations by ancient visitors to our planet? Where did the pharaohs get the idea of having themselves mummified so they could wait for the "gods" to come back and revive their bodies? Did they witness the "gods" being revived from a state of suspended animation after a lengthy space voyage? Any of this farfetched stuff was just barely *possible*, Jenny thought, even though her intellect rejected it. It was the kind of speculation that couldn't be disproved by analysis or investigation. Kollar's extraterrestrials were like ghosts: he admitted they weren't around anymore, so you couldn't show they didn't exist by not finding them. You had to let them dwell in a tiny space in your imagination.

Kollar was seeming more like a ghost, too. It was half past six. Where was he? Jenny's eyes kept darting up and down the street. Traffic was thinning out. Should she leave or should she stay? When Kollar pulled over to the curb in his tan Volksbus, she almost jumped out of her skin because she had come so close to giving up on him.

He was smiling. He didn't seem at all scared. Did this mean nothing had gone wrong? Or nothing had happened?

As she climbed into the Volksbus, he reached across the empty passenger seat for her maroon overnight bag and tossed it in back. She almost stepped on a Coke can with her high heel, which could have twisted her ankle. "Sorry," Kollar said. "My young assistant—you'll meet him—is a bit sloppy. He seldom cleans up after himself." She slammed the door and buckled herself in. "You look lovely," Kollar said, pulling out into sparse traffic. "Your father will be proud of you. He's less than a half hour away, and very anxious to see you."

Jenny caught her breath. The mere mention of the possibility of seeing her father sounded strange and thrilling, far stranger than any of the bizarre notions in Kollar's books. To what extent did she dare believe in him? She reminded herself that he was the type of person who might be easily fooled. A large part of him probably wanted to be fooled because he ached so hard for proof of his theories. As they zipped across a bridge, heading out of town a different way from the way she had come in, she let her breath out slowly and forced herself to resume breathing normally, as if nothing extraordinary was happening to her. "Are you sure it's him?" she asked Kollar, trying to sound calm and levelheaded.

"Of course!" he proclaimed zestily. "There is no question! Vickers and Thompson, too. You will see, they are with him. They were all imprisoned for the same reason. What a marvelous event they took part in, Jenny! Wait till they tell you about it. I know you won't fully believe it till you hear them with your own ears, see them with your own eyes."

"Tell me," she pleaded, no longer able to remain as calm as she wished. "Give me some idea what to expect. How should I deal with…with my father?" She wondered why she couldn't think of him as "Daddy." It was what she had always called him and how she had always thought of him, as a little girl. Was this an indicator of how far she had grown away from him? Of her inability to believe in him? If he came back to her, would she be able to close the emotional gap?

"Deal with him?" Kollar asked, repeating her own doubtful-sounding words. "Show him that you care, that you are on his side. It is what he craves. He kept asking for you, he wanted so badly to see you right away, but it was important to get the videotapes made first."

"What videotapes?"

Jenny listened with mounting incredulity as Kollar rambled ecstatically about the "corroborative testimony" Teague, Thompson and Vickers had given him, "an irrefutable confirmation" of a tremendous government cover-up of a UFO crash. "I still have to get more information on tape," Kollar said. "I didn't have time to do it all—but there is enough to protect us. The CIA won't dare harm us once they realize they won't be able to get their hands on all the copies of the tapes, they can't prevent our story from being told. Tomorrow I'll record more data—details of scientific knowledge gleaned from the crash—discoveries far in advance of anything previously known on this earth. No one will be able to seriously doubt its extraterrestrial origins. If we can force the government to release photographs of the wreckage and the corpses being kept in cold storage at Wright-Patterson…"

"Corpses in cold storage?" Jenny mumbled.

"In liquid helium," said Kollar. "Cryogenically frozen,

the way some rich earth people have themselves preserved after they die, in hopes of being revived in the future, when we learn how to do so."

Modern mummies, Jenny thought. Cryogenics. The latest brand of hope for an afterlife. Technological hope for immortality. To Kollar, it must make perfect sense. It lent a symmetry to his theories. If we had pharaohs today, they'd have themselves cryogenically frozen after death, instead of having their organs scooped out and their skins dried and stretched over their skeletons. "My father believes in this stuff?" she muttered, her voice so faint it might have been coming out of a foggy dream of the past or the future.

"He *corroborates* it!" Kollar boomed. "All three of these great scientists back each other up in every detail, even when interviewed separately. I tried hard to trick them, to trip them up, but I could not do it, and I assure you I'm a skilled interrogator. You will admit I got things out of *you* that you didn't want to give, won't you? I am sure these men can pass a lie detector, and they will, as soon as I can get them into a closed session with a polygraph expert. They've all three agreed to be tested, Jenny." He turned his head for a moment while he was driving and peered at her so intently it made her hands twitch. "Don't be scared. Your father is *normal*. He was put away because of what he *knew*, and for no other reason. You'll soon see for yourself, he is in full possession of his mental faculties."

Jenny wanted desperately to believe him. But now she was more confused, more panicky and scared than ever. Was Kollar crazy or not? "The safe house," he pointed out, as he pulled the Volksbus off the two-lane blacktop onto a long, rutted, dirt-and-gravel driveway. She stared at the plain, white, two-story farmhouse beckoning in the distance, shadowed by several tall old poplars, like a ghost house in a horror story. She tried to soothe her jumbled emotions by telling herself that most of the mystery and suspense would soon be over. The unimaginable was actually going to happen: her father was going to come to her like a corpse back from the grave.

Kollar hit the brakes so hard they screeched, the Volksbus lurching so violently that if Jenny hadn't been buckled in, she'd have hit her head against the windshield. "Christ!" she snapped, glowering at Kollar. But his face was ashen, his jowls clenched, and she whirled to see what he was staring at. A sick feeling hit her in the pit of her stomach. The screen door was ajar, held open by a pair of legs sticking out onto the front porch. The legs were perfectly still, one buckled under the other in a jutting angle, an odd angle, that made Jenny know that the person whose head she could not see was no longer alive. Her father? She was scared to make a move, scared to go and find out. Maybe if he stayed in the Volksbus this moment would stay forever frozen in time and she'd never have to face whatever horrors were yet to come.

"Not your father," Rolf Kollar blurted, as if he had read her mind. "Not one of the escapees. It is Jason Rawlings...my assistant...1 can tell from here."

But Jenny wondered who else might be dead inside the house. And she still didn't dare to move a muscle. "Don't!" she cried when Kollar opened his door. His eyes flickered, but he ignored her and got out. Now she was terrified of being left alone in any one spot. So she opened her own door and got halfway up, but her legs were so rubbery she fell back. Summoning a curious, contradictory mixture of fear and courage to impel her to action, she made herself climb down from the vehicle and stand on the gravel in her wobbly high-heeled maroon shoes. Kollar was already up on the porch, and she followed him as though something awful would happen to her if she didn't—but she knew something awful was going to happen anyway.

She heard the flies buzzing and swarming and smelled the cloyingly sweet puddle of warm blood that had attracted them. Nausea overpowered her and she staggered a couple of steps and vomited on the grass. Thankfully, not much came up but stomach acid since she hadn't eaten for a long time, hadn't yielded to the temptation to buy a hot dog to kill time in town. She blotted the sourness from her lips with a hanky from her jacket pocket, then let the hanky drop from her fingers.

She crept up behind Kollar, startling him as he put his fingers on the screen door. He stopped what he was doing long enough to look at her, then look back. She hovered close to him, shielding her body with his, not only because she was afraid something might jump out at her, but because it seemed easier to look at the corpse over someone else's shoulder. The screen door creaked open in Kollar's fingers, and she saw the head half blown away in the thick red puddle, the inner door splattered with gore. But Kollar was looking past that awful sight... toward something else. Jenny forced herself to peek around his shoulder and shuddered when she saw two additional corpses back in the shadows, lying face down on the bloody linoleum floor.

"I think it's Thompson...and Chaney," Kollar murmured in a hoarse whisper. "We've got to go in and see. Oh, God, this is terrible," he moaned. "Maybe they're all..."

All dead, Jenny finished the thought. Maybe they were all dead. Even her father. And who had killed them? Kollar? No. She denied that splinter of fear even as it pierced through her. How could Kollar be the murderer? He had seemed genuinely excited over the information he had gotten from the escapees and he had said he needed to get more, so he would have wanted to keep them alive. But if he were insane? Then nothing about him might be as it seemed. And Jenny might be next to die. She jumped back as Kollar turned toward her. He let the screen door go shut on the dead body wedged in the doorway. She wished she could close her ears on the mad buzzing of the blood-hungry flies.

Kollar said, "We'll go around back, in through the living room. This old house is laid out strangely. When you approach from the road, you enter the kitchen first. Probably the farmers wanted it that way so they wouldn't have to always track mud on their living room carpets."

Jenny barely heard him. She dimly realized he must be babbling to allay fear, his own fear as well as hers. He, too, was shocked and dumbfounded—scared. So he couldn't be the murderer, and she felt almost guilty for entertaining the suspicion. They had to go into the house together. They had to find out for sure which ones were dead. Since there was too much blood and gore to step gingerly around the bodies in the kitchen, they would have to go in through the living room. Dreading what else they might find, she followed him around the side of the house.

There was no screen door on this side, just ripped-out holes where the hinges ought to be. The old, weather-beaten wood door was locked, and Kollar fumbled for a key as he and Jenny stepped up onto the back porch. It wasn't in as good repair as the other porch, and she had to be careful not to poke a high heel through one of the holes in the rotted floor boards. The door was warped tightly against the jamb; Kollar had to slam it with his shoulder to make it open. The noise sounded obscene to Jenny; it was as if they were forcing their way into a tomb. Trying not to tremble, she followed Kollar in, glancing warily all about her as she moved past the blue armchair, the camera, and the rest of the video equipment.

In the hall between the living room and kitchen, Kollar said, "Wait here. I'll check out the upstairs."

His footsteps creaked up the dusty, uncarpeted stairs. Her eyes stayed with him, obsessively following him—so she wouldn't have to look the other way, past the hallway, into the kitchen. She stayed rooted in one spot, listening to him moving around up there. Finally, he appeared on the landing, towering above her, silhouetted against a grimy, uncurtained window. "Nothing," he announced with a hoarse sigh. He came softly down the stairs and placed a hand on her shoulder. She had always thought of him as a cold-hearted man, but she knew that now he was making an effort to comfort her a bit, and she appreciated it.

"I'll go in first," he said, his eyes flickering toward the kitchen.

She nodded meekly. She understood that he was trying to make it easier for her by not obliging her to look closely at any of the dead men until he could tell her exactly what she was going to see. He had jumped the gun by saying that none of them was her father, but he wasn't quite sure, and he was doing his best to prepare her for a greater shock than what she might already be expecting.

He went into the kitchen, leaving her standing there, and shortly she heard some ugly, bone-chilling noises, and she knew he must be turning two of the bodies over. "I was right," he called out hoarsely. "Chaney, Rawlings and Thompson. The other two are gone. Vickers and your father."

He tiptoed toward her. Her eyes darted downward, then jerked back up—he was making bloody footprints on the linoleum. He stooped and took off his shoes before stepping onto the hallway carpet.

Jenny shuddered. She entertained a flicker of hope that since her father hadn't been killed in this house, maybe he was still alive. "Is it really Kevin Thompson?" she heard herself asking, her voice little more than a croak. The answer was keenly important, of course. If she could positively identify Thompson's body, then she'd know for sure that at least there was a grain of truth to the stories Kollar had been telling her.

"You'll have to go in and see for yourself," he said. "I know what you are thinking. I didn't see any of the videotapes anywhere, so they must be gone. For the time being, unfortunately, there is only one way for you to sample a small measure of the proof you are seeking."

He slipped his feet back into his bloody shoes, and she knew what he was going to do. She turned her head away while he dragged the dead body across the floor, sliding it close enough to her that she wouldn't have to walk in the mess made by the murderer.

Her peripheral vision took note of the gaping, bloody chest wound as she made herself look down at the dead face, grimly contorted in its final agony. It was Kevin Thompson. That she was sure of, much surer than she'd have imagined she could ever be. Somehow, finding him in this condition helped confirm her belief in his identity. His facial features were slacker and fleshier than she remembered them, his body heavier, almost corpulent. But he was the same man who had come to her home often seven years ago as her father's friend, and had played with her and teased her and even brought her birthday and Christmas gifts.

"It's him," she told Kollar. She sounded astonished, even to herself. The astonishment came from having her doubts converted to belief all in an instant, when such a large part of her had been expecting something quite the opposite to take place. However, her conversion extended only to the acceptance that this was Kevin Thompson. She still wasn't ready to swallow the bulk of the wild scenario that Rolf Kollar had spouted while driving her out. here. He had plunged her into a nightmare far worse than anything she had bargained for. And despite her effort to remain rational, she had the sense that in this nightmare, even more bizarre things, things that her intellect was still refusing to believe, might yet be possible.

"Since you admit this is Thompson," Kollar said, "you will concede the likelihood that the other two who escaped with him really *were* Norman Teague and Abraham Vickers."

"I...I guess so," Jenny stammered.

He took off his shoes, carrying them as he led her back into the living room. She stood like a zombie by the blue chair while he put the shoes out on the porch, then rummaged through some boxes near the television monitor. "The tapes are gone," he mumbled. "So is the money, from upstairs. There is one more place we have to look."

"Where?"

"The barn. I am sure the car will be gone, too. Wait here. I will check it out myself."

Not taking no for an answer, he went out through the still open door. He didn't put on his shoes till he was down on the grass. Jenny watched him, wanting to follow, not wishing to be left here alone. Mostly the thing that kept her from tagging after Kollar was her fear of what additional discoveries might be waiting in the barn. Staying by herself in the house was horrifying, but at least in here all the deaths were known. She kept staring at her wrist watch, promising herself that if ten full minutes went by, she'd jump in Kollar's Volksbus and take off—if the keys were still in it. But it only took him six minutes to come back. He was wearing his shoes. They were wet. He must've hosed them off.

"Gone!" he fumed. "I told you so! I'm the fool for letting Chaney screw up the whole works. But the money was already his—he didn't need to do this!"

"Since he's dead," Jenny said, "how can you blame *him*? How could he have been responsible?"

"He must've gotten careless, overconfident. He figured he was the pro, we were the amateurs. He thought he could bump us all off and be safe with my money. He didn't want to leave anybody alive who might finger him. Once a snake, always a snake, and it's the way the snake would think. But somebody turned the tables on him—probably Thompson. When Chaney shot Rawlings, Thompson must've jumped on him. He got shot, too, but at least he managed to stick a knife in Chaney's gut. Then Vickers and Teague must've finished Chaney off."

"Then you think they're still alive?" said Jenny. "Where do you think they are?"

"Who knows?" said Kollar. "Running like scared rabbits, I suppose. Wouldn't you? They're probably so confused, the CIA will nab them easily. Then they'll come after me and you."

"How will they know we're involved?"

"Hmph!" Kollar snorted. "They have ways. Torture. Truth serum. Vickers or your father will talk. It won't be their fault, they won't be able to help themselves. Damn it: I was on the verge of a great coup, and now it may never come to light. The CIA will do their job much better this time."

"Look," Jenny murmured through her fear, "I don't know exactly what's going on here, but I still don't believe in anything so weird as a UFO cover-up."

"Oh, don't you?" Kollar snapped. "You should have heard Thompson, Vickers and your father telling about it. If I only had those tapes!"

Jenny stared at him, amazed that he could still be ranting about his lost triumph. "Rolf, you and I are in a lot or trouble," she told him, "and we had better think clearly enough to bail ourselves out. We do know that the government imprisoned three men illegally and had them declared dead. Now, what if we call the Wheeling Police, or even the West Virginia State Police? I can identify Thompson's corpse. His fingerprints will prove he didn't die seven years ago when his plane supposedly crashed. Once we get civilian police in on this—"

"No!" Kollar interrupted. "We can't afford to notify *anybody*! Not if we value our personal safety. The CIA will invoke 'national security' against us. It always takes precedence over police matters. If you and I stick around here, we'll find ourselves in Blue Ridge sanitarium, and nothing we know or suspect will ever disturb anybody else's peaceful dreams."

Taking a deep breath, Jenny said, "I guess I really don't share your belief that civilian law enforcement departments can be so easily manipulated and silenced."

"How naive you are!" Kollar mocked. "Have you learned absolutely nothing from what was done to your own father? If you phone the police, they'll slam you in a cell until the CIA requests that you be turned over to them. You won't be doing your father any good, you'll be *hurting* him. So far, he and his pal Vickers are probably still safe, even if they're confused and scared. Do you want to be the one to put the CIA hot on their trail? They'll land in the sanitarium or the morgue!"

"Then what can we do?" she moaned.

"Jenny, my advice to you is to go home. Sit tight and wait. If your father manages to stay alive, he'll be paying you a call by and by, because he'll be driven by his desire to see you."

11

B rian Meade, the commander of the CIA team sent in to put the lid on Blue Ridge, was forty-two years old, big, baldheaded, slow-moving but not slow-witted. In his eighteen years with the Agency, he had always been a field man, had always plugged away getting his hands dirty instead of hiding behind a desk. He could be counted on to clean up any kind of mess, to do whatever task he was assigned, to the best of his ability. Moral qualms didn't enter in. Long ago he had decided that he was on the right side and that it was absolutely necessary for the right side to sometimes do wrong things in order to survive and win. His baggy, sleepy-looking brown eyes and his fat, droopy jowls, coupled with his slow, plodding manner, often gave others the mistaken impression that he was either lazy or dumb. When the people on the wrong side underestimated him that way, they usually paid.

Blue Ridge was one of the messiest clean-up situations Brian Meade had ever seen. Nothing had gone wrong there before, and now it had gone wrong in spades. Good thing the place was so isolated from the rest of civilization. On the other hand, its very isolation had made the chopper attack possible.

Looking down at the scene from a second-story window of the administration office, Meade found the devastation impressive, rather than terrible; it was a wild chess move made by a resourceful antagonist, and now it was up to him to counter. If he made the right moves, snagging all the errant little pieces, he'd be one of the few people to ever know that a pitched battle had taken place today on American soil.

Down below, bulldozers were working, churning up thick clouds of dust, clearing the rubble of the demolished lookout towers, so that they could be quickly rebuilt. Helicopters were circling low in the sky, making sure no one came close enough to spy or to launch another attack. Meade had two hundred men working for him. First thing they had done was cordon off the whole area—a square mile, all around the sanitarium, fenced in with gigantic rolls of brand-new concertina wire. This newly established perimeter was being patrolled by dozens of armed guards on the ground, backed up by the circling choppers.

Before Meade had arrived at Blue Ridge, guards had shot five inmates and rounded up half a dozen more who had tried to escape into the woods by climbing over the rubble of one of the flattened towers. Two inmates had burned themselves up on the fence; its voltage supply came from a system independent of the towers, so even though they were knocked out, the current in the fence was still hot. The pattern of the char marks showed that the two inmates had actually jumped up and gotten hand holds and toe holds before they were electrocuted.

It was now seven o'clock, almost dusk. It had taken

Meade till just a few minutes ago to establish for sure that there were only three inmates still on the loose. He had had to wait for all the bodies and pieces of bodies to be dragged out of the rubble and identified. Thirteen guards and fifteen inmates were dead. The rest of the inmates were in their cells or in the infirmary being treated for wounds. Except for Haskell, Perry and Blake. They were the birds who had flown the coop. Meade knew this, not only by counting heads, live ones and dead ones, but by listening to a stool pigeon named Chudko who swore those three had shoved him down in the dirt when he tried to stop them from escaping in the assault helicopter.

"Here you are," Dr. Melvin Lieberman said, slamming the drawer of a tall steel file cabinet.

Brian Meade turned from the window. He took the dossiers on Haskell, Perry and Blake from the hairy little hand of the director of Blue Ridge Hospital. Lieberman was small, bony, hirsute; if he shaved twice a day, his face would probably still be tinted black from his pointy cheekbones to his protruding adam's apple, making him look unclean.

"I don't know if you really have to read everything in the folders," the doctor said. "I've been ordered to give you all the essential facts, holding nothing back."

"Are you uncomfortable with that?" Meade asked in his most casual, unthreatening way. Not only did he speak slowly, but he gave his voice a soft, sonorous rumble, as if he might doze off if he became any less interested in the matter at hand.

"What I think about it doesn't matter, I follow orders," said Lieberman. "I assume those in charge are correct in entrusting you with my secrets."

"*Our* secrets," Meade corrected.

The doctor tugged nervously on the knot of his tie.

"So why don't you just tell me what I need to know," said Meade. "I'll still need to read it all later, but this way I can learn enough to get started on the manhunt."

So far, it hadn't been a manhunt, it had been a helicopter hunt, because Meade hadn't known precisely who he was after. The first thing he had done was to order his own choppers to comb the area, fanning out, flying in ever widening concentric circles, in hopes of spotting the machine that had spirited the three inmates away. He had hoped it would have been ditched someplace nearby, if not in a clearing in the forest, then at some small West Virginia landing strip. He thought he knew which machine he was looking for, because two months ago an assault helicopter had been stolen from a National Guard motor pool in Ohio. But so far his knowledge hadn't helped him. If the machine couldn't be found, it couldn't be tied to the pilot by evidence such as fingerprints or maybe abandoned personal belongings, and the pilot couldn't be pounced on and made to rat on the escapees.

"Let's go into my office," said Dr. Lieberman, glancing all around nervously, as if there were prying ears in the immediate vicinity, even though the six steel desks normally occupied by administrative personnel were all empty at the moment.

Meade followed him and sat in a brown leather armchair in front of the doctor's large glass-topped desk. His furniture was civilian rather than military issue like the other stuff around here, but still his office had a cold, institutional feeling because there were no ornaments or paintings on the walls. After shutting the door and locking it, he sat down behind his desk, sighing, rubbing his bony thumbs together. He took off his thick eyeglasses and pinched the bridge of his nose. Then, when Meade was just about out of patience, Lieberman started to talk in a squeaky monotone as devoid of wit, charm and vivacity as the sanitarium itself.

"The human brain," he droned, "is like a marvelously complex, unbelievably miniaturized computer with literally millions of electrochemical circuits. There are areas of the brain that seem to be specifically wired for logical thought, and there are other areas more loosely wired, so to speak, more susceptible to flights of fancy. Some of these loosely organized areas contain receptors that bond readily with potent psychoactive drugs—PCP, for example—angel dust. Ten years ago, I started asking myself, why should the brain have specific receptors for a drug that causes people to act crazy? I decided it might be advantageous to promote the breakdown of normal channels of thought, to allow for revelry, dreaming and imagination. If there were receptors for man-made angel dust, that should mean that a natural angel dust with the same chemical structure and function must already exist somewhere in the brain, and we might tap mankind's creativity in new, exciting ways, if we could find the substance and activate it at will."

Dr. Lieberman paused and cleared his throat. He took off his glasses and rubbed his tired, bloodshot eyes. Then, when it became obvious that Meade wasn't going to open his mouth to either console or accuse, he went on with his confession. "My ideas failed to excite research foundations in the private sector, so I eventually accepted CIA funding. It took me two years, but my experiments finally produced a promising new drug. It seemed more powerful than PCP, without any of the undesirable side effects. I named it 'quantalibrium'. It has the ability to provoke quantum leaps of creative imagination. It acts like a catalyst, unleashing the ninety percent of the human brain's intellectual capacity that nature seems to hold in reserve, untapped."

"Then where's the problem?" asked Brian Meade. "Sounds like a success story to me. How does all this info help me find the three guys who got loose?"

"Because to find them you need to know who they are and how they might behave," Dr. Lieberman said with as much forcefulness as his squeaky monotone could muster. You are *not* looking for three men named Haskell, Perry, and Blake. Those are false names, phony identities. You are really looking for three men who disappeared and were declared dead: Dr. Norman Teague, Dr. Abraham Vickers, and Colonel Kevin Thompson."

Meade blinked his sleepy-looking eyes a few times, but other than that he gave no indication of being startled by any of the doctor's revelations. "I see," he said calmly. "I need to be brought up to date. Tell me the rest of it"

"We had every reason to believe that quantalibrium was perfectly safe," Lieberman said. "We didn't just charge blindly ahead. First we tested it on Federal prisoners, volunteers. It actually raised their intelligence quotients, without apparently harming them in any way, but of course they lacked the training and the formal education to use their heightened intellects in ways that could be called optimum. We felt we had to go on to the next stage, in order to give quantalibrium a real proving ground. That was when we presented our data to Universal Dynamics, Inc., a think tank based in Washington, D.C., where Teague, Vickers and Thompson were working. They volunteered to enter the quantalibrium program, which we still considered experimental, but not especially dangerous. At this point, I was riding high, brimming with great expectations. I was convinced that my new drug would enhance the already outstanding mental processes of the think tank members, inspiring them to new inventions, new discoveries, and new insights of political, economic and military significance."

"But something went wrong," Meade guessed.

"Yes," said Lieberman, shaking his head dolefully.

"What?" asked Meade.

He listened with a placid, noncommittal expression while the good doctor told a sad tale of the unfortunate long-range side effects of quantalibrium dosage, which were not apparent on the prison volunteers because their part of the study hadn't gone on long enough. By the time they started exhibiting bizarre symptoms, it was too late for the volunteers from Universal Dynamics, also. The drug did indeed produce the quantum leaps of creative imagination that were desired. However, after repeated, prolonged use of the man-made angel dust, it caused certain brain functions to disintegrate, producing paranoid reactions. And, if the mental degeneration was not arrested by "control" drugs administered regularly, those who had taken quantalibrium would become hopelessly, permanently psychotic.

"Last week, for instance," said Dr. Lieberman, "we had an inmate who had become immune to his control medication. He started burning off his fingers one by one by touching them against our electrified fence, laughing idiotically the whole time, till finally he killed himself by hurling his body against the wires."

"In other words," said Brian Meade, "we have three loonies on the loose at this very moment, and you're telling me that without the drugs you'd have them on here in the sanitarium, they're just going to keep getting loonier and loonier."

"That's correct. Unless you can recapture them in

time, and we can get them back on their control medication."

"How rapidly will the mental deterioration happen?"

"It's highly unpredictable," said the doctor. "Quantalibrium affects different individuals differently, and at different rates. For some, the regression into complete paranoia takes only a day or so once control medication is withdrawn. And stress seems to be a factor. It seems usually to speed up the deterioration."

Brian Meade eyed the doctor, disliking him but not showing it. He mostly didn't resent his clean-up work. Some messes were unavoidable, even in the most rational kinds of operations. But this mess at Blue Ridge was the work of a half-mad tinkerer. It reminded Meade of the time the Army had driven some of their own troops insane, causing several of them to even commit suicide, by putting LSD in their food without their knowing it. It was a "mind-expanding" experiment, just like this quantalibrium thing. Meade thought the tinkerers ought to have learned their lesson *that* time. But he would keep his opinion to himself. And no matter how the mess got made, he would clean it up ruthlessly and thoroughly, so it wouldn't be a stain on the nation's honor.

There was a rap on the door, and Dr. Lieberman got up to answer it. He let in Wayne Dorsey, Meade's second-in-command, an ex-hillbilly from Arkansas who always wore expensive, tailored suits and had his blonde hair fashionably styled and sculpted, but still managed to look like a yokel because of his long arms, big hands, and protruding front teeth. "I think I figured out who the inside man was," he announced boisterously. "I told you there had to be one, remember?"

"I didn't disagree on that," said Meade.

"Well, anyway, I was right," said Dorsey. "We found a nylon rope tied to a chunk of steel that was part of the railing at the top of one of the towers. Two guards were on duty up there this afternoon, Clarence Corrigan and Bernard Philips. When we dragged their bodies out, we thought at first that both of them must have been crushed in the rubble 'cause neither of them had gunshot wounds, but I was anxious anyhow to find out what the autopsy reports would show. I just got them. Philips had a concussion, not bad enough to kill him, and a whole gang of internal injuries from being crushed under a pile of rocks; he died of bleeding and suffocation. Corrigan was all mangled up, too, plus his neck was broken. But here's the kicker." Dorsey smiled, revealing his protruding upper front teeth. "Corrigan had rope burns on his hands. He must've been rappelling down from the tower after knocking out Philips, when the guy in the assault chopper decided he wasn't taking Corrigan along for the ride."

"What can you tell me about this Clarence Corrigan?" Meade asked Dr. Lieberman.

"Not much. I can get you his file. He's been working at the sanitarium for, oh, roughly seven years, I suppose. As far as I know, he's always been considered an efficient and trusted member of our staff."

"What a coincidence," said Meade, "that Corrigan should be hired here at about the time that all three of our escapees became inmates. Could be he was an agent-in-place, a mole, waiting to be called upon to perform this particular assignment."

"Who would plan that far ahead?" asked Dr. Lieberman.

"Us," said Dorsey. "Or the KGB."

"Get some men on Corrigan," Meade told his second-in-command. "Tell them to dig up everything they can. Maybe they'll find something that'll lead us to the pilot, or to somebody we don't know about yet. Somebody has to be pulling the strings."

"Right," said Dorsey. "If it's the Soviets…"

Meade interrupted him to brief him on the true identities of the three escapees. "We'll put all their friends and family members under tight surveillance," Meade said, "in case Teague, Thompson and Vickers try to get in touch with anyone from their past lives."

"You'll want to alert Dr. Gary Cameron," Dr. Lieberman advised. "He knows that Teague, Thompson and Vickers were inmates here. He ought to be told they've escaped."

"Dr. Gary Cameron?" asked Meade, surprised. "Of the Cameron Foundation? Martha Teague's fiancé?"

"Yes. He was the one who suggested the sanitarium… as an alternative to…er…harsher measures. He knows about the quantalibrium experiment… and that the drug was responsible for the aberrant behavior that made the three men a security risk. Since he's about to marry Martha Teague, he's in a perfect position to help you prevent Norman from getting to his ex-wife and his two daughters."

Meade said, "Tell me something, Doctor. How can Gary Cameron intend to go ahead with his marriage to Teague's wife when he knows full well that Teague is still living? He's not worried about committing bigamy?"

Lieberman smiled insipidly. "I imagine he doesn't view it as bigamy. After all, Norman Teague has been declared legally deceased. Even if this hadn't been the case, the marriage could have been annulled because of his insanity, his legal incompetence. So the end result is the same, despite the differing technicalities. I would suppose that this is how Cameron views the matter."

"But I wonder how Martha is going to view it, if we don't prevent Teague from getting to her," said Meade.

"That is the least of our worries," said Dr. Lieberman. "If the KGB has Teague, Thompson and Vickers for sure this time, they will glean a lot of useful information and a lot of disinformation as well. They'll have to sift through it like hens pecking through a haystack, but much of what they'll find will be pure gold. It's why the three men had to be locked away. They couldn't be trusted once they started losing their sanity."

"I almost hope that the KGB *does* have them," said Wayne Dorsey. "They might think they're getting nothing but gibberish, and bump the three escapees off. That way, at least we wouldn't have to worry about the shit hitting the fan when the American public finds out they're still alive."

"We won't let that happen," Meade said. But he knew he was going to need a lot of luck in order to keep his promise.

Privately, he wasn't quite buying the quantalibrium story. A shrewd, pragmatic man who had survived eighteen years of back-biting and intrigue, both internal and external to the Agency, he knew full well that his superiors didn't always tell him the truth. Often they had good reasons not to. They told him what they needed to tell him to enable him to do his job. Usually a lie was as good as the truth, sometimes better. He didn't mind the lies as long as they weren't the kind that could hobble him or place him in danger. Sometimes the lies protected him by keeping him from knowing too much for his own good.

He figured he had probably been told the truth about

the three escapees' identities, but he wasn't entirely convinced that they had taken some kind of crazy drug. There could be some other reason why they had been locked up. Maybe, if Meade captured them and they started spouting off certain things, Meade's superiors wanted to make sure he wouldn't pay too much attention. Well, they needn't have worried. All he cared about was doing his job, cleaning up the mess. He didn't intend to open up any fresh cans of worm.

12

Cleaning up the mess stirred up all the old, hated Auschwitz images in Rolf Kollar's mind. For more than forty years he had not had to put his hands on dead bodies, and now fate had brought him full circle. This time there were only three bodies, instead of thousands. He tried to tell himself he ought to be able to deal easily with so few.

In his last two months in the concentration camp, when he was nearly dead himself, he was made a member of the *Sonderkommando*, the Special Work Detachment of eight hundred prisoners who worked in and around the crematoriums, helping to dispose of what the Nazis called "the garbage"—the human victims of the gas chambers. By then he was eighteen years old, a camp veteran, a walking skeleton with a few strings of muscle still working, keeping him from being extermi- nated. He and his father, both husky and strong at the outset, because they had worked together as bricklayers back in Germany, had managed to survive for almost four years. His mother, an asthmatic, unfit for hard labor, hadn't passed the first "selection". Rolf Kollar had just turned fourteen a few days before being "resettled" at Auschwitz, or else he would have been gassed with his mother, for no child, male or female, under the age of fourteen was allowed to live. Many times he had come close to undoing his "good luck" by hurling his emaciated body against the electrified fence that surrounded the camp. But once he was assigned to the Sonderkommando, he knew he would not have to commit suicide; every four months, after helping to gas others, each Sonderkommando would in turn be gassed, so that none of them would be around after the war to tell what had been done to six million European Jews and other "undesirables".

Kollar was utterly resigned to his fate, and yet something kept him going, in the smoke and stench of the flesh-burning ovens, a crazy, tenacious spark deep within him, a soul maybe, that wasn't quite ready to be sent up the chimney. He wondered why he was cursed with this spark of irrational hope that had stopped him from hurling himself against the fence, and was still making him go on, helping the Nazis do their ghoulish work. How could he know that before his Sonderkommando could be liquidated, the Nazis would flee and American soldiers would liberate the camp? How could he know that before he was saved, he would have to help cremate his own father?

On the day his father died, the Americans were only a hundred miles away, the gas chamber had claimed some of its last victims. But to Kollar it was another day among the dead and the living dead. Wearing a gas mask and some rubber boots that came up to his hips, he entered the vast chamber, two hundred yards long, where three thousand men, women and children had just been "processed". The bodies weren't evenly scattered, but were in tangled piles as high as the ceiling. This was because the deadly gas entered through perforations in the pillars, near the floor, then rose, so that in the five minutes it took to paralyze the lungs of all three thousand people they clawed and trampled one another, trying to reach higher levels of air, where they might manage to live a few seconds longer. The bodies of old people and children were always at the bottom of the pile, the strong young men at the top, covered with scratches and bruises. All of their faces were bloated and blue, horribly contorted.

Kollar's Sonderkommando squad moved around and around the mound of bodies, squirting water on them, powerful blasts of water from big rubber hoses. They had to wash away blood, urine and feces—everything excreted in the last act of dying. After that, they started untangling the slippery pile of flesh, by tying leather thongs around the dead wrists and ankles, then dragging the bodies across the concrete floor and loading them two dozen per load on large freight elevators that would take them up to the ovens.

Kollar did these macabre chores by rote, his mind numb, working mechanically, unfeelingly. But he got a terrible jolt when he suddenly saw his father's face staring glassily up at him, the bald head sliding across the slick concrete in a watery trickle of blood. The face was so swollen and misshapen that it should have been unrecognizable on a conscious level, but the realization struck deeper than that, struck at feelings of grief and loss he thought the Nazis had killed. His knees buckled and he would have fallen on top of the corpse he was dragging, but another Sonderkommando man grabbed him and held him steady for a few seconds, till he was able to make himself continue. If he had fallen, it would have been all over for him, a bullet in the back of his neck from one of the 55 guards. Why didn't he let himself be put out of his misery? The instinct that made him cling to life under these conditions seemed hideously perverse, grotesque, degrading. But years later he came to believe that a Higher Power must have wanted him to live and accomplish something wonderful, something special. He had been chosen to reveal the mysteries of the "gods from other galaxies".

Why, when once he had dealt with thousands of corpses every day, was he now so sick and shaky over the three in the farmhouse kitchen? Apparently he was no longer as numb to the presence of death as he had been forty years ago. Maybe the difference was that this time he must keep his wits about him, the clean-up job had to be thorough, he couldn't leave any incriminating evidence. Today he had no crematorium to turn every-thing to smoke. He'd have to dig a deep grave in the woods behind the barn.

Before he had driven Jenny Teague into Wheeling, where she got a taxi to the airport, he had dragged Jason Rawlings' body all the way into the house and had locked both doors. He had half expected to find CIA men crawling all over the place when he got back, but instead he had found everything as he left it.

At a paint store in Wheeling, he had bought three big plastic drip cloths. The first thing he did, while it was still dusk, was to wrap each of the three bodies in a plastic sheet and push them one at a time, in a wheelbar-row, out to the place where he intended to dig the grave. On one of his trips back and forth, he spotted a hanky that had to be Jenny's lying in the grass, so he wrapped it up with Thompson's corpse. He didn't want to leave any trace of her here to be discovered by the CIA or the civilian police. He was pretty sure she was frightened enough to keep her mouth shut. He had told her he would deal with the "problem" at the safe house. She hadn't ventured to ask how. Obviously she didn't want to know. He was only too glad to spare her the grisly details.

The worst part of it, worse than wrapping the bodies up and dragging them out, was swabbing the blood and gore out of the kitchen. Kollar kept seeing himself hosing down mounds of naked bodies, hauling them to the elevators. Even as they lay on iron racks in front of the roaring ovens, their blood continued to run in watery trickles on the concrete. This time it was old, cracked linoleum. Kollar scrubbed and mopped till the floor was clean and shiny, but he still couldn't shake the old memories, ingrained in his soul, of splashing through puddles of blood in high rubber boots, knowing it wouldn't be long before his own body was dragged from the gas chamber to be cremated.

Meticulously he wiped everything down, every household article, every piece of video equipment, every door, mirror, doorknob, every stick of furniture that might yield a fingerprint. Even though the deed was in a phony name, he still had to make sure he couldn't be connected to the place through Chaney or Rawlings. He had to "sanitize" everything the way the CIA might have done if they had committed the murders themselves. That very thought had panicked him when he had caught his first glimpse of the carnage—Rawlings' legs sticking out onto the front porch. But after seeing all three dead men, he knew that a struggle must have taken place among them. It was even possible that Chaney's intention hadn't been to merely wipe everyone out. Maybe he was trying to pull a fast one—like taking the videotapes for himself, to sell them to the media or to some foreign power—when Rawlings and the three escapees turned on him and overpowered him. Perhaps Rawlings was even in on the scam with Chaney, in which case he got what he deserved.

So far, the fiasco had put Kollar in the red over six hundred thousand dollars, half a million of it presumably still in the hands of Vickers and Teague. Maybe he'd never get any of it back. He had figured it as a good investment, since film and book rights to the story would have fetched millions. Well, losing the money was the least of his worries; thanks to his previous books and movies, he was many times a millionaire. Even the prospect of losing his life was secondary, for in his mind he was in a sense already dead, he should have perished forty years ago, and each day since then was a gift he almost didn't deserve. He'd gladly die if he could first get those videotapes back and show them to the world. But the chance of doing that seemed depressingly slim.

He told himself not to despair, not to lose hope, but to keep on doing whatever he had to do, living from minute to minute, the way he had done in the concentration camp, and maybe in the long run he would survive and triumph. He had to keep believing he had been spared for a higher purpose. His work was not yet finished.

It was pitch dark by the time he started digging the grave, so he had to do it by lantern light. At first it was fairly easy, cutting through sod to a soft layer of earth underneath. But then he ran into hard yellow clay and rocks. He knew he'd be out there most of the night, sweating and struggling to make the hole deep enough for three corpses. Since he was working behind the barn, the glowing lantern shouldn't be visible from the road, and no one should hear the thuds and scrapes of the pick and shovel.

After he dumped the bodies in the hole, before covering them with dirt, he intended to douse them with kerosene and set them on fire, so that someday, if they were ever exhumed, accurate identification would be exceedingly difficult. In the years before the cremating ovens were fully operational, a similar method had been used at Auschwitz. Thousands of corpses had been dumped into huge trenches and burned.

At the Wheeling Airport, waiting to board a shuttle plane that would take her to Pittsburgh, where she would transfer to a flight bound for Washington, D.C., Jenny Teague was a nervous wreck. In the ladies' room she dropped the figurine of an astronaut carved in anthracite coal into a rubbish barrel; once she got out of West Virginia she did not want to carry any evidence that she had set foot there. She had no way of knowing how much immediate danger she might be in. The police might pounce on her at any moment and throw her in jail. The false name on her tickets—Jenny Trask—seemed too obvious, too close to her own name. How could she have been so stupid? Miraculously she had made it through the baggage check without being put in handcuffs. But when two men in dark suits, carrying briefcases, kept staring at her as they approached, she almost bolted and ran. They went past her and sat down, chatting, and she made herself relax a little. She knew she had to act like a normal everyday person so she wouldn't draw suspicion. A cigarette would help. But she refrained.

Because of seeing Kevin Thompson's corpse at the farmhouse, she was absolutely convinced that her father was still alive or had been, up until a few hours ago. She had always thought that whatever his fate had been, the KGB must have been behind it. But now she was wrestling with the shocking notion that her own government had been sinister enough to make three noted citizens "disappear." Before this, even though she understood they weren't perfect, she had always believed in the basic goodness and rightness of her government and her country. She had been proud of her parents' scientific achievements. The fact that her mother worked with NASA on spectacularly successful space projects had strengthened her patriotic feelings and helped assuage the emptiness, the void in her life, that she had felt ever since losing her father.

When Rolf Kollar had first come to her with his incredible scenario—the stuff about the CIA-run sanitarium—she had thought that he must have some of his facts twisted, and even if they were partially true, the government might have a good reason for isolating some men from society. Now she felt an impulse to latch onto this explanation more strongly. If her father—a pragmatic, analytical, rational man—was now babbling about UFOs, perhaps he was no longer in full possession of his faculties—much as Jenny hated to admit it might be so. The way things were falling to pieces, it seemed even more likely to her now, that he might be recaptured or murdered before she could find out the truth.

Jenny didn't think she could go on living on pins and needles without confiding in anybody. Maybe she should break down and tell her mother everything. But would Martha believe her? Or would Martha turn against her, convinced she was becoming just as schizophrenic as her sister Sally?

Her actions had put her in terrible danger while accomplishing nothing. Although she believed that a sanitarium break-out had taken place, she couldn't prove it to anyone else. Without hard evidence, no one would believe her, not even her mother. Ironically, she and Rolf Kollar were perpetuating the cover-up by keeping quiet about what had happened at the farmhouse. She figured that at this very moment he must be hiding the bodies, wiping away clues. Out of fear, he was inadvertently helping the CIA. But if they caught him, they wouldn't shake his hand. He'd probably tell on Jenny—they'd have ways of making him talk. They'd come for her. They'd deal with her swiftly and efficiently, like blotting up a stain. She wouldn't ever find her father. She'd never see him again. Like him, she'd simply disappear and no one would know where to look.

13

In the blue Oldsmobile, Norman Teague and Abraham Vickers were heading east toward the Pennsylvania Turnpike. Teague was glad he was behind the wheel and glad he had the big .45 automatic tucked in his belt. It was making his stomach hurt by rubbing against the bottom of his rib cage, but he didn't dare lay the weapon on the seat. He had gained a new respect for his traveling companion, and a new fear. Back at the safe house, Vickers had certainly proved that the quiet ones were the ones you had to watch.

When Thompson went to the sink to get a drink of water, Teague was ready to spring into action because he had seen the ex-test pilot undo one of his shirt buttons first. It didn't look like Vickers was ready to do *anything;* it seemed like he didn't even know what was going on. Sitting at the big kitchen table, his head was nodding, his eyes half closed. Teague wondered how he could be so complacent, as if he couldn't sense the hostility all around him, coming from Rawlings, Kollar and Smith. It was all too clear now that they must be working for the KGB.

Teague could tell from the sneaky way his videotape interview was conducted, the kinds of questions that were asked.

Thompson tossed his ice cubes into the sink, a hard toss with a loud clatter that made Smith look in that direction as Thompson whirled and plunged the steak knife into Smith's gut. Smith already had the .45 out, firing, as Thompson fell on top of him. Some of the splatter from the huge exit wound caught Teague in the face, making him blink, slowing him down. But he threw himself across Thompson, hoping by the pressure of their two bodies to keep Smith from jerking the .45 into position to fire again. It fired anyway, sideways, blowing a hole in the bottom of the refrigerator. The recoil probably helped Smith get the weapon unpinned from beneath Thompson's body. Teague clawed and scratched and got hold of Smith's wrist.

At the same time he heard glass shattering. Then, when he was sure his strength was no match for Smith's —the gun would soon be pointed at him, blowing his head off—Vickers knelt with a broken ginger ale bottle and brought the jagged thing down hard into Smith's face. Blood started spurting all over—the glass must've ripped the jugular vein. Smith let loose a gurgling scream and his grip loosened on the gun and Teague was able to wrench it away from him. Thompson's dead weight held Smith down while Vickers kept chopping with the broken bottle, over and over, chopping at Smith's face.

Somebody said, "Oh my God!" and Teague whirled, pointing the .45. It was Rawlings, frozen in the doorway, a sick look on his face. Teague's finger tightened on the trigger, but then he hesitated, and Rawlings ran. He almost got out the door before Teague fired, aiming for the middle of the fleeing man's back, but hitting high, at the base of the skull. The upward trajectory blew away most of Rawlings' head. The impact spun him sideways, slamming him against the wooden door before his feet kicked out and ended up ahead of him, on the porch.

Teague was half sick. He had never seen so much blood. He got to his feet, letting the .45 drop to his side. Then he turned, jerking it into firing position in case the fight wasn't quite over. But apparently it was. Vickers had stopped chopping at Smith, but was still kneeling over his inert form, slowly grinding the broken bottle around and around in Smith's face, methodically shredding his features as if they were exotic ingredients to be ground up in a pestle.

"Vickers!" Teague yelled in an effort to jar the little fat man to his senses.

Vickers looked up, saw the big .45 pointed his way and apparently leapt to the conclusion that Teague meant to shoot him. He got halfway up, a silly smile on his face, ready to come at Teague with the broken bottle, a disgusting implement, dripping blood, with pieces of skin hanging from its jagged edges. Taking a big chance, Teague dropped the .45 to arm's length, shouting, "Vickers! Stop! They're all dead! You and I have got to get out of here!"

Vickers hesitated, shaking his pale, bulbous head as if he were coming out of a trance. He brought his improvised weapon up, chest high, and for a moment Teague thought he might have to use the .45. But Vickers merely blinked his eyes, staring at the bloody piece of green bottleneck as if seeing its true character for the first time. Then he let it drop. "All dead, all dead..." he muttered.

"Yes," said Teague. "You and I are free. We've got to stick together, make the right moves, or else they'll catch us and put us back in the sanitarium."

"Gotta get cleaned up," Vickers mumbled, staring at his bloody hands.

"You're right," said Teague, encouraging coherent thought that might help bring Vickers out of his daze. "You certainly acquitted yourself well. I didn't imagine you had it in you. If you hadn't jumped in the way you did, I think Smith would've shot us all, even with that knife in his stomach."

Vickers smiled. It was a faint smile, but an obviously pleased one. He wasn't normally a man of action. All his life he had shunned physical activity. He hated sports, even spectator sports. Now he couldn't help being proud that he had not only done something physically violent but had done it well when the chips were down. Teague had the eerie thought that maybe a new appetite had been awakened in Vickers, an appetite for violence. Maybe he would grow to like it more and more, if the opportunities kept arising. Teague had to admit that he also felt a certain macho pride. An exhilaration. He remembered how skeptical he had been, back in the sanitarium, when Kevin Thompson had told him how exhilarating it could be to put one's life on the line and then use one's skills to the maximum to survive the danger. Now Teague thought that maybe he understood, just a little, why Thompson had enjoyed being a test pilot. Well, for him all danger was over, while for Teague it wasn't. Survival wasn't yet guaranteed from one moment to the next.

Teague and Vickers were blood-soaked, not just their faces and hands, but their clothing. "Upstairs," Teague said. "Maybe there's a shower...clean stuff to wear."

"We should wash our hands here first," Vickers suggested. "And take our shoes off before we go up."

"Yeah, right," said Teague. He was pleased at this further evidence of rational thought coming from his ally. It made perfect sense not to track blood all over the house, so if they did find clean clothes to change into, they'd have a chance of keeping them clean. But first Teague had to roll Thompson's body off of Smith. He had to feel in Smith's pockets for the keys to the Oldsmobile. Then he washed his hands and the keys in the kitchen sink. By that time. Vickers was already rooting around upstairs. They found suitcases in three of the bedrooms, some on the beds and some on the floor. One of the suitcases looked brand new, so they opened it first. Jackpot. It was full of new clothes, still in their store wrappers. "Must be more stuff they bought for us," said Teague. He and Vickers checked and found the sizes right for themselves and Thompson. Under the bed in that particular bedroom, there were even some new pairs of shoes—a pair of loafers and a pair of sneakers for each escapee.

"What do you make of this?" said Teague. "Looks like they were fixing to treat us pretty nice."

"At least they wanted to make us think so," said Vickers, "till they got what they wanted out of us."

"That's the way I figure it," said Teague.

They went from room to room, opening all the suitcases and looking under all the beds. They dumped stuff out as they went, but most of it was useless to them—clothes and personal articles that must've belonged to Smith, Kollar and Rawlings. However, under one of the beds they found what turned out to be a bonanza: a big, beat-up, leather suitcase that was locked. It was the only one that had been locked, so that alone was enough to make Teague and Vickers extremely curious. Plus, they found it in the room they had figured out must be Smith's. "Probably full of guns and knives," Vickers joked. "But let's break it open anyway."

For a moment Teague pictured himself drawing the .45 from under his belt and shooting off the lock. Then he remembered the keys he had taken from Smith's pocket. He got them out and sure enough there was one that looked like a suitcase key. It fit the lock. He turned it and opened the lid. All he saw at first was a folded-up garment bag. But when he unzipped the bag, Vickers let out a long, low whistle. They both stepped back and stared at the stacks of greenbacks. They looked at each other in disbelief, then back at the treasure.

"I guess neither one of us will be letting this out of our sight from now on," was Vickers' comment.

"Nor one another," said Teague.

"Oh, I trust you," said Vickers, jokingly. "I might as well. After all, any time you wanted to, you could shoot me.

"You know I wouldn't do that," said Teague. "Any more than you'd stick a knife in my back. We've been through a lot together. I don't know how much money is there, but we'll split it fifty-fifty."

They still hadn't counted it. It was locked in the trunk of the Oldsmobile. Having it in their possession had perked their spirits up and made them work faster cleaning themselves up and getting clear of the safe house that had turned out not to be so safe for Smith, Rawlings and Thompson. All the money packets Teague had seen had been wrapped in thousand-dollar bank wrappers. If the stacks underneath were the same, there could be a quarter million dollars or even a lot more than that in the suitcase, he figured. Enough to start a new life. Providing his life as a fugitive didn't get "terminated with extreme prejudice." The CIA jargon for politically motivated murder almost made him laugh. Terminated with extreme prejudice. He wondered why they hadn't done it to him seven years ago. Probably there was no logical explanation. Over the years he had learned that there was much less rhyme and reason than one might suspect in so-called "intelligence" operations.

While driving, Teague and Vickers didn't converse very much because the radio was on. Teague wanted to soak up as much as possible of the current feel and flavor of the world in which he had been set free. He assumed that Vickers was doing the same, although from the complacent look on his face Vickers might have been merely daydreaming. Nightdreaming. It was eight o'clock, already dark. That was good. It'd make the blue Olds harder to spot if anybody was looking for it. Glaring headlights and tail-lights speeding through the night looked pretty much the same on *all* cars. After a seven-year absence from the world, Teague found everything on the all-news station interesting, even the commercials. He no longer expected to hear anything about a sanitarium break-out. It had been hushed up, as he had expected it to be. So far there was nothing about the killings at the farmhouse either. This seemed to confirm his hunch that Kollar, Rawlings and Smith were KGB agents. And what about Jenny? Was she working with them willingly or unwillingly? Teague might have been able to find out by sticking at the farmhouse and getting the jump on her and Kollar when they came back from town—but he had been scared of learning the truth that way. If he'd have learned for sure that Jenny was his enemy, he'd have had to kill her. So it was best to evade the issue for now. He didn't want his own daughter's blood on his hands. But he was more suspicious of her than ever. It seemed clear to him that he and Vickers would have perished along with Thompson if they hadn't taken Smith and Rawlings by surprise.

"Truck stop," Vickers said. "Let's pull over and get something to eat."

"It's a big, conspicuous place," Teague said, but he slowed down anyway. The idea of going into a public place and ordering food off a menu, like a regular person, had a powerful allure that blunted his sense of danger.

"That's why it's perfect," Vickers said, chuckling. "Whoever's looking for us is never going to figure we'd be dumb enough to loaf around in a big place right on a main highway. As far as they know, we're in a helicopter, bound for Timbuktu. Besides, there are only two of us now, and they're looking for three."

"Not if Kollar has players in the game. He could've passed out enough information to nail us. The car, the license number, everything." But even while he was making his argument, Teague's willpower was weakening. He put the right-turn signal on and pulled off the highway. It was as if he was only in partial control of the decision. The part of him that disapproved of what he was doing twisted his face into a worried grimace.

"Worry wart," Vickers said with a giggle, as Teague drove up a ramp, passing under a couple of streetlamps that splashed his face with light, enabling Vickers to see his expression. He found Vickers' mirth disconcerting. The circumstances did not seem to merit it. But in Teague's experience stress often produced strange reactions in people. Strange and sometimes dangerous.

It was a huge truck stop, not just a diner, but a full-fledged restaurant coupled with a Boron station, a motel and a general store. The business enterprises were surrounded by a couple of acres of asphalt parking lot, currently occupied by maybe a hundred parked cars and fifty big rigs. The whole area was floodlit. The place was in West Virginia, but only a mile from the Pennsylvania line.

———

TEAGUE BACKED the Oldsmobile into a slot so the rear end was tucked up against the hood of somebody's red pickup, hiding the license plate. "Lot of trouble for nothing if the pickup pulls out before we do," Vickers said, laughing.

"I wish you'd cut the levity," Teague snapped, adjusting the .45 under his belt so hopefully it wouldn't keep rubbing against the same sore spot. He considered leaving it in the car, but then all Vickers would have to do would be to ask him for the car keys on some pretext, maybe to put a package inside, and he wouldn't be able to say no, and Vickers might grab the gun. Why was he becoming increasingly distrustful of Vickers? He couldn't exactly say. He told himself it was only prudent to be exceptionally careful with a gun on hand— and a huge amount of cash. "Let's not lollygag around in there," he said, slamming the car door. "The more we keep on the move, the better off we are."

"We're going to stay and eat, aren't we?" Vickers said, almost whiningly.

"Take-out food. Buy what we have to buy and get out. If you have a different idea, we can split up the money here and now and go our separate ways."

"That would be dumb," said Vickers. "We need each other to corroborate our stories if we can get the tapes to the right people."

"We can always get in touch later," said Teague.

"How?" asked Vickers.

Teague couldn't come up with an immediate answer. Too much stress, too much danger, he told himself. Too much time in the institution, other people pushing him around, doing his thinking for him instead of letting him think for himself. His brain was fogged. His reflexes were rusty, despite his effort to maintain them. Maybe he was no longer equipped to survive. "Pay phones," he said, passing some outdoor booths. "Maybe we can make some calls."

It dawned on him that he and Vickers hadn't so much as discussed who they might try to get in touch with in order to obtain help. Did they both have to automatically distrust all their old colleagues, friends and relatives? Wasn't there anybody who might believe in them?

"Who?" asked Vickers, echoing the thought.

"Our wives," said Teague. "We could phone them… without letting them know where we are. That way…"

"Maybe," said Vickers. "I'd like to at least hear Helen's voice again, even if she won't care to hear mine."

They each had several hundred dollars in their pockets, folding money taken out of the suitcase. They entered the restaurant, trying not to act nervous even when they saw two West Virginia state troopers sitting at the long plastic counter. Sipping coffee and dunking doughnuts, the troopers didn't so much as look up at them, didn't even bother to check them out. This seemed to confirm what Teague had felt all along, that ordinary police officers would be the least of their worries. The KGB and CIA were quite accustomed to battling each other covertly, like vicious parasites in America's underbelly, with the general public largely oblivious to exactly what was going on.

HIS WORK at Universal Dynamics had opened Teague's eyes to some of the stuff. And Blue Ridge Hospital had given him his PhD. If he told what he knew to most people, they'd call him paranoid. But he'd be shocking them with pure facts.

Sitting at the counter, he kept looking in the mirror at what was going on behind him. He didn't want to be caught gawking. But Vickers had no such qualms, apparently; he kept swiveling his pale high domed head around like a con fresh out of stir. Teague nudged him to get him to stop. He grunted and acted mad. There wasn't much to see anyway—it was just that ordinary things became novelties after not seeing them for seven years. The restaurant was big, clean, fluorescent, with a pastel decor, orange, brown and tan. In the mirror Teague could see that most of the customers sitting at tables and booths were men. Some looked like truckers and some didn't. It seemed odd that there were so few women, and no mommies and daddies with their kiddies. But then it struck Teague that most of the women in the place could be hookers, acting rather demure for the time being because of the presence of the state troopers. Most of the women weren't eating, just sipping coffee and smoking. A lot of the guys were chowing down on hamburgers and French fries or fried chicken and mashed potatoes.

Teague noticed another oddity. The waitresses working the booths and tables were all elderly women, no competition for the ones he had pegged as hookers. Perhaps it was hoped they would lend the establishment a disarming, grandmotherly air—one of the functions performed by madams in the old-fashioned bawdy houses. The counter was being worked by a waiter who seemed to be more than a waiter, more than a restaurateur. He wasn't wearing an apron. He was about forty, almost handsome, except his skin was too swarthy and his black hair was too oily. He had on an expensive-looking blue polo shirt, black trousers and shiny black patent-leather shoes. On his fingers were a couple of gold rings set with big stones, a diamond and a ruby. He was built like a weight lifter; his wrists and forearms were especially massive and hairy. Smiling didn't seem to be in his repertoire. His deep-set black eyes fixed Vickers and Teague with a cold stare as he snapped a couple of menus in front of them.

"I just want two cheeseburgers, an order of fries and a large black coffee," said Vickers.

"I'll take the same," said Teague. "To go."

"Both orders?" asked the counter man.

"Yes.

"Cheeseburgers with the works?"

Both Teague and Vickers said yes.

"It's gonna take ten or fifteen minutes," said the counter man. "Coffee while you wait?"

"Yes, please," said Teague.

Vickers said, "No, thanks."

The counter man gathered up the menus and poured Teague his coffee. Vickers got up without a word and wandered away. One of the portals that led out of the restaurant was a wide archway with an overhead sign: General Store. In the mirror, Teague saw Vickers going through the archway. He had an urge to follow immediately, to see what Vickers would buy; some kind of weapon, for instance. But he didn't want to let his distrust show. So he made himself sit still and drink his coffee. He felt better when the two state troopers got up, paid their bill and left. One reason he had restrained himself from following Vickers was his fear that the troopers might notice the bulge under the front of his shirt, telling them he was "armed and dangerous."

The take-out order came quicker than he expected. The counter man set it in front of him in two white paper bags, and he paid the tab. While waiting, he had noticed that he was very hungry, and the more he thought of the cheeseburgers and French fries, the more he craved them. He decided this sort of appetite wasn't so strange; after all, he hadn't had anything from a grill or a deep fryer in the past seven years, any more than he had had anything on the opposite extreme—gourmet. The Blue Ridge Hospital cafeteria mostly served food that could be prepared in bulk—like soups, stews and casseroles out of institutional-size cans.

He started to head for the general store to get Vickers, but then he remembered he had to have plenty of change for the phone booths outside. The counter man scowled when Teague asked for five dollars' worth of quarters, dimes and nickels, and when Teague told him what he wanted them for, the man said, "I can only let you have three dollars' worth. You don't even need that much. Once you get through to the operator, she can bill your home number."

"Of course. I didn't think of that," Teague said. He wondered if the counter man or whoremaster or whatever he was would finally crack a smile if Teague told him that the cells at Blue Ridge didn't have any "home phones".

He passed through the archway and found that the general store was certainly comprehensive, even to the inclusion of a large section behind a coin-operated turnstile where one could purchase pornographic magazines and videotapes. Apparently some of the truckers holing up for an overnight stay might prefer taking something vicarious to their motel rooms instead of some of the live fleshpots loitering in the restaurant.

Vickers had just paid for some purchases, and was turning away from the cash register with a big brown paper bag. "Let's go," Teague told him. "I already paid for the food."

"Don't you want to look around?" Vickers said, grinning. "There's some interesting stuff in here."

"I can see that. But we'd better clear out, keep on the move." Teague was glad he could carry the white bags in front of the bulge from the .45. He was dying to ask Vickers what he had bought. But he figured that if Vickers had anything to hide he could easily lie. Right behind the cash register there were rifles for sale, in racks on the wall, and pistols in a locked showcase. Did buying a firearm require a waiting period in West Virginia? And if it did, could the waiting period be eliminated by a bribe? Teague liked the idea of being the only one with a gun between him and Vickers, but he could see that if they stuck together he'd have to constantly worry about preserving his supremacy. He smiled wryly. It reminded him of Russia and the United States worrying about who possessed the most atom bombs.

"Something funny?" asked Vickers.

"No, not really," said Teague.

They were crossing the lot, toward the car.

"You had an odd look on your face," said Vickers. He chuckled. "I thought maybe you were thinking about getting laid. We could do it if you want to stick around for a while. You take notice of all the prossies?"

"All the more reason to clear out," said Teague, "before we find ourselves caught in a vice raid."

"Did you get plenty of change?"

"Yes."

Teague put the bags of food in the Oldsmobile, and he thought it curious when Vickers hung onto his brown bag instead of tossing it in the car, too. They split up their change and went into the phone booths. There were four, and they took the ones at the ends. Teague took a deep breath, preparing himself mentally for the attempt to reach his wife. Just then, out of the corner of his eye, he saw Vickers take something out of his bag of purchases and slip it under his shirt. What was it? A gun? A knife? Whatever it was, Vickers felt a need to conceal it, so he must be up to no good.

Maybe using a telephone was something you never forgot how to do, like riding a bicycle, but it still felt awkward after not doing it for a long time. Put in the coin—a quarter instead of the dime that Teague remembered. Listen for the dial tone. Then dial. And hope to hear a familiar voice. Martha. If Jenny answered, Teague would know for sure that Kollar had been lying about bringing her to the farmhouse. If she had been in Wheeling, she wouldn't have had time to go back to Manhattan even if her co-conspirators could have taken her by private jet.

"One dollar and twenty-five cents, please."

Jarred by the voice of the operator, Teague plunked in the coins. He was sure he still knew the number of his apartment in Manhattan. He waited through five rings. Then someone said hello. A man, young or old he couldn't tell. Panic struck him and he perspired profusely—more shook up than when he had been fighting for his life. Of course he had often considered that his wife might have found a new man, but thinking about it in abstract terms didn't diminish the impact of finding out it was true. "May I please speak to Dr. Martha Teague?" he asked, his voice quavering.

"I'm sorry, you must have the wrong number," the man said. "Nobody by that name here."

"Is this apartment number three, Washington Court?"

"Yes…but…"

"Martha Teague used to live there. Apparently she doesn't any longer. I'm sorry to bother you," said Teague. He was actually tremendously relieved to find out Martha wasn't involved with this guy. The intensity of his reaction surprised him—was it because his nerves were frazzled? Ever since escaping from Blue Ridge. he seemed to be living in a world of heightened colors, heightened sensations. Maybe it was only the contrast with his previously drab existence. But it made it hard for him to view everything in its proper perspective. When he was living with Martha, he hadn't thought of himself as an especially jealous spouse; he could even have forgiven a casual affair, probably, if such a thing had happened under circumstances that could be considered "understandable." But now he found himself clutching at some pristine image of his wife, as if common sense didn't tell him it would be completely unreasonable to expect her to have remained celibate during his long absence, his presumed death.

"You could try phoning the building supervisor," the man on the line suggested. "Ask him if your party left a forwarding address.

"Thank you, that's a good idea," said Teague. "Can you give me his phone number, please?"

Luckily the building supervisor was in, Mr. Benvenutti. He had an Italian accent. He wasn't the same person who had held the job when Teague lived there,

and that was good because it was in Teague's best interests not to be talking to anyone who might recognize his
voice. "Dr. Martha Teague," Mr. Benvenutti said,
repeating her name fondly, excitedly. "She did live here
for sure. I see her come and go every day pre' near. You
did know her, sir?"

"I'm a close friend of hers...but we haven't stayed in
touch lately."

"Well, she move away about three year ago. I was
sorry to see her go. Very nice lady. No trouble, no
complain. She's an important scientist, everybody tell
me. Her husband disappear, leave her with two young
girls. But I see in the paper she gonna get married
again...next month, I believe...to another famous scientist, Dr. Gary Cameron. I see them on TV together."

Teague clenched the telephone receiver so hard it
made his knuckles hurt. *Cameron.* That know-it-all. That
upstart! Did he actually have his own foundation now?
Teague and his wife had worked with Dr. Gary Cameron
at NASA and at Universal Dynamics, Inc. Back then,
Teague had noticed the way Cameron would scope
Martha out, but he didn't think Cameron would dare
make any moves. In fact, it had amused Teague to see his
wife coveted by a lesser man, a man to whom Martha
surely would never stoop. But now Teague was stunned
and was seeing the light, as if the cardboard had been
whipped back to reveal the worms crawling underneath.
It was suddenly clear to him that Gary Cameron might
have had a stake in his disappearance. Maybe Gary was
even part of the plot.

"Do you have a forwarding address and phone
number for Martha Teague?" Teague asked.

"No, sir, I'm sorry, I like to help you," said the
building supervisor. "She work for the Cameron Founda-

tion now, the newspaper say. Maybe you try there tomorrow."

"Thank you very much. I'll do that."

After hanging up the phone, Teague wandered dejectedly over to the Oldsmobile and got behind the wheel. He stared at Abraham Vickers, who was still in one of the booths, plunking coins in the slot. Vickers stood still for a long time, probably listening to unanswered rings, then he cradled the phone and gathered up returned coins. He didn't give up even though that particular call hadn't gone through. He inserted another coin and dialed another number—or maybe the same number. Pause. More coins. Then a long wait, a hang-up, another gathering up of the money from the coin-return slot. Teague grimaced and shook his head, utterly annoyed. He wondered how long Vickers would keep on putting in coins and dialing old out-of-date numbers like an idiot trying over and over to fit a square peg in a round hole. There was a bulge in the front of Vickers' shirt, and he was so caught up in what he was doing he wasn't aware he was letting the bulge show. How stupid! Did he actually think that Teague wasn't wise to him? He was hiding a weapon, probably a gun. No doubt he had bribed the guy in the general store to sell it to him without proper registration.

Teague moaned inwardly. *Why oh why is the whole world against* me? Clutching the steering wheel, he leaned his forehead against it, feeling the veins throbbing in his temples, his heart pounding with anger and frustration. He was a fugitive, unjustly imprisoned and stripped of his dignity, fighting to stay alive and keep his sanity, while less deserving people, inferior people, lived like kings and queens. They had stolen everything from him —his wife, his daughters, even his rightful name.

Vickers finally left the phone booth and came toward the car, reaching for the door handle, yanking on it only to find it locked. Teague didn't pull the button up. Instead he started the engine, put the gearshift lever into drive. Vickers stared at him, his mouth gaping open, forgetting to hold his brown paper bag over the bulge in his shirt. For a moment Teague was sure Vickers would reach for the gun. So Teague peeled out, racing across the asphalt, catching a glimpse of the little fat man frozen like a dummy in the rearview mirror.

Teague sped down the ramp, back onto the highway, headed toward the Pennsylvania Turnpike. Now he was on his own. He had a gun, a car and a suitcase full of money—he should do okay. The videotapes were in the trunk, too. Teague's heart was hammering, his foot heavy on the gas. He had to make himself ease back to the speed limit, remembering that the two state troopers who had been in the restaurant could be lurking nearby. He was scared, excited, maybe a little guilt-ridden, but sure he was doing the right thing. Now he didn't have to worry about treachery from anyone close to him.

14

At first Vickers couldn't believe that the Oldsmobile wasn't coming back. He paced around the lot, staring out past the ramp and its rows of lights, into the darkness of the highway. Then he started to laugh. Three truckers stomped past him, giving him a wide berth, eyeing him with suspicion and anger. He put his hand over his mouth, stifling his mirth like a child caught giggling in kindergarten. The truckers piled into a big rig, slamming the doors. Their grizzled faces peered down from the cab, looking at Vickers as if he weren't quite all there. He reached into the front of his shirt, fondling the deck of pornographic playing cards he had bought in the general store. Watching the big rig pull out, he sat down on a bench and picked at the cellophane wrapper around the deck of cards. The top card, face up, clearly visible through the wrapper, showed a couple of nude young women performing fellatio on a couple of nude young men.

Vickers had developed a secret taste for pornography even before he got stashed away at Blue Ridge. Now his libido was being fanned by seven years of abstinence. Like a red-faced adolescent he had concealed his purchase of erotica from Norman Teague, out of fear that Teague might have scorned him. High and mighty Teague always acted as if he was above ordinary human concerns like the need for orgasms. He wasn't even attracted to the prostitutes in the restaurant—maybe women no longer fazed him after not seeing any for such a long time.

For most of Vickers' life his sex drive had been low, abnormally so, if he could believe the statistics put out by researchers like Kinsey and Masters and Johnson. He had no desire to produce children; his work in astrophysics was all the reward he needed. He and his wife Helen made love about once a month. Then, in the year immediately prior to his incarceration at Blue Ridge, his sexual appetites suddenly, unexplainably rose to a fever pitch. To say the least, it wasn't the sort of mid-life crisis he was expecting. Helen just couldn't keep up with him. His work suffered; he knew it, though he kept trying to cover. He began furtively to keep a library of pornography and to frequent prostitutes. He wasn't good at being deceptive, so Helen found out about his extramarital activities and filed for divorce—two weeks before he was forcibly taken out of her life.

Some of the things he did with prostitutes were positively kinky; he would have been ashamed to have anyone find out. He simply couldn't help himself; his tastes kept getting more and more bizarre. Near the end, he knew he wasn't any longer in control of his drives, he was a prisoner of lust. It wasn't even much fun except during the brief moments of consummation. The rest of the time he was a wreck, worrying himself to a frazzle over his lack of interest in science, which had virtually been his god. Ironically, before this crazy sex fever set in, he had made some of his most striking achievements; but now he no longer cared.

He almost accepted his term in the sanitarium as a penance he deserved. The treatment he received there, the sedatives and the "isolation therapy", succeeded in reducing his libidinous urges to their formerly low, easily managed level.

But now the animal in him was loose again.

He supposed it was guilt that had made him try calling his wife. It certainly wasn't pent-up desire, even now he had glowing memories of her frigidity. He had dialed the number he remembered from seven years ago and had gotten a recorded message that it was no longer in service. That was that. He wasn't even very disappointed. He tried a couple of numbers that had belonged to his favorite call girl. One of the lines kept giving him a busy signal, and the other belonged to a total stranger—a drunken, half incoherent Puerto Rican. Vickers stopped trying the line with the busy signal when he saw Teague giving him the evil eye. Then high and mighty Teague took off and stranded him. Funny, he hardly gave a damn. His mind was becoming like it used to be, focused on getting laid to the exclusion of all other concerns, even those normally deemed major. Chuckling to himself, he went into the phone booth again, to have another shot at phoning his favorite call girl, Sally Davenport, the one with the busy signal. Hearing her voice might fire him up enough to take a crack at one of the beat-up prossies hanging around in the restaurant.

For the umpteenth time he went through the rigma-role of dialing and plunking in coins. To his surprise, Sally Davenport really did answer this time. He brought out his pornographic cards, wanting to look at them while he talked to her. But when he told her who he was, she got scared, called him a weird bastard with an even weirder sense of humor, cursed him for mocking the dead, and hung up on him. He sagged against the corner of the booth, laughing pretty hard, appreciating the humorous aspect of the situation.

He came out of the booth and sat back down on the bench, looking at his cards one by one. Sally Davenport would do anything for a price, even S&M. He hoped he hadn't frightened her so badly that she'd have her phone number changed, but he doubted it—she was used to putting up with all sorts of freaks. Now that he knew he could reach her, he'd surely try to spend some time with her when he got back to New York. The scenes on the playing cards were pretty tame compared to what Vickers was into just before he got put away. The only apparatus involved was a plastic vibrator. Everything else was just straight sex, oral and genital, between couples, three-somes or foursomes. No gay stuff. No S&M. Nothing to get Vickers totally turned on. He could almost picture the cards being used as an ice-breaker at some dull, tacky, middle-class party. Everybody pick a card and you have to do whatever is shown on your card to the person sitting on your left.

Vickers giggled, picturing how his wife would've reacted to his imaginary party game. But his mirth was cut short when a brown Chevy pulled up parallel to the bench he was sitting on. He jumped—his first thought was "police." Trying to act nonchalant, he gave his deck of cards a slow shuffle, keeping the backs facing outward so the pornographic images wouldn't show.

If the driver of the car was a cop, she was out of uniform. A peroxide blonde, not bad looking, not too old either. Vickers looked up at her, still shuffling. "Hi, honey, my name is Mary Jo," she said in a hoarse two-pack-a-day voice that she probably hoped sounded low and sultry. "I was wondering if you could use some company."

Vickers smiled, fanning the cards and turning them toward Mary Jo so she could see the pictures. "Actually," he said, "I'm awfully tired playing solitaire." He got up, clutching the brown paper bag full of purchases from the general store.

Mary Jo laughed. "I'll bet you are, honey," she said, wetting her lips with her tongue. "Hop in, and we'll change the game to stud poker."

She sprayed a can of violet scent around the inside of her car before Vickers got in. Now it smelled like plastic violets and stale cigarettes. There was a quilt in back. The lighter popped and Mary Jo got her cigarette glowing, then pulled into a parking slot. Negotiation time. Vickers had expected her to zip right over to the motel next to the restaurant, but she told him she was a free-lancer, not one of the stable of girls working out of the truck stop. "That way I get to keep all the cash I earn, instead of cutting in those pimps. But if they catch me horning in on their turf they'll break my legs, maybe even kill me," she said, her eyes darting all around the lot while she took short, deep drags on her cigarette.

"Sure you're not a vice cop?" Vickers asked, pointing at the short-wave radio on her dash. "If so, what you're doing to me is entrapment, it'll never stick." He wondered where she was hiding her gun and badge. At least he had something to protect himself; one of the things in his brown paper bag was a big, sharp hunting knife. The rest of the stuff was innocuous: chewing gum, candy, breath mints. He reached into the bag.

"Oh, that!" Mary Jo giggled nervously. "That's my

C.B. It's not police issue—it's how I land my tricks, honey. I cruise the interstate, and when I pull up behind some trucker's big rig, I get him on my wavelength. If he's lonely, I make a date, just like I did with you. But I can get busted, too, if the cops happen to tune in on my pitch, so I have to watch what I say and how I say it. You can trust me, honey. The only cop about me is I'm real good at copping a joint. Twenty bucks for that or you can have a half-and-half, same price. I know a place we can park, cozy and private. I can't use the motel, and I can't hang around here and let the pimps get me."

Vickers had been trying to pop the snap on the leather sheathe for the hunting knife inside the bag. He let go of it, felt for the package of breath mints, pulled it out, opened it, popped a mint into his mouth. He offered one to Mary Jo, hoping she'd take it for her cigarette breath, but she declined. She put her hand on his thigh. "C'mon, honey, I can't stick around! Twenty bucks for a half-and-half, okay?" He nodded. She knocked ash out her window, stuck the cigarette in her mouth, put the car into gear and pulled out.

It alarmed Vickers when he saw they were heading west on the highway, back toward where he and Teague had come from. Was this some kind of trick? Was Mary Jo CIA? Taking him back to Blue Ridge? He reached into his paper bag, used his thumb to pop the snap on the sheathe, and got his fingers around the handle of the hunting knife. *No*, he told himself, *stop* thinking so weirdly. She was just a highway whore, nothing more. He giggled at the accidental rhyme. Highway whore, nothing more. It had a reassuring lilt, he decided.

"Something funny, honey?" Mary Jo asked, stubbing her butt in the ashtray.

He giggled again. Funny honey. Stubbing her butt.

"I like a good dirty joke," she told him. "Help us get to know one another. What's your first name?"

"John," he lied wittily. *He* thought it was witty.

"Well, John," she said, apparently not seeing anything funny about it, "are you married or single?"

"Single."

"What do you do for a living?"

"I'm an astrophysicist."

"Now I *know* you're putting me on," she said, chuckling, lighting up another cigarette.

"No, I'm perfectly serious," he said, offended.

"Well, I didn't mean to hurt your feelings. I'm sorry, I mean it. It's just that you look so ordinary. Mild-mannered. Like a shmoo. Remember the shmoos in the Lil Abner comics? I used to love them! Chubby little things that never hurt anybody, just kept giving themselves to people. That's what you remind me of, Johnny, cuddly as a shmoo, prob'ly not an unkind bone in your body. Right?"

"That's what my wife used to say about me," said Vickers.

"I thought you said you're not married," Mary Jo pounced, flashing him an askance look.

"Helen died…seven years ago."

"Oh…I'm sorry, foot in my mouth again. Haven't you been able to find someone new?" the highway whore said with great sympathy.

"Not where I've been." Highway whore, nothing more. Did she think he might fall for her and marry her? One thing, he was better off in her car than with one of the whores back at that big, conspicuous truck stop. If the CIA had it staked out, he had fooled them. Unless she *was* the stake-out. And even then he could get the jump on her. She didn't know he had the hunting knife, did she? No, she *couldn't* know.

"Where on earth have you been?" she laughed. "Alaska? Even in Alaska they have women, don't they?"

Was she toying with him? Did she know he had been in stir? In Blue Ridge? "I mean my work keeps me busy," he said evenly. "I wanted it to, after Helen died."

"Better to be hooked on work than on drugs," she said, using the dash lighter to get another smoke going. "I've got a hundred-dollar-a-day coke habit. It's not what's making me sell myself, I'd be doing that anyway, I don't have the education to do any kind of work that's not drudgery, minimum wage. I make lots of good, easy money, but cocaine sucks it up. I know I have to get off it, but I can't, John." She took a deep, quick drag. "What's an astrophysicist do, give physics to the Houston Astros?" She cracked up over that one, and he giggled right along with her. She had a clever streak in her he would not have anticipated. But laughing too hard made her cough on her cigarette smoke. "No, seriously," she said, coughing.

"As an astrophysicist," he told her soberly, "I study the physical laws that govern the movements of the heavenly bodies. The workings of the universe. Our own universe…and others."

"What do you mean? There's no other one but ours, is there?"

"I've seen first-hand evidence that we're not alone," he intoned ponderously.

She laughed gleefully. "You're a big put-on, Johnny! You sound like a supermarket tabloid. I buy them 'cause they're so outrageous, they take my mind off of things. Last week there was a big headline about Russian doctors delivering an alien baby! A starship supposedly crashed in Siberia and nine injured spacemen were rescued. They looked like little kids except they were sexless and had green skins and no mouths. One of them was pregnant, but don't ask me how that could be if she was *sexless*," said Mary Jo. "And, get this, her baby came out looking like a *reptile*—it had a lizard head, tiny black eyes and no nose, just a little hole for a nostril. Its skin was blue and scaly instead of green like its parents'." She stubbed out her cigarette. "That makes *no* sense. Why shouldn't the baby look human if the big space people did? Whoever makes up these articles doesn't even use logic!"

"What does a baby butterfly look like?" said Vickers.

"Oh...a caterpillar," said Mary Jo, getting his point.

"You see?" he told her. "It does not resemble its parents. Fuzzy worm turns into butterfly. These extraterrestrials might go through a similar gestation."

"You're not going to get me to believe in them," said Mary Jo, laughing again.

"No, I don't suppose so," Vickers said resignedly. He was convinced now that she knew who he really was. She was playing cat-and-mouse with him. She was CIA. Her superiors, her control, had told her that Dr. Abraham Vickers was crazy, likely to babble about extraterrestrial visitors. What was she going to do? Park somewhere on a pretense of giving him sex, then kill him and leave his body to rot in the woods?

She had already turned off the main highway onto a narrow, rutted dirt road. The bottom of the car bumped over the ruts. Trees were so close their branches scraped the car windows...whisk, whisk...setting Vickers' teeth on edge. He felt claustrophobic. A man being pulled into a trap. An ambush maybe. Inside the paper bag, his hand tightened around the handle of the hunting knife. His fingers cramped. The narrow, bumpy road ended in a tiny clearing, a cul-de-sac. Just enough room to swing the car back and forth to turn around and go out. But the CIA highway whore wasn't going anywhere yet. She cut the engine. She turned toward Vickers and smiled, sure she had him where she wanted him.

He jumped when she moved toward him.

"My, my, Johnny," she teased. "Take it easy, honey. Has it been a long time for you?"

He thought that she knew damn well how long it had been. She had read his dossier.

"A little kiss," she said. "Don't be shy. Then we can get out under the stars, spread the quilt on the grass."

How far was she going to take her perverse game? Was she actually intending to make love to him before whipping out her gun and shooting him? He had to admit it was a hell of a good idea. The ultimate S&M.

Her lips found his. Her tongue went deep, tasting of sour smoke. His fingers stayed in the paper bag, clutching the knife. Shake it, shake it, shake it out of the sheathe. Too tight. He needed his other hand, if he could reach around her...

She pulled away, smiling her coyest, sexiest smile, trying to look damn near virginal. An impossible task. She began to unbutton her blouse. What the hell, he took off his shirt. He realized suddenly that she wasn't about to kill him in the car; she needed it to escape in, she wouldn't want it full of bloodstains. That was why she had mentioned making love in the grass, under the stars. He could've stabbed her while they were kissing. He owned the element of surprise, she didn't know about his knife. He squirmed out of his pants while she undid her skirt.

When she was naked, he saw that she wasn't carrying

any gun on her person. Where was it? Under the car seat? In her red purse, red the color of blood? Yes, red made sense, He let her get the quilt and lead him to a grassy spot in the clearing. "Breath mints," he said, carrying his bag. She brought her purse, red, red, the color of blood. She had her gun, he had his knife, they were circling each other like two sly, murderous animals. Who was going to strike first? The thrill, the suspense, the scariness of it gave Vickers a powerful erection. He dived on Mary Jo, entering her without any preliminaries. His orgasm came quickly, shudderingly, even before she got started. He had the jump on her, more ways than one. As he climaxed he jerked the hunting knife free of its tight leather sheath. It sprang up, big and hard, as his knife of flesh went soft. Mary Jo never even tried to grab for the gun in her purse. She knew her game was up, her cover was blown. "CIA whore!" he screamed, his blade flashing downward. Her scream melded with his as the big heavy knife pierced her breast.

He stabbed her again...and again. "There...there... there...there..." Patiently, he continued to puncture her, the way he had ground the broken bottle into that man's face. In the end his stabs were weak, almost tender little pricks, barely piercing the skin. A myriad of wounds evolved on her naked body, some huge and gaping, some entirely superficial, hard to even discern in the starlight...aesthetic little red marks on her arms and shoulders and back.

Vickers wondered why he was compelled to minister to her in this way. He liked the style, the feel of it. The final pricks and scratches were like the dying tremors of a great orgasm.

He dumped her blood red purse out. Onto the blood-soaked quilt tumbled lipstick, cigarettes, comb, keys, chewing gum... No gun. The clever bitch probably had it hidden under her body. Or else maybe she would've killed him with her hands. Pressure points. Thumb pressure on his carotid artery. He shivered, realizing how narrowly he had averted his own demise. He looked down at himself. He was covered with blood. He backed away from the ugly remains of the CIA whore. He started walking, looking for some clean water, maybe a gurgling stream in the woods, where he could wash himself off. Cleanse his body and spirit. Then get dressed, get in her car and drive away. He needed a car to catch up with high and mighty Teague, who had deserted him.

Worse, he realized. Teague had betrayed him. Teague was the turncoat, the worm in the woodwork. Last man in on the escape plan. Teague was CIA. Working with the dead bitch. Highway whore, something more. But Vickers was too smart, he had smoked her out. He giggled, reliving her death.

No stream nearby. He couldn't hear any gurgling water. He kept walking, naked and barefooted. Twigs and stones hurt his feet, but he was a man with a mission, beyond pain. Soon he came out onto the blacktop road. Had he been wandering in circles? No, he knew he was too smart. He'd catch up with high and mighty treacherous Teague and kill him the way he had killed Teague's partner. Then he' d tell the world about the crash of the saucer, the autopsies on the extraterrestrials. First he'd take a shower, then he'd put on clothes and shoes.

Naked, the bloody knife in his hand, he started walking down the blacktop road.

———

IN A GIFT SHOP at Pittsburgh International Airport, Jenny Teague bought a paperback entitled *UFO Encounters*. If she couldn't smoke, she'd read; it'd help her look like an innocent traveler. Unless some CIA agent saw the title. She chuckled inwardly, trying to dispel the irrational fear. Normally she would never have bought such a work of supposed "nonfiction" because she'd be embarrassed to have anyone catch her reading it—they might suspect her intelligence. But now she found herself irresistibly drawn to the subject matter. It seemed bizarre that things that had *never happened* could have such a profound effect on people's fate. UFOs—or the belief in them—had been a major factor in the horrible murders back at the farmhouse. Was Rolf Kollar telling the truth when he said Jenny's father had spoken, on videotape, of examining UFO wreckage and extraterrestrial corpses? If so, could there be some kind of rational explanation for what he was claiming to have seen? Or was he really insane, like Jenny's sister Sally?

Jenny read the UFO book on the plane. Luckily she got a window seat next to a portly man who spent most of the flight dozing. Still, she hid the book's cover when any of the flight attendants passed by. She felt as sheepish and foolish as she might've felt reading pornography in public.

To her consternation, she discovered that in reports of extraterrestrial encounters, even if the purported contactee could be proven insane the absence of perfect sanity did not serve to discredit testimony. On the contrary, mental deterioration following one of these encounters was to be expected, and could serve as an indication that a genuine encounter might have taken place.

It was common for contactees to exhibit some or all

of the following symptoms when examined medically
and psychologically:

1. Loss of all memory of the encounter until it
   was remembered in dreams or in hypnotic
   regression.
2. Visual and auditory impairment, sometimes to
   the point of hallucination.
3. Burning eyes, headaches, stomach pains.
4. Unusual skin burns, marks or discolorations.
5. Extremely high levels of radiation in the blood
   or major organs.
6. Loss of physical coordination, mental acuity.
7. Tingling or numbness of fingers, toes and
   limbs.
8. Episodes of neurosis or even psychosis.
   Theoretically these side effects could be due to
   the electronic or antigravitational "force-field"
   of the UFO or the telepathic energy generated
   by the extraterrestrials themselves. According
   to the accounts Jenny read, the force-field
   could linger for twenty-four hours or more
   after the UFO disappeared or stopped
   operating over a particular geographic area.

What it all seemed to mean was that, if her father had
actually examined UFO wreckage and alien corpses, the
exposure could have physically altered his brain waves.
He could be telling the truth about what he had seen,
and it could have quite literally driven him insane.

At 9:45 that Saturday night, Brian Meade got a phone
call from CIA national headquarters in Langley, Virginia.
"One of our birds has apparently been spotted," Meade's
case officer told him. "Vickers. He was seen wandering

down a country road, stark naked. A big knife in his hand. West Virginia state troopers got after him, but he scrammed into the woods. It's too dark to track him right now. Those woods are thick and rugged. The troopers are bringing in reinforcements with blood-hounds. First light of dawn they'll go in."

"How do we know it's Vickers?" Meade asked.

"We don't know for sure, but who else could it be? A loony with a knife. Some farmer phoned in the first report—he and his wife almost ran the loony down, they had him in the head-lamps of their pickup truck just after they rounded a bend on their way home from a shopping trip. They said the guy they saw was short, bald and pear-shaped, like a nebbish. It's got to be Vickers. In case it is, we can't afford not to be on the scene."

"Right," said Meade. "Dorsey and I will go. How do we play it? What's our cover story?"

"You'll liaison with the commander of the Wheeling Barracks of the West Virginia State Police, a Lt. Cargill. I ve already set you up with him. He knows you and Dorsey are CIA, and that you're working on a matter vital to national security. Everything else he 'knows' is a he, but the lies sound plausible—he seemed to buy them. You're after Vincent Blake, James Haskell and Charles Perry, renegade CIA agents recently caught selling secrets to the Soviets. Before we could roll them up they disappeared and were presumed to be either dead or in the process of defecting to Moscow. But just this morning, one of our moles in the Russian Embassy informed us that Blake, Haskell and Perry were heavily drugged by the KGB, then turned loose somewhere in West Virginia. The drug they were given, haloperidol, is the same one the communists give their dissidents when they lock them up in insane asylums. It produces psychosis. So, when the West Virginia State Police bulletin turned up on our computer scan, we thought the description of the suspect and the type of incident indicated it could be Blake."

"CLEAN?" said Meade, asking if the bulletin had come over the Civil Law Enforcement Assistance Network, a computerized nationwide criminal data system monitored by the CIA, as situations called for it, from the Langley headquarters.

"Yes," said the case officer. "That part of our story is of course true."

"Will Lt. Cargill turn the suspect over to us if his troopers make the arrest?" Meade asked.

"Well, it's a murky issue. So far the state of West Virginia doesn't have anything substantial on him, only the indecent exposure. We're wiring a federal warrant to Cargill, charging Blake, Perry and Haskell with espionage. But for obvious reasons we can't follow through and put them on trial, even if they're delivered into our hands. That's why the key aspect of this is so dependent on you and Dorsey."

"I understand, sir."

"Very good. Excellent."

What Meade understood, without putting it into incriminating words, was that he and Dorsey were to make sure that Vickers was not taken alive by the West Virginia State Police. How Meade and Dorsey would accomplish this was up to them. The only prerequisite was that "Vincent Blake" must die in a way that would make his death appear "regrettable but unavoidable".

"Hopefully you'll get to question him first," said the case officer.

"That part might be tricky if not impossible," said Meade, "But I have faith that somehow you'll find a way," said the case officer. "If we get Vickers, it'll be one down, two to go. Making him talk first is our best shot at quickly wrapping up all three."

"I'll do my best," said Brian Meade. After getting off the phone with his case officer, he went across the hall from Dr. Lieberman's office, which he had been using in the doctor's absence, to another of the Blue Ridge Hospital administrative offices, where Wayne Dorsey was leaning back, behind a gray steel desk, smoking a cigarette. Meade briefed Dorsey on what they had to do. There was no time to waste. They couldn't wait around till morning; they had to liaison with Lt. Cargill tonight if they expected to join his troopers in the manhunt at the first light of dawn.

"I like our cover story," Dorsey said, smiling, showing his protruding front teeth. "It doesn't inhibit us. We can seem on the level and still do our job. Nobody can prove the three targets aren't who we say they are or that we don't have a good reason to be hunting them down."

"It's a Pulitzer Prize scenario," Meade said, sarcastically. But privately he thought the cover story sounded better than the so-called real story and he'd sooner believe the former if he had to take his pick.

"Wheeling's only about an hour away by helicopter," Dorsey said, looking at a wall map. "If I didn't know better, I'd be tempted to think maybe we're getting a big break, maybe putting the lid on this thing will be a snap. But I know all three guys aren't going to fall into our lap tomorrow. We'll be damn lucky if we wrap up the one."

"Right," Meade said. "For once you're making perfect sense, Dorsey. Must be because you're in the sanity ward."

"Huh?"

Amused but not betraying his amusement, Meade

watched Wayne Dorsey using one finger to scratch the top of his sculpted blonde head, making a cowlick, while his mouth gaped open like a cartoon hayseed. Meantime, Dorsey thought that if Meade had tried to crack a joke, it wasn't funny. Joking was something Meade seldom did, so he didn't exactly know how.

"The sanity ward," Brian Meade said dryly. "That's what Dr. Lieberman calls this particular wing. It's where he keeps the quantalibrium patients. The treatment he gives them while they're here keeps them from going totally bonkers, so he calls it the sanity ward."

Abraham Vickers was terrified of the smoky-black forest. He had found his way in by star light, working his way in deep, till a moist, clinging fog had materialized like a shroud out of nowhere, enveloping his naked skin, forming glistening droplets on the long, thick blade of his knife, turning its red blood-streaked gleam a shimmering pink. His eyes were burning from exhaustion but he stayed on his feet, the soles hurting, his shoulder rubbing the rough bark of a fat tree trunk, as if it were his anchor, scared to sink down into wet weeds where spiders, snakes and other fanged animals might crawl over him in the dark.

He was hopelessly lost and confused. He'd be unable to find his way out even if the sun were shining. His common sense was dribbling away in helpless little spurts—and he knew it. In his brief, lucid moments he tried to soothe himself, working hard not to panic, to stay calm. He'd manage for a few seconds, then the next hot flash would come and his heart would pound so hard he could feel his flabby pectorals quivering and his thought processes would disintegrate like soapy bubbles gurgling down a drain. Just when he was ready to just take off running blindly, a brief calm would come over him, but he couldn't explain why or make it last, though he tried desperately, like a rabid animal in fleeting remission with enough momentary intelligence to grasp the insidious nature of the horrible disease that was relentlessly eroding his mind.

The lucid moments started disintegrating faster and coming over him less and less often, till finally they were replaced by a pervasive sense of humor. Everything was simply funny. Vickers giggled. Pure unadulterated glee percolated through the cells and synapses of his chubby little body. He kept right on giggling, finding the sense of his own doom especially hilarious. He sat down, leaning against the rough bark, laughing so hard he was almost too weak to hold the knife steady.

He had to forcibly concentrate, biting his lip bloody to slow his giggles, using the hunting knife to methodically slice off his left index finger, using the tree trunk as a cutting block. He drolly watched the blood spurt, unable to hold in an explosive spate of giggles.

The blood stream slowed, and he was getting weak, ever so weak, from bleeding and giggling. At last he knew pure freedom and joy, utter release from any caring about living or dying, like the inmate he had seen burning his fingers on the fence. He must start on the next finger before he became too weak from laughter. No, the thumb. The thumb should be next. The notion tickled him, and he had to control his mirth to steady the sharp blade and make it slice cleanly into the web of flesh at the thick, chubby joint. He hoped he would have the strength to do all the rest of his fingers. Wondering how he could hold the knife to do the other hand made him laugh harder and harder and harder…

15

Teague woke up groggily when the muted sunlight got hot enough to make him sweat. The rays were slanting through a grimy, uncurtained window near his bed. He let his eyes go shut and was scared to open them again—he might find himself back in the sanitarium. But, no. His sanitarium cell didn't smell musty and the mattress on the steel, bolted-down bunk was hard as a board, not squeaky and saggy like *this* mattress. He got the courage to look around. He never dreamed he'd be this overjoyed to awaken in a fleabag hotel room.

For a long time he made no move to swing his legs out of bed. He kept going over and over everything that had happened in the past twenty-four hours. At least three people that he knew of were dead, in addition to the guards and inmates who had perished at Blue Ridge before the helicopter got out of there. Teague now realized he probably should've killed Vickers instead of merely ditching him. The situation was dog eat dog, a primal struggle for survival. If the little fat man fell into enemy hands, he could tell them the make and license number of the car Teague was driving, if they didn't already know.

The car would have to be ditched. Belatedly this had dawned on Teague last night when he was racing toward the Pennsylvania Turnpike, and at the last instant he had bypassed the turn-off to the toll ramp. He couldn't understand how he had almost made such a dumb mistake. He should've automatically known he'd have to avoid all major highways till he got another car. His thinking must be sluggish from seven years of not having to deal with the real world. He had to remind himself that the real world was full of a lot of nice things, a lot of pretty things, but also a lot of things that were ugly and dangerous.

What was the name of this little town? Washington, Pennsylvania. Only about thirty miles from Wheeling. He had come into it by a back road after getting enough sense to get off of the interstate. Then he had decided to hole up till morning. The Lafayette Hotel. Yes. Remembering the name of the town and the hotel was a good sign. He was already thinking better, after a few hours of fitful sleep.

What day was it? Sunday. He had in mind to ditch the Oldsmobile in the woods somewhere, then pay cash for some kind of used car. But no car dealerships would be open on Sunday. So, think. *Think.* All right, get hold of a newspaper and check the classified ads. Buy a car directly from the owner, greasing the deal with a hefty chunk of cash from the suitcase under the bed.

Remembering the cash made Teague's heart skip a beat. What if it was gone? His eyes snapped toward the bolt on the warped, chipped-varnish door. The bolt was still secure, thank God. The one tall, narrow window by the bed was still locked. Apparently nobody had sneaked in during the night. But Teague was alarmed enough to get up and drag out the suitcase, brushing dust balls off of it as he tossed it onto the squeaking bed. His fingers shook as he fumbled in his trousers pocket for the key, and when he pulled the key out the trousers fell onto the dirty linoleum floor. He unlocked the suitcase and opened it. Then, his eyes feasting on all those green-backs, he was overcome by a compulsion to count them.

He dumped the bundles out, using the sagging mattress as a trough, making an enormous overflowing pile on the squeaky bed. The bundles were wrapped with thousand-dollar money wrappers. He checked three bundles and found that each one really did contain a thousand dollars. He scrutinized a few bills and found no ink smudges, no blunt or sketchy engraving, no indica-tion of counterfeiting. Then he counted the bundles as he packed them back into the suitcase. There were four hundred and ninety-nine. The five-hundredth one would have been the one he and Vickers had split up for pocket money before going into the truck stop.

He was rich, if he could stay alive and hang onto his fortune. But it was a case of double jeopardy. The suit-case full of money was enough, in and of itself, to make him a hunted man, even disregarding questions of ideol-ogy. He couldn't trust anybody—everybody was either a traitor or a potential traitor. Even his daughter Jenny. And especially his wife Martha. She must have been involved in the plot to commit him to the sanitarium. She and her adulterous lover. Teague could see clearly now how his wife and Gary Cameron must have conspired to make his blood boil. He couldn't wait to get back to New York and confront them.

Perspiring and grimacing with rage, he groped under the limp, yellowish pillow and pulled out the big .45

automatic that had already blown two of his enemies away, back at the farmhouse. Clutching the weapon, he vowed that nobody would silence him this time, nobody would stifle him and betray him, not even his own flesh and blood.

————

"IT'S CALLED LESCH-NYHAN SYNDROME," said Dr. Lieberman, referring to what Abraham Vickers had done to himself.

He was talking to agents Meade and Dorsey, who had just returned from Wheeling. Not long after sunup that Sunday morning, West Virginia State Police led by Lt. Cargill, with Meade and Dorsey tagging along, had found the hacked and mutilated body of Mary Jo Means, a known prostitute; then they had used bloodhounds, giving the dogs a whiff of Mary Jo's blood and Vickers' cast-off clothing, to track Vickers to where he had died, deep in the forest, with most of his fingers and toes cut off. Meade and Dorsey had identified the body of "Vincent Blake" and had presented Lt. Cargill with official documents enabling them to claim it. The corpse and its severed digits were now being consumed in the crematorium maintained at Blue Ridge for the disposal of deceased inmates.

"Lesch-Nyhan syndrome," Dr. Lieberman explained, "is caused by a mutant gene, a fact that was discovered about twenty years ago by Drs. Michael Lesch and William Nyhan of the Johns Hopkins medical school. The syndrome was first noticed in certain children suffering from cerebral palsy. As they became older, they began to exhibit aggressive and self-mutilating behavior. If they weren't restrained, they would compulsively chew off their fingers, lips and tongues. Or they would ferociously attack other children, biting, kicking and scratching like demons. Often they would howl with laughter as if the most striking thing about their sado-masochistic behavior was its humorous aspect."

Meade cleared his throat and rubbed his drooping jowls between his thumb and fingers. "Are you saying that your drug, quantalibrium, produces the Lesch-Nyhan syndrome in previously normal adults?"

"Not always," said Lieberman. "But sometimes. In fact, in about ten percent of the cases. We're trying to get at the root of the chemical reactions involved, and eliminate all the undesirable side effects. We know that in the Lesch-Nyhan children the mutant gene inhibits the production of a specific enzyme that's necessary for normal brain development. Somehow quantalibrium also indirectly destroys this enzyme in some adults whose genes give no evidence of being impaired."

"What are the chances of Thompson and Teague going totally bonkers like Vickers did?" Wayne Dorsey asked, cigarette smoke furling between his protruding uppers. "If we can't find them our own way, I wouldn't cry myself to sleep if they cleaned up their own mess by bumping themselves off."

"Well," said Dr. Lieberman, "neither Teague nor Thompson ever exhibited any tendency toward the Lesch-Nyhan syndrome when we experimentally withheld or moderated the dosage of their control medications. Like Vickers, they were both paranoid schizophrenics, but without self-destructive tendencies. Their delusions will gather force the longer they stay on the loose, but all of their rage and aggression will be directed toward others. They may become serial murderers. Their behavior will have a certain deranged logic, with a rationale and motives that they find perfectly comprehensible within the framework of their own psychological warp. They will be able to scheme and plan and take steps to elude capture, just like any ordinary homicidal maniacs."

"Could they have turned against whoever busted them out?" Dorsey asked.

"Quite possible," said Lieberman with a thin smile. "The more they deteriorate mentally and emotionally, the less they'll trust anyone, even each other. Anybody who befriends them will be in mortal danger."

Brian Meade's dislike for the director of Blue Ridge Hospital took on a new aspect. He could see that Dr. Lieberman was enamored of the strange manifestations produced by quantalibrium and proud of his part in unleashing them. He liked to see his creation at work, even if the work was sometimes destructive. He was a modern conjurer whose mumbo-jumbo had set loose some evil demons, and there was a dark side of him that could appreciate what he had wrought as good, scary entertainment.

"What a weird situation," Dorsey said. He leaned forward and stubbed out his cigarette. "Tell you what, I have a funny hunch Teague's the only one of the three still alive and kicking. Thompson's body is gonna turn up somewhere just as dead as Vickers. Lt. Cargill's men talked to folks at that truck stop who saw Teague and Vickers come in and buy stuff and then leave together, but they didn't see anybody who looked like Thompson. So where the hell was he all that time?"

"Could be he was asleep in whatever kind of car they were driving, which I wish some witness would've seen," said Meade. "Right now we don't know exactly what we're chasing or what direction to look. All we can do is guess. That's why we've got to rely on our stake-outs."

Dr. Lieberman's intercom buzzed. He picked up the phone. After a short listen he said, "It's for you," and handed the phone to Meade.

A secretary put Meade on hold, then in a few seconds his case officer got on the line. "It's confirmed," the case officer said with a triumphant snap to his voice. "Jenny Teague was in Wheeling yesterday. Our guy showed her picture to the airline clerks. He got a positive I.D. I want you to roll her up. How soon can you be in Georgetown?"

Meade took his good old time replying, letting long seconds of silence dull the thrust of his case officer's impulsiveness. At times like this, Meade's reputation for thinking and acting slowly was a quite useful ploy, giving him the necessary time to dope out and slow down other people's hasty moves. It was always very tempting to react to every little apparent break in a frustrating case, whereas often it was wiser *not* to react. Just keep a poker face and don't prematurely lay all the cards face up.

Late last night, agents watching Jenny Teague's Georgetown apartment had seen her coming home carrying a traveling bag. That had prompted a computer search of airline reservations, and the name "Jenny Trask" had popped up. Most criminals had a tendency to choose aliases that let them keep at least the initials of their real names, but Jenny had gone to a ridiculous extreme. Meade almost found her ineptness touching. After all, who could blame her for wanting to help her own father? The question was, who had enlisted her and why? She must have known in advance about the Blue Ridge escape. But how much more did she know? Maybe nothing. Her father, in his deteriorating mental condition, might be running from her and everybody else. Just because she went to see him didn't mean that she succeeded.

"I don't think it'd be smart to snatch her," Meade said. "Just keep her under tight surveillance. She's more valuable as bait."

"No," said the case officer. "We have to find out everything she knows. Then either give her a snow job that'll make her work for our side, or..."

"Or make her disappear."

"Yes."

"Two disappearances in the same family, even with a seven-year gap, are going to stir up a whole other can of worms, and we might find that we've gained a big fat zero." Meade said. "At this point there's no guarantee Jenny Teague can tell us where her father is or where he might be headed. According to Dr. Lieberman, quantalibrium makes people run around like chickens with their heads cut off. It could be that Jenny made a wasted trip and had to go home without ever laying eyes on her father. But if he stays on the loose he may eventually search her out. We should stick to her like glue, day and night, but don't do anything to rattle her."

The case officer took a deep breath. "Okay," he said with great reluctance. "We'll play it your way for now. I'll give you a week. Till next Saturday. If the mouse doesn't come for the cheese by then, we're going to roll her up."

"Agreed," said Meade. But he hoped some other angle would break first. He hated to have a case running him instead of the other way around. It made him feel like he was trapped in the middle of a big cold snowball gathering momentum, rolling downhill. If the damn thing hit a boulder and broke apart, he could be the only one who got smashed while his superiors looked on from a high, safe hill.

He didn't especially want to see Jenny Teague destroyed, but he didn't see how he could prevent it. She was probably innocent of any evil intentions other than the zeal to be reunited with her "dead" father. Meade could empathize greatly with that kind of wistful impulse, that kind of unrequited longing. His own daughter, Sarah, would have been about Jenny's age by now, if she hadn't died with her mother in a car accident. Sarah and Jean were on their way home from a supermarket. Sarah was only three years old, strapped in her car seat. They stopped at a red-light and a punk kid high on speed slammed into them. The gas tank exploded. Lot of good it did them to be buckled in. To this day, Meade could never bring himself to wear a seatbelt, even though he knew it was the safe, smart thing to do, Jean and Sarah couldn't have escaped the instantaneous inferno, buckled or unbuckled.

He wasn't a profoundly introspective man, yet he sometimes wondered if his refusal to use a seatbelt meant that he had a secret, subconscious desire to end the sadness and loneliness that often overwhelmed him when he wasn't working hard, cleaning up other people's messes. But if part of him didn't want to go on, why did he conscientiously protect himself on the job when he could purposely make some dumb move that would cause his superiors to have him eliminated? Or why didn't he just let somebody on the other side plug him? More than once there had been chances where he could have let himself be a fraction too late squeezing off a round from his Colt Cobra.

But the death wish scenarios repulsed him. Maybe they were subtle forms of suicide, but still suicide no matter how you cut it, and Meade didn't want to die dishonorably even if he'd be the only one to know. He had too much pride, too much patriotism. Staunch Catholic beliefs were deeply ingrained in him, even though he hadn't been to mass since the day of the double funeral, fifteen years ago. He liked to think his loved ones were waiting for him and watching over him. Maybe someday he'd join them, if he managed to die with his sins forgiven, and if he didn't take his own life, an act which the Church said would keep his soul forever in limbo, eternally separated from God and from his cherished wife and daughter.

Dr. Norman Teague arrived in New York City on Sunday night, after making an eight-hour drive in the five-year old rusty green LeMans he had bought for three-thousand dollars cash from a retired schoolteacher in Washington, Pa. He checked into a Holiday Inn on West 57th Street, below Ninth Avenue. He was scared to go out of his room, scared to even temporarily abandon the suitcases containing the videotapes and a fortune of almost half a million dollars. So he ordered a steak dinner from room service, cased the hallway through the peephole before opening the door, and stayed alert to whip out his .45 automatic at the first sign that the bellboy might be anything but a real bellboy. Nothing fishy happened. Teague gave the bellboy a proper fifteen percent tip, not too high, not too low—he wasn't about to draw attention to himself by coming on too stingy or as too much of a splurger.

The steak dinner was passable, the porterhouse not too tough, the baked potato warm but not hot. He wished he had ordered a bottle of scotch and considered remedying the oversight, but he decided not to have another go at room service. At least he had a carafe of coffee and a glass of ice water. When he finished eating, he did another careful check through the peephole before easing the door open and depositing the tray in the hall.

He stayed up late reading and watching television. He had to voraciously devour current events in order to reassert his place in the world, to capture the scope and breadth of everything that had transpired during his absence. He had bought piles of popular magazines —*Time, Newsweek, U.S. News, Omni, Penthouse, Playboy, Scientific American, Reader's Digest*—at various points along his journey, including the newsstand in the motel lobby. While he read he thought of many, many things, including disguises. What should he do to make himself look different? Grow a mustache or a beard? Buy a wig? Shave his head? All of that stuff seemed not only silly but of dubious effectiveness. Anyway, he didn't want to change his appearance, did he? He wanted to look as much like himself as possible so he could convince others of who he really was. He had to get his videotapes on the air. He had to latch onto somebody who might help him, somebody he might trust. The world wouldn't believe one lonely voice crying in the wilderness. They'd dismiss him as a nut. They'd have a vested interest in keeping him dead, if only to protect their own sanity, so dependent on the false reality that had been painstakingly constructed for them.

The following morning, he left the Holiday Inn, carrying two suitcases. He trundled them to the nearest branch of the Manhattan National Bank, where he opened a savings account by depositing two thousand dollars cash in the name of Norman Thompson. He hated using a false name, but he had no choice. There was little doubt in his mind that the CIA would be scanning America's vast computer networks for any new transactions by Norman league. The bank manager let him open his account and also reserve two safety deposit boxes when he explained that he had lost his Social Security card but would furnish the number in a few days, after he received his duplicate card in the mail. The address he used on all the bank forms was fictitious, but the important thing was that he now had keys to two safety deposit boxes, where he stashed most of his money and his tapes. He felt freer than he had felt for days as he carried the light, empty suitcases back to the Holiday Inn.

After a room-service lunch, he took a taxi to the New York Public Library where he took out and paid for a library card under the name Norman Thompson. He looked up his real name in the card catalogue and checked out books and periodicals to begin reading up on his own disappearance. He learned many news-worthy facts and semi-facts about his wife and his two daughters. To his surprise. Martha by now was well known as a rocketry expert, almost a celebrity in her own right, whereas seven years ago she dwelt in his shadow. Apparently Dr. Gary Cameron was stroking her ego by allowing her to be his collaborator on a number of important projects. It was probably how he had won her over and seduced her. Teague seethed with rage when he pictured himself as their cuckold. Researching his own life as if he were a stranger to himself, he found out that his daughter Jenny was a student at Georgetown University and Sally was supposedly suffering from a psychosis. No wonder. They had ripped her father away from her and made the poor child grow up in a miasma of lies and hypocrisy.

In a *New York Times* interview that Teague read, his daughter Jenny sounded quite intelligent, honest, charmingly sincere. He felt a surge of pride in her that he could not wholly suppress. Was it all too pat? Or did it make perfect sense that his eldest daughter would become a journalism major with a probing, fact-seeking mind and a zeal to be reunited with her father? Teague yearned to believe in her. Yet he knew it was wiser not to. But wasn't he only human, after all? Didn't he need a friend? An ally?

In his desperation, he rehashed his impressions of Rolf Kollar, who had presented himself as the prime mover behind the escape from Blue Ridge. Could it be that Kollar really wasn't in on the KGB plot that caused the deaths at the safe house? Could he himself have been a victim of the treachery?

Over the next two days, returning several times to the library, Teague researched Kollar's background and even read some of Kollar's books. It was clear that the man had built an extraordinary career on the study of extraterrestrial encounters; and as a prime result of his work he had been vilified by the military and scientific establishments. His enemies were Teague's enemies. Perhaps his motives had been genuine and he was suffering as much as Teague from the traitors all around them.

Jenny Teague got four B's and one A on her final exams, when normally she should have expected straight A's with maybe, at the worst, one B. The only good thing about this week was that it *was* final week so she didn't have to go to regular classes and she didn't have to sing in public. She was able to stay in her apartment, seldom venturing out except to take the five tests, but no matter where she was, she felt that ghosts were looking over her shoulder. She wondered if she was being watched by government agents—or even by her father. Somehow she managed not to go back to chain-smoking, even though her nerves were a total frazzle. She kept thinking about Rolf Kollar's prediction that if her father remained alive and on the loose he would eventually try to contact her. If he did try it, government agents or even foreign agents might pounce on him. Jenny could very well get caught in the middle. Whoever didn't want it to be known that her father was still alive might have to dispose of her, to keep her mouth shut.

She was glad that her finals were all crammed into the first half of the week, because now she was anxious to go home, where at least her misery could have company, even though she couldn't share her secrets. Right after her last test was over, on Wednesday, she lost no time packing up her personal belongings and piling them into her little red Toyota hatchback. She had already notified her landlady that she wished to reserve the apartment for next school term, in spite of her promise to her mother that she'd think about transferring. That promise had been contingent upon her hopes of having her father back home, and now those hopes seemed somehow shakier and illusory than ever.

She could have driven the Toyota down to Wheeling last Saturday but Rolf Kollar had told her not to. He had said it was bad enough *she* might be recognized, let alone having one more vehicle on hand with a traceable license plate. As harrowing as going by plane had been, it would've been far rougher on her if she' d have had to drive back alone from the scene of the disaster.

On Thursday morning she drove home to New York, a five-hour ordeal at 55 mph on the interstates where most of the other vehicles kept zooming past her as if she were standing still. The creepy feeling that she was probably being tailed made her stick tenaciously to the speed limit, fighting the wild itch to floor it and get the damned trip over with. At one point she was pretty sure she had picked out the man following her in a black Nova, but then he disappeared from her rearview mirror, and she wasn't sure whether she was wrong about him or if he was replaced by another agent.

She didn't stop to eat. She only stopped once for gas. It was a lovely spring day, but for her its beauty didn't matter. She didn't feel any of the exuberance she normally would've felt with a year of school over and finals over and passed with good grades. She couldn't stand the idea of going into a restaurant and wondering about every pair of eyes behind her back. So she ignored her hunger pangs and told herself she was too nervous to hold any food down anyway. She kept trying to piece together everything that had happened to her, kept dwelling on it and rehashing it, to the point where she was worried she might have a wreck from not keeping her mind on the road. She decided that she simply couldn't believe her father had been a traitor. If somebody had to be blamed for whatever had happened, why not Thompson and Vickers? Maybe they were spying for or attempting to defect to the Soviets, and somehow implicated her father—and that's why the CIA made them disappear. That kind of thing would be more plausible than a UFO cover-up. Her father was an innocent victim caught in the middle, and now she was caught too. She was on his side but he didn't know it. They were together against the same frightening odds.

She remembered Rolf Kollar's promise to get in touch with her, should he learn anything new and important. She half hoped and half dreaded that somehow this would happen. He was perhaps her closest living link to her father, but it was a link that seemed to have been severed.

Feeling utterly powerless, Jenny tried to think how she might use her college-acquired journalistic skills to follow up the leads and get at the truth. But she would probably have had to start at the safe house in Wheeling, and to have kept going from there, wherever the pursuit would have taken her and no matter what the cost. She hadn't been brave enough to even consider doing it at the time. And now the scary opportunity was gone.

The closer she got to home, the more edgy she became. Zooming into Manhattan through the long white fluorescence of the Holland Tunnel was like burrowing into a brightly lit unknown. All her life she had enjoyed the immense power, the bustle and jangle, the thrilling promise of the vast city, but now she found it threatening. She dreaded what might happen to her here, as if she were a timid, frightened tourist from the boon-docks instead of a proud, confident native. Most of outsiders' fears were exaggerated, built of lurid publicity, but hers were not—she had seen the dead bodies to prove it. The ogres set loose at the so-called "safe" house probably weren't going to leave her alone. She didn't know how she'd be able to carry on blithely in the presence of her mother, grandmother and sister. And her intended stepfather.

Sally was home from St. Francis Hospital. Jenny knew it from talking to her mother on the phone Wednesday night. But now coping with her younger sister's mental state was the least of her worries. She'd consider it a triumph if she could cope with her own.

Half a block from her home, instead of being in a light, happy mood, she was clenching the Toyota's steering wheel so hard her knuckles were bloodless, her palms slippery. A white Corvette ahead of her stopped for a red-light, and she jammed on the brakes, narrowly screeching to a stop in time to avoid a rear-end collision. The other driver glowered at her and she shrugged apologetically, rubbing her hands on her jeans, leaving sweat marks. If there had been a pack of cigarettes in the glove compartment she might've dived for them; after all she had been through, it seemed weird that public embarrassment, not fear, might have driven her to start smoking again.

The guy in the Corvette swiveled his head around and peeled out angrily, and she followed at a much slower pace, leaving a longer gap than usual. She had timed her arrival for mid-afternoon so she wouldn't have to fight the rush hour, but now she'd almost prefer to be hung up in traffic a while longer. She had little doubt that the building she lived in, Park West Apartments on the corner of West 70th, would be under surveillance. Half a block from home, she got stopped by another red-light, and she looked all around at familiar sights that were suddenly threatening. A loiterer on a park bench could be covertly watching her from behind his newspaper. The man selling hot dogs and soft pretzels under the Cinzano umbrella across the street could be a secret agent. Throngs of people loafing at the fringes of the park— joggers, frisbee tossers, binocular wearers—all were suspect.

For all Jenny knew, her father might even be lurking somewhere, watching her and trying to outfox all the other watchers. Every time she went out from now on these kinds of jittery thoughts would be tumbling through her head—she wondered if she could stand it.

Sucking in a deep breath, trying to resign herself to putting on a cheerful face for her welcoming family, she pulled the red Toyota around the corner to the side entrance of Park West Apartments and clicked on her left-turn signal to go down the ramp into the huge underground parking garage reserved for residents of the building.

She looked all around before sticking her pass card in the slot. When the corrugated steel door lifted far enough, she pulled right in. Then she stopped, turned her head and watched the door go shut, so she would know that no one had slipped in behind her.

Security was tight at Park West, but there were still ways that a determined intruder might sneak in. Always before now she had entertained some slight fear that one day somebody might be lurking behind one of the white-washed pillars in the subterranean garage. Today her eyes darted all about as she selected a parking slot, and she didn't even try to convince herself that her fear was probably irrational.

16

The teenage clerk in the registrar's office became very cooperative when she was told that the man on the line had to talk with Jenny Teague about a summer job on his small-town newspaper. "Sir, will you please hold for a moment?" she said perkily. "I'll punch up Miss Teague's file."

"Jenny gave me her Georgetown University phone number," the man explained, "but I haven't been able to reach her there, and if I can't get in touch with her I'll have to hire someone else."

"Oh, we wouldn't want you to do that, sir. Just a moment, I'll try to help you." After a couple of minutes, the clerk got back on the line. She sounded puzzled. "According to our computer, Miss Teague's final exams were finished yesterday. And she's already accepted summer employment with the Cameron Foundation in New York City. That's where she lives, so with her finals over she might be on her way home."

"What number do you have for her campus residence? Maybe I made a mistake jotting it down. As I said, I've tried calling there but I get no answer."

The clerk hesitated. "Well...I suppose there's no harm in giving out the number, since it's in the Student-Directory anyway. Here it is..."

Norman Teague already had his pen ready. He copied down the number. "Thank you very much," he said cheerfully. "You may have done your university a service, miss, because if I can't hire Jenny, the next person in line comes from a school that's one of your archrivals in basketball—St. John's."

"Oh! We certainly wouldn't want you to hire anyone from there!" the clerk said, giggling.

"Thank you for your help," Teague said, and hung up.

He was a little concerned that he may have been on the phone long enough for his call to be traced. But he didn't figure that the registrar's office would be wire-tapped. Probably the only tap would be on Jenny's line. He dialed the number the clerk had given him, only to get a recorded message that the number was no longer in service. If his daughter would've answered, he would have hung up. At this point he only wanted to pinpoint her whereabouts, not try to make contact. He had to play everything close to the vest or else he might walk into a trap.

Since her final exams were over and her campus phone number was already disconnected, odds were pretty good that Jenny must have already left for home. If so, she could be there now. She *must* be there. Teague could feel it in his bones. He had been scared that the computer read-out from the registrar's office would say that she was dead or missing—somehow a victim of whatever had gone wrong in Wheeling—but apparently she had returned safely to college, if she had ever really been in Wheeling, and now she'd be home for the summer. Unless the CIA had screwed with the computer read-out. Which Teague doubted. He seemed to be developing a sixth sense regarding matters vital to him, and more and more he was relying on his animal instincts and believing in them as a special kind of ESP born out of his need to exist on the razor's edge of the struggle for survival. He believed that all his senses and all his wits were unnaturally sharpened so he could outfox his enemies and turn the tables on them. He could feel Jenny's presence, less than a hundred miles away. He knew she must have gone home to her mother, grandmother and sister...and she must realize that he was alive. But he could not go to her. He couldn't phone her. Not unless he wished to be caught.

Today Teague was in a hotel in East Point, Long Island, the beach town where Rolf Kollar lived. He had been here since noon, and had already scouted Kollar's large Victorian house, two blocks from the shore. Somewhat to his surprise, the place did not appear to be under surveillance by anyone other than himself. Apparently Kollar was not suspected for his involvement in the Blue Ridge break-out. Teague considered that this tended to prove what he already was inclined to assume: that Kollar had taken part in the plot out of personal motives and was not working for the KGB or the CIA.

This morning, Thursday morning, Teague had checked out of the Holiday Inn and had taken his last ride in the rusty green LeMans. He chanced his first and only cruise past Park West Apartments and past the Cameron Foundation on West 82nd Street. He kept his eyes straight ahead like a disinterested ordinary citizen as a thrilling surge of panic shot through him at the thought of how close he was to his family and to his enemies. How easy it would be for some stake-out man to pick him up through a hidden lens! But it didn't happen. He got by. Panic turned to exhilaration over the close call. He warned himself not to become addicted to those kinds of thrills.

He drove out to LaGuardia and abandoned the LeMans in the vast airport parking lot, then tore up his ticket stub and dropped the pieces into a rubbish barrel. Odds were that the car would sit there for weeks without attracting any special attention—after all, there wasn't a smelly corpse rotting in the trunk. Eventually it would be towed to the auto pound and if nobody claimed it, it would be crushed into a lumpy block of metal and plastic. Probably nobody would take the time and trouble to trace the registration back to the retired school teacher in Washington, Pa. Anyhow, the worst that could happen would be that the CIA might end up dusting the car for fingerprints and then they'd learn that Teague had driven it to New York. So what. They already knew the Big Apple was his likely destination, and finding out how he had gotten here wouldn't help them a bit. It was still a cat-and-mouse game for him not to fall into their hands, and he had a city of eight million to scurry around in, looking out for the hunters and listening for the bells on their necks. Lying back on his comfortable hotel bed, he chuckled to himself. His enemies didn't literally wear bells, but they might as well. They often moved slowly and clumsily and bureaucratically, while his moves by comparison were sleek and smart.

This morning he got away from LaGuardia soon as he ditched the car, because he was wise to the fact that all airline terminals would have been put under heavy surveillance right after the Blue Ridge escape went down. Nobody pounced on him, though. He took a taxi to East Point. Tonight he intended to pay Rolf Kollar an unannounced visit. But first he'd have to dope out a way to deal with Kollar's big, mean German Shepherd. Through a pair of binoculars bought at an East Point sporting goods store, he had observed the beast prowling behind a cyclone fence and going into a wild slavering frenzy, rattling the fence with the weight of his lunging body, when some kids came by on their way to the beach. Apparently the animal was trained to viciously attack anybody but its master; it didn't bark and growl when Kollar came out to feed it, but just wagged its tail merrily like a tame, innocent pup.

"Come here, Taurus," Kollar cried out. "That's a good boy! Are you hungry?"

Teague didn't stick around long, even though he had a good hiding place back in the woods. The vicious beast might sniff his presence and somehow let his master know where to look. The whole setup—the guard dog and the fence—sent shivers up Teague's spine, reminding him of Blue Ridge.

———

JENNY'S GRANDMOTHER, Helen Dudley, cooked a wonderful meal in celebration of her homecoming. All of Jenny's favorite things were on the menu: ziti macaroni with meatballs, chicken and spareribs cooked in the red sauce, fried eggplant, spinach salad, espresso coffee and homemade cannoli. Mrs. Dudley's maiden name was Helen Corsini, and she had been raised on fine Italian cooking in a large family that operated a successful restaurant in Brooklyn. Her husband, an electrical engineer, had met her when she was nineteen years old and waitressing in the restaurant. It always amazed Jenny that her grandmother was such a refined and worldly woman, sophisticated beyond her level of formal education. In fact, she seemed wiser, more gentle and understanding than Jenny's mother a lot of the time, although Jenny tried to think that this was because her mother was so busy with her work and so traumatized by the events of seven years ago. Still, there was no denying that she could relate more easily to her grandmother than to her mother. In appearance, Mrs. Dudley wasn't the stereotype Italian grandmother with black hair up in a bun and fat jiggling under her upper arm when she waved her wooden spoon. She was neat, trim and fashionably slender, her gray curls crisply permed, her complexion slightly ruddy from makeup tastefully and judiciously applied. Somehow her white apron didn't even seem to get any spots on it, she was so skillful and efficient when she worked in the kitchen.

Today being a Thursday, a regular work day, Jenny's mother wouldn't be home till six. Often she worked later than that, but for this festive occasion she had promised to be home. Gary Cameron was coming for dinner too, pushing the point that he was part of the family. Wonderful, Jenny thought. On her first day back, in fact within the first few hours, she'd have to put on a false face for everybody and pretend that all the lovely, delicious food wasn't sticking in her throat.

The cooking odors filled the small apartment, even drifting back to Jenny's bedroom as she unpacked the luggage she had brought home from college. Her sister Sally sat on the bed watching her, not saying a word, not jumping up and down asking what this was and what that was, the way any ordinary seven-year-old sister should have behaved. She was tranquilized into stone-faced placidity, like a gargoyle sitting cross-legged, her green plaid skirt hiked up in a way that would've been lewd if she hadn't been wearing panties. Her freckled face was cute, surrounded by light brown hair done up in bangs and ponytails, rather it would have *been* cute if it hadn't been so oddly expressionless. Jenny felt guilty admitting it to herself, but Sally gave her the creeps. It was hard to treat her like a normal little girl, which was the way one was supposed to treat her as much as possible, on the theory that it would encourage her to *stay* normal instead of lapsing into one of her recurrent schizophrenic episodes. Thank God that although this apartment wasn't huge, it did have three bedrooms. In the old apartment Jenny and Sally had slept in the same room. If that were still the case, Jenny certainly would've found some excuse not to come home for the summer. As it was, she would lock her door at night, scared of what Sally might do to her in her sleep.

"Are you going to be here all the time now?" Sally asked suddenly, startling Jenny. The child sounded as though she very much wished the answer wouldn't be yes.

Jenny almost dropped the sweater she was refolding. "I think just for the summer," she said. "Unless I transfer back here for next semester…the way Mom wants me to."

"Why does she want you to do that?"

Sally's tone indicated that she found the notion of having her big sister around all the time perfectly dreadful, and so should everyone else. Jenny wasn't far from agreeing out loud.

But she refrained. "It's nice to have the whole family

together," she said, grimacing at the double entendre only she could understand.

"You don't like me watching you, do you?" Sally asked, and continued to sit and watch even after Jenny did not reply. She could have said she didn't mind, but it would have been a lie, and she was perversely glad that she had chosen to keep at least that one little lie off the books. If anybody was Up There counting, which she very much doubted.

She considered pleading sickness so she wouldn't have to sit down to a big "happy" meal with the family. When she had first arrived, after hugging and kissing her grandmother and her little sister, she had said that she was tired from her trip and not feeling well, thereby laying the groundwork for copping out of anything that became too unpleasant.

"Oh, dear, I hope you're going to feel well enough to eat!" Grandmother had said. "Why don't you just lie down for a while, Jenny? Take some aspirin. You don't have to be in a rush to unpack. It can wait till tomorrow, can't it?"

"I'd rather get it out of the way," Jenny had said. "Then I can rest without worrying."

"A young girl like you worrying about such a little thing?" Grandmother had said, smilingly raising her eyebrows.

Jenny got all her stuff put away, then told Sally that she wished to take a nap.

"You just don't want me around," Sally accused. She took her good old time swinging her legs over the edge of the bed, standing up, bending and straightening her knee socks, plucking imaginary lint from her skirt, and finally leaving the bedroom.

Jenny shut the door, bolted it, sliding the bolt home very softly, and stood there breathing deeply, trying not to cry. She didn't completely succeed and had to reach for a tissue to blot her cheeks. Looking at herself in the dresser mirror, she thought she was about to fall to pieces. How could she possibly pull herself together? The whole ordeal was getting to be way too much for her to handle.

It dawned on her that so far through this crazy mess she had been almost entirely passive. Instead of acting on her own hook, she was a pawn, pulled this way and that by strangers and strange chains of events of which she had barely a glimmer. If she had some plan, some logical goal, maybe it would help her cope. Maybe it would be better than floundering helplessly in a dearth of facts, waiting for the roof to cave in instead of helping to shore it up.

But what could she do to better her situation? How could she escape the void or at least make it more habitable? She lay down on her bed, staring up at the white ceiling, working hard to concentrate her thoughts without using cigarettes as a crutch. A couple of times she glanced at the nightstand, seeing the clean glass ashtray, figuring she'd have to get rid of it now because she didn't need it and didn't want to ever need it again. It occurred to her that if she had to play a role, if she had to wear a mask in the presence of her family members, then maybe she should actively determine what shape the role should take. Don a mask of her own choosing. Decide to become a spy in a hostile camp. Instead of unwillingly harboring her secrets, maybe she should covet them and use them as a basis to discover even more. If her father stayed alive, he would have to prove his identity. He'd have to convert the disbelievers. He would need help. Someone to lay the groundwork. Somebody like Jenny.

Buoyed by a new sense of purpose, she sprang to her feet and started undressing to take a hot, relaxing bubble bath. She intended now to make herself attractive and charming for her welcome-home dinner. She vowed to eat and drink heartily. Be nice to Gary Cameron. Disarm everybody. Make them glad to be with her, so they wouldn't suspect that she was on a mission to pave the way for her father's triumphant return.

———

JUST BEFORE DUSK, Teague was hiding in the woods watching the large Victorian house. He was waiting for it to get a bit darker before he would make his move, when Kollar made it easy by coming outside, petting the dog, , and driving away in his tan Volksbus. At this point, with the sun almost down, nobody was heading toward the nearby beach, so there wasn't much reason to wait any longer.

Teague strode boldly toward the house, and the German Shepherd charged madly across the yard, barking and salivating, anxious to chomp his fangs into warm flesh. Teague had just the thing. He tossed a recently killed rabbit over the wire fence, and the dog was confused and stopped to sniff. Grinning slightly, Teague leaned over the fence and shot the dog with a steel-tipped hunting arrow from the same East Point sporting goods store that earlier today had sold him a pair of binoculars.

He had once been a decent archer, but of course he hadn't been able to practice for seven years. However, the target was at close range and was quite large. From roughly seven feet away, leaning sideways, Teague managed to sink his shot just behind the animal's shoulders at a downward angle. It missed the heart, though, resulting in a furious howling and whimpering. But the dog wasn't moving much—all it did was scrabble its paws.

Teague was wearing rubberized gloves, and he touched the fence with an arrow tip to see if it would shoot sparks. It didn't, so it wasn't electrified like the one at the sanitarium. Why did Kollar live this way after being an inmate at Auschwitz? Didn't he want to forget about fences and guard dogs for the rest of his life? Or had his ordeal turned him into some sort of masochist?

Since he had seen Kollar padlock the gate, Teague climbed over the four-foot-high fence, and by now the dog was almost dead. A clean death would have been preferable, a heart shot, instead of all this bleeding and whimpering. He drew another arrow from his quiver, notched it, and administered the coup de grace. Then he looked around. It didn't appear that anybody had been disturbed by the commotion. Lucky that Kollar's house was rather secluded, an expensive piece of property, perfect for someone who liked a degree of isolation but wasn't willing to entirely forego the amenities of urban civilization.

Stooping to examine the dead dog, Teague saw that his first arrow must have partially severed the spine, which accounted for the lack of movement afterwards. He complimented himself on his own ingenuity. He supposed he could have used poison, had even considered putting some into a hunk of steak, but he wasn't at all familiar with toxic substances and had certainly never poisoned anything but a few insects or a mouse. He had never shot anything with an arrow either, except targets.

But he felt more comfortable employing an old skill, one of many that would have to be redeveloped now that he was free. He had bought the rabbit in a pet store and had wrung its neck himself. He got no thrill out of doing it, but he couldn't afford to be squeamish. Was he becoming brutalized? Finding it easier to kill? Maybe so, but everything he was doing had been forced on him.

There were nightlights on inside the house, which was quite handy, enabling Teague to reconnoiter with relative ease. The huge wraparound porch was sheltered by tall shrubs and an old, fat weeping willow tree. But the tall, narrow windows were tightly shut even though there were screens to take advantage of the breeze from the ocean. Teague skirted around the porch to a side window and peeked in. The filmy curtains were slightly parted and the room was dimly lit. It was a study, with a rolltop desk, an easy chair, and tall shelves full of books. Teague figured this would be his point of entry, so he laid down his bow and quiver. But, whoops, he had almost forgotten something, almost made a dumb move, putting the cart before the horse. What was the matter with him? Was it the pressure? Yet outwardly he felt perfectly calm. Cart before the *dog*, he corrected himself with a faint chuckle as he crept back out toward the yard. He dragged the dead animal around the side of the house and hid it behind a mulberry bush, leaving the arrows in the carcass. The broad, wedge-shaped tips couldn't be pulled out without widening the wounds with a good sharp knife.

Back at the side window, Teague took a glasscutter and a roll of duct tape out of a small leather pouch on his belt. He no longer believed this special equipment was absolutely necessary, though. If the cops weren't coming after what he had done to the dog, then he could probably with impunity simply take a piece of brick from the tulip bed and smash his way in. But he found the cleverness of his prepared method of entry aesthetically pleasing. Besides, why should he make jagged shards of glass to cut himself on? The glasscutter was neat and efficient. It made a tiny squealing noise as he cut a circular pattern two inches wider than his hand. He spread a strip of duct tape across the circle, tapped it with his rubber-gloved fist, and the circle hinged inward without falling and breaking, since it was held by the tape. He reached in through the neat hole in the glass and unlatched the window. He was afraid the sash would be varnished shut or even nailed, but to his satisfaction it slid open easily. First he put his bow and quiver inside. Then he climbed into Rolf Kollar's study.

———

AT THE SUPPER TABLE, Jenny Teague was a perfectly charming young lady. In the long dining room mirror above the oaken buffet, she occasionally stole reassuring glances at herself, taking comfort in the way the candle-light flattered her soft black curls and deep-set black eyes. She wore a low-cut white cocktail dress with a pearl necklace and matching pearl earrings. She could tell that her mother and grandmother were proud of her, and Gary Cameron was impressed, too. Sally was jealous and kept glowering at her, but she shrugged it off. Even though her insides may have been churning, she found that her newly contrived sense of mission gave her strength and helped funnel her energy. She was going to try to be as calculating, as objective as her ex-lover Professor Aaron Stasney always preached one should be when homing in on a news story. This one was a potential blockbuster, she thought with a certain smugness; it was bigger than any scoop Aaron could ever have dreamed about, and when it came to light it would show him up for belittling her and casting her aside. But she couldn't dwell on revenge. She must subdue her emotions even though she was personally involved in her investigation. Deeply involved. At last she had found a way to try to use her journalistic skills to uncover the truth. Or to help her father reveal it.

Several glasses of Chianti during the delicious Italian meal aided her lugubrious mood. She warned herself not to lose control by becoming too tipsy. But so far, all things considered, she felt fine.

"A toast!" she said, raising her glass. "Here's to all of us! To our family, reunited!" They all drank. Even Sally took a sip of root beer. And Jenny got a secret thrill out of knowing what her toast really meant. Was it her imagination, or did the great Dr. Gary Cameron seem unduly nervous sometimes when his eyes met hers? Could it be that on some level he wasn't totally buying her act? Was there any way he could possibly suspect what she had been involved in over the past few weeks? *No.* How could he? More logically, he must be worried that she might be coming on too strong, pretending to welcome him as a stepfather when she didn't feel it in her heart. That kind of suspicion she could live with; it wasn't a dire threat. But it wasn't comfortable either, so she had better tone herself down.

Her eyes went to her mother's face. Martha seemed relaxed and happy, unusually so. Definitely not as nervous as Gary. So far, neither one had said a word about the wedding, though if it should come off, it was only a month and a half away. They must be purposely avoiding the subject on Jenny's first day back. She had to admit Gary and her mother made a handsome couple, sitting side by side at the lace-covered table. He was wearing a dark three-piece suit and she was in an emerald dress with ruby necklace and earrings. Her hair was lighter than Jenny's, purposely lightened to conceal gray. Her complexion was smooth and youthful; she was often taken for thirty-five or so when she was actually ten years older. Gary Cameron was fifty and looked it, but he was still an attractive man, slim and broad shouldered. He looked fine on TV. His face was dimpled and artificially tanned. His thick shock of auburn hair was gray at the temples. He had green eyes magnified swimmingly by the steel-rimmed spectacles he was wearing for nearsightedness tonight, instead of the contacts he wore on camera.

Suddenly a brand-new alarm went off in Jenny's mind, prodding her to a heightened inner level of alertness. How much did Gary Cameron actually know? Could he be CIA? Far out as it seemed, could he have had a hand in her father's disappearance? Taking another sip of wine, she told herself to calm down. She must guard against being irrationally motivated to pin blame on her mother's fiancé. If he was usurping her father's place, he was doing it unwittingly. Jenny had never doubted that Gary sincerely loved her mother, even during her period of deepest resentment.

To chase away tension, she got up and dutifully helped her grandmother serve coffee and cannoli. Over dessert, she asked Gary and Martha what they were currently involved in at the Cameron Foundation. "I mean, if it's something you can talk about," she added, since so much of their work was government stuff, confidential or top-secret.

Martha turned toward Gary, wanting him to take the

lead in the conversation, letting him warm to Jenny's attempt to be sociable. "Well," he said, after chewing and swallowing a bite of cannoli, "one of the most exciting things doesn't look like much, but it's really going to do a big job for us. We're developing a small portable receiver for use with radio telescopes that will then be stationed around the world to try to pick up intelligent signals from outer space."

"Isn't that a bit farfetched?" asked Jenny.

"Not at all," Gary said, smiling. "Although we don't have proof that anybody else is actually out there, we do know that there are literally millions of galaxies in the universe, so the odds must be rather good that some of them have inhabitable planets. It's not going to cost much to go exploring with radio signals, so it's just something we should do. Think of how awesome it'd be if we actually someday made contact."

"I don't believe there's anybody else out there," Sally suddenly piped up, her mouth smeared with creamy white filling from her third cannoli. "I know there is," she added somberly, and resumed eating avidly. She didn't say another word, just kept stuffing her face. Every time she came out of one of the spells that put her in confinement, she had a tremendous craving for sweet stuff. Yet she never became plump, probably because she was still growing. Or because her fits burned up the calories.

"Delightful meal, Helen," Gary said, patting his stomach. "But I'm afraid it's going to put me on the handball court for some extra hours."

They all laughed and heaped additional compliments upon Grandmother Dudley.

"You know," Jenny said to Gary and her mother, "I'd like to interview you two. You're involved in some pretty exciting stuff at the Foundation, and you're both celebrities, too. I've gone and written about other people for my journalism assignments, and ignored you two because you're so familiar it's almost like I couldn't spot a good story right under my nose. I could write an article, use it for one of my classes next semester, and maybe even submit it to a magazine in the meantime and get it published." She stopped talking, pretending to catch herself and control her' excitement. "I'm sorry," she apologized. "You probably have tons of more important things to do. You've both been interviewed so often I guess you're sick of it. I shouldn't have asked."

"Well…" Martha began, looking at Gary imploringly.

Grandmother Dudley looked at him, too.

"Of course we'll grant you an interview!" he declared magnanimously. "Want to do it tomorrow? You ought to come down anyway, Jenny, for a bit of job orientation."

"Gee, we haven't even talked about that," said Jenny. "Mom told me I'd mostly be doing technical writing— manuals and reports and so on. Do you think I can handle it? Maybe it would have been better if I had at least minored in science, instead of literature."

"Oh, it's not that way at all, dear," Martha consoled. "Our people will supply the proper technical terminology. But it'll be up to you to express what we have to get across in writing, in laymen's language, actually, to the politicians and businessmen we must depend on in order to fund our projects."

"I'll do my best," Jenny said. "But don't go easy on me. Promise you'll tell me immediately if I'm not doing as good a job as anyone else you might've hired."

"We promise," Gary said, smiling. "But I'm sure it's a promise we'll never have to keep."

———

ROLF KOLLAR CAME HOME at eleven o'clock from a speaking engagement in front of the American UFO Congress. There were only about three hundred members in the Manhattan chapter, but for tonight they had sold enough extra tickets to fill a three-thousand seat high-school auditorium. Kollar of course had been the draw, not their usual jibber-jabber about sightings real and imagined. He had pocketed fifty percent of the gate, which came to seventy-five hundred dollars. The check was in his wallet, and he intended to deposit it bright and early tomorrow morning, hopefully before it would have a chance to bounce.

Normally he would've felt quite satisfied with himself. It was easy money, and at his advanced age it was lovely to possess such a powerful earning power in a culture where money was a vital measure of a man's worth. Acquiring lots of money used to be extremely important to him, as if he might be able to become worth so much that nobody could ever again try to send him up a chimney. But now that he was rich and in his so-called golden years, money wasn't so important. One could be sent up a chimney in spite of it. Or because of it. Had the Jews been gassed because they were Jews or because the Nazis needed an excuse to take all their money and possessions, even their gold teeth?

These kinds of abstrusely morbid thoughts had been running through Rolf Kollar's head ever since the debacle at the safe house. He had been living on edge, wondering exactly what was going to happen to him. Would he be found out? Would Jenny Teague cave in and talk to the CIA? When would the other shoe drop? One thing about the gas chamber, one got used to not wondering. In there, even death had been stripped of most of its uncertainties.

His dawn-to-dusk gas lamps were burning as he pulled into his gravel driveway. The house looked okay. He didn't feel especially uneasy till he got out of the Volksbus. Where was Taurus? He should've been running and lunging against the gate, panting and clambering to be petted. Of course pedigreed dogs were sometimes stolen, put to sleep with tranquilizers and then loaded into trucks to be sold to scientific laboratories. Kollar shuddered. Somehow he knew that Taurus hadn't been merely stolen. No. This had something to do with Blue Ridge. He could feel it in his bones, with a resurgence of the finely honed instincts of one who had once called upon every innate resource in order to play the odds and survive. Should he cut and run? He grimly decided against it. He mounted the porch and unlocked his front door, steeling himself to face whatever might be lurking in his own home. After all, how could it be worse than the Gestapo?

He swung the door open and reached for the light switch.

"No lights!" a voice hissed. "Shut the door and come in! Keep your hands out in front of you!"

Kollar obeyed. Beyond the foyer, the living room was dim, lit only by a nightlight. The man the hissing voice belonged to couldn't be fully seen—just his eyes peeking and his hand holding a gun, pointing from behind the archway. Once the door was closed, the whispering voice said, "Now you can turn the lamp on." Kollar did so, and Dr. Norman Teague stepped into the foyer. In one hand he held the gun and in the other a tumbler of scotch. "I helped myself," he said, jiggling the ice cubes. "I hope you don't mind. You made me wait for a long time."

"Taurus…" Kollar said. "What did you do to him?"

"I'm sorry," said Teague. "I don't like to kill animals."

"Then why did you do it?" Kollar demanded, his heart pounding angrily, making him want to lunge for the gun. To his surprise, he was hit with grief as well as rage. He had never expected to be grief-stricken over the loss of the dog, whom he had regarded more as a protector paid in food and water, than as a pet.

"Stay where you are! Don't do anything rash!" Teague said. "Put yourself in my place, Rolf. I couldn't just ring you on the phone or come striding up to your gate. What if you're being watched or wiretapped? What if you're not really my friend? After all, your associates turned on us at the safe house. Smith and Rawlings. They were just waiting for you to leave, so they could tie us up and turn us over to the KGB. We managed to get the jump on them. Then we took off. We couldn't be sure that you and my daughter Jenny weren't part of the plot."

"Rawlings couldn't have been working for the KGB," Kollar said, shaking his head. "Blair Chaney—that's Smith's real name—is a different story. I wouldn't put anything past him. Maybe he figured he could get paid by me *and* the Russians. If so, he got what he deserved. But Jason Rawlings didn't need to die. I assure you he was innocent. So is your daughter. She loves you, and you ran out on her after she made a leap of faith and took a great risk by coming to meet you."

"I guess I believe you now," Teague said. "I need to put my trust in somebody. I want you to help me reach Jenny. She can vouch for me, I have to tell my story. I'm the only one left who can do it."

"Where's Vickers?"

Teague shook his head sadly, sticking his gun in his belt. "Abe is dead. He was badly wounded in the fight at the safe house, and he died on the highway, in the car. I had to bury him in the woods."

"Why are you suddenly ready to trust me?" Kollar asked.

"I read up on you during the past four days, since I've been in New York. The government is against you, like they're against me. You're an iconoclast, a maverick. I didn't know anything about you before. But now I see that you're not the type of man to trust governments whether capitalist, communist or fascist. I believe you're working on your own hook, Rolf."

"I wish you had realized it earlier," Kollar snapped. But despite his losses, he was glad to have Teague back. It seemed to mean that he would get a brand-new chance to astound the world with the story of the UFO cover-up.

Teague swished the melting ice cubes in the tumbler, then took a sip of scotch. "I don't love or trust my wife anymore," he confessed sadly. "All I want to do is leave the country to live with Jenny and Sally. But first I have to bring my story out into the open, so I can live freely. They won't be able to lock me up in a sanitarium again.

"Where are the tapes?" Kollar asked.

"I have them in a safe place. I'm hanging onto them, Rolf, I hope you understand that. They're my insurance policy."

"Okay, but we' 11 have to get them on the air. Unfortunately, two of \he people backing you up are now dead. If Jenny will go on television and identify you as her father, that helps. But it would be even better if we could get corroboration from your wife. Are you telling me you don't want Martha to be involved?"

"Let her stay with Gary Cameron!" Teague said bitterly. "That's who she supposedly loves! She won't say that I'm her husband because she wants me to stay dead!"

"You can't know that for sure," said Kollar.

Teague grimaced, eyeing Kollar calmly. In a chillingly flat tone he said, "I believe that my darling wife was involved in the plot to have me confined."

17

J enny focused her Nikon and snapped a picture of Gary, Martha and Sally standing beside a ten-inch-high model of a one-thousand-foot radio telescope. "This is the kind that will be hooked up with our portable receiver," Martha had explained. "It's a scale model of the radio telescope at Arecibo, Puerto Rico. With it we can scan about eight hundred stars, all within eighty light-years of earth, and all similar in size and age to our Bun. If these stars have planets, then there's a reasonable likelihood that some of the planets might have intelligent life." The telescope model was in the ultramodern reception area of the Cameron Foundation, which occupied the fourteenth and fifteenth floors of a huge Manhattan skyscraper. The plush carpet was bright red, the walls were flawless white, and the desks, sofas and lounge chairs were composites of blue vinyl and curved, transparent plastic. The fluorescent ceiling was high enough to accommodate not only the telescope but the huge canvasses spaced all around: magnificent, brilliantly colorful renderings in oil of visions of planets and asteroids beamed back to earth by NASA satellite probes. The paintings were interspersed by potted trees and shrubs and sunrays streaking through tinted glass, so that the decor overall was a curiously beautiful mixture of terrestrial and extraterrestrial scenery.

The human subjects of Jenny's camera were backlit by shimmering sunlight, so she took several back-up shots, bracketing her exposures. She was approaching this "assignment" as professionally as possible, as if she didn't have an ulterior motive.

This morning she had relaxed and "opened her mind" by playing her guitar and singing some lovely old folk ballads. To her surprise, Sally had crept into her room and listened quietly, with a transfixed, serene expression on her face. Gone was the animosity of yesterday, as if music really could soothe the savage beast. But Jenny knew that Sally's serenity was probably temporary, in fact likely to represent a lull before a storm. Her mood swings were so extreme, so unpredictable, that at times they could seem positively demonic,

After putting her guitar away, Jenny had asked for privacy (Sally had gone quietly enough), and had locked her door to spend several hours reading up on Dr. Martha Teague and Dr. Gary Cameron. She tried to think of them as interview subjects only, not as people close to her, as she went through an inch-thick collection of articles and clippings provided by her mother. The stuff was arranged chronologically, the earliest material in the back; but none of it pertained to Dr. Norman Teague; and none of it went back farther than three years. So it all dated from about the time when Gary and Martha came out in the open with their plans for betrothal.

In one of the more recent articles in the file, Dr. Martha Teague talked fondly and respectfully about her father, who was of course Jenny's grandfather. "Engineering seemed so exciting, so adventurous," Martha was quoted as saying. "My father always knew how to answer my little-girl questions about how things worked, what made the world tick. I guess I was a tomboy—I never cared much about playing with dolls, instead I fooled around with toy microscopes and chemistry sets. I loved science. I knew that my father was esteemed in his profession, and I could see that my mother also looked up to him. Her family, the Corsini family, owned a fantastic Italian restaurant, and I adored what they could do with food, but I had no interest in doing it myself. To this day I'm not a very good cook—I can't even do an egg over easy without cracking the yellow or making it turn hard."

Martha said she didn't want to *exactly* follow in her father's footsteps, so she decided to become an aeronautical engineer instead of an electrical one. She started dating Norman Teague while she was working on her master's degree at Columbia and he was earning a doctorate in physics. Two years later they were married, and both accepted positions at Manhattan University. That's where they met Dr. Gary Cameron, a prominent faculty member who already was building a national reputation as the head of the University's prestigious Laboratory for Planetary Studies. Through Dr. Cameron, Norman and Martha Teague were commissioned to work on various space exploration projects for NASA. They also joined Cameron in a part-time association with Universal Dynamics, Inc.

For Jenny, skipping through the file and reading the highlights was like picking up jigsaw pieces and seeing how they fit into patterns that illuminated aspects of her own life. As she took mental notes on astronomer Gary

Cameron, it seemed more and more that his close involvement with her family was no accident, instead it was almost preordained.

According to Cameron, the direction his life would take was determined at age eight, when he made "the marvelous discovery that stars were really far-away suns." The idea that some of those suns might have planets like ours, teeming with life, enflamed his boyish imagination with a fervor that continued to burn brightly, enabling him to captivate others. He felt a driving need to let laymen know "there's something else out there" and to whip them up so they'd pay for his quest in tax dollars and private grants. By hyping the media and capturing the popular imagination with attention-grabbing gimmicks like the "interstellar messages" he designed to be carried aboard the Mars and Venus probes, he achieved celebrity status and eventually made himself rich. His books, movies, lecture tours, radio and television programs, and numerous other ventures brought him millions of dollars each year, most of it funneled through the "nonprofit" Cameron Foundation.

Despite his personal attractiveness, Cameron apparently wasn't a womanizer and had never married. He seemed to have few interests outside his career, except for his interest in Jenny's mother, and even that was career-related since their jobs had brought them together in the first place. Martha had joined the Cameron Foundation five years ago after Grandfather Dudley died of cancer and the family was strapped by hospital bills and funeral expenses. Now Jenny was going to work there. Probably if her father hadn't disappeared he'd be working there, too. It was almost as if Cameron had some kind of hold on the Teague family, drawing them to him like a huge planet capturing a cluster of asteroids in its much stronger gravitational field.

It struck Jenny that Gary Cameron and Rolf Kollar were like flip sides of a coin—the shiny side and the tarnished side. Both were pitchmen, but Cameron was selling science and Kollar was selling pseudoscience. Or were they both pitching the same thing? Or stirring the same brew? In one of the articles Jenny read, Cameron's contributions to astronomy were labeled "competent but less than brilliant" by colleagues who openly wished he would use his enormous fund-raising talents for projects that were more worthwhile. At first Jenny thought these kinds of comments might be dismissed as sour grapes.

But on her job orientation tour this afternoon, she saw that the Cameron Foundation was not only a base for legitimate scientific inquiry but was also a gigantic, well-oiled money machine. She was shown a large, efficient staff industriously pursuing an amazing variety of ways in which man's intellectual curiosity could be marketed and exploited. Under the auspices of the Foundation, an astonishing array of "intellectually stimulating" products were developed, manufactured and sold, not only books, slide-shows and videotapes by and about Dr. Gary Cameron, but also scientific games for children and adults, solar-system maps and lightshows, models of artificial satellites and space modules, deeds to stars and planets, and expensive memberships in an Interstellar Society.

After taking her photos in front of the model of the Arecibo radio telescope, Jenny interviewed Dr. Martha Teague and Dr. Gary Cameron on tape in Cameron's plush office, with Sally present, sitting on the sofa, swinging her legs back and forth idly, a rather blank expression on her face. The first few questions were designed to be relaxing. Then Jenny decided to take off the kid gloves just to see what kind of reaction she could provoke. "You realize," she said, "that your critics consider the Cameron Foundation a commercial sell-out. They say you can't possibly give paid testimonials for scientific products, contribute research material to a Hollywood science-fiction movie, and sell mail-order toys and games without compromising your principles and integrity."

"I'm afraid I already don't like the tone of this interview," Martha Teague blurted. "Let's cut it short." She was smiling, as if cracking a joke, but it was clear that her feelings had been hurt. She wasn't prepared to be skewered by her own daughter.

"No, no," Gary Cameron protested. "Jenny is being a good journalist, asking us some hard, tough questions. We oughtn't to be insulted. Not if we're perfectly comfortable with our own motives."

"How do you respond to your critics, then?" Jenny asked, trying to sound open-minded and fair.

"We're pragmatists," Cameron answered. "We're not holed up in some ivory tower, some genteel bastion of academia, we're in the arena fighting the good battle. If hype is what sells scientific endeavor in this country, we have to be willing to resort to it when necessary. Judge us by our accomplishments, not by our methods. Who's done more to stimulate public interest in computer technology, anthropology, medicine and space exploration? We're sowing the seeds that will inspire more and more young people into fields where we desperately need intelligent, innovative minds."

"What do you consider the most important project that the Cameron Foundation is engaged in right now?" Jenny asked.

Cameron leaned back, thinking, taking off his steel-rimmed eyeglasses and rubbing the bridge of his nose. During the tour, when Jenny had photographed him, he had also removed his eyeglasses.

"The Soviet-American Mars landing," said Martha Teague. "Wouldn't you agree, dear?"

Jenny always got a funny feeling when she heard her mother address in romantically intimate terms this man who was not her father. But she had thought she was growing used to it—up until a few weeks ago.

Cameron nodded, still pinching the bridge of his nose, as if he had a headache. "Tell Jenny about it," he told Martha.

"Well, we've been working hard trying to break down political opposition on both sides of the Iron Curtain so Russians and Americans can launch a joint mission to Mars."

"A manned mission?" Jenny asked.

"That's the only kind that'll accomplish our objectives, which are rather altruistic." Martha smiled, then went on. "We want the astronauts' lives to depend on each other, and on support from millions of people in both countries. If the two superpowers could cooperate on a big space adventure, maybe they could set aside some of their mutual paranoia. We did it in a small way on the Apollo/Soyuz linkup in 1975. The idea is to turn space into a territory for peaceful exploration, not a battlefield. Cooperation, not competition, should be the objective. Maybe a successful Mars mission would spark other joint enterprises on earth. It could deflect our energies from the arms race by using the same technologies to a higher purpose."

"With or without us, the Soviet Union is going to Mars anyway," said Cameron, "They've been practicing keeping men in orbit for six months, eight months, and more. We also know they're preparing a gigantic new rocket for launching sometime in the year 1992, which just happens to be the seventy-fifth anniversary of the Russian Revolution."

"But it's also the five-hundredth anniversary of Columbus' landing in the New World," said Martha. "What a beautiful opportunity for joint exploration and development of another New World! And for a resolution by the two superpowers to continue to use out tremendous technological prowess for the good of all mankind instead of for destruction

"It's possible there was once life on Mars," Cameron added. "A billion years ago, rivers flowed there, and there was oxygen. Now it's hot and arid and there's no atmosphere. We should find out what went wrong. Is the same thing likely to happen to our planet? If so, we had better figure on colonizing other worlds, or else we're doomed to become extinct."

Jenny found herself liking and respecting her mother's professional motivations—and those of Gary Cameron. Maybe some of the tackier stuff they were into really could be justified on the grounds that it helped support their overriding goals which, Jenny had to agree, were undeniably altruistic. But a part of her didn't wish to empathize with them so unreservedly. She had to remember she was working for her father. "Since you obviously believe that it's within our present means to send manned rockets to other planets," she said, "do you give any credence to the notion that extraterrestrials may have visited the planet earth in times past, or are doing so now?"

Sitting next to Jenny in front of Cameron's palette-shaped glass-topped desk, Martha Teague leaned sideways and stared at her eldest daughter in a frankly patronizing way. "Now you sound like Rolf Kollar!" she quipped sarcastically.

"I'm merely playing devil's advocate, Mother," Jenny replied coldly, trying not to lose her temper.

"I'm sorry," Martha apologized. "I didn't mean to sound so scornful, dear. It's just that serious scientists find this UFO business so preposterous, yet we get asked about it all the time. Conventional evolutionary theory adequately explains the genesis of man, thank you! We don't need to suppose that some so-called 'gods from outer space' came down here to take a hand in it. That kind of babble belongs in *National Enquirer*. All it does is distract people's attention from the more important business at hand—which is to explore and colonize our own solar system, and to do it in Partnership with the Russians instead of remaining locked in a horrifying arms race that's blanketed the earth with sixty-thousand nuclear weapons.

"What do you say to the hundreds of UFO reports that appear to come from reputable sources?" Jenny asked. "For instance, Colonel Kevin Thompson. Supposedly there are Air Force documents that say he sighted three saucers and fired at them before his plane crashed. Do you believe this could be possible?"

"I certainly do," Dr. Gary Cameron stated flatly, startling Jenny with his admission. But then, turning toward him, she saw that he was smirking. "I mean I believe it could be possible that he saw flying saucers in his mind. Something was terribly wrong with his airplane, he was going down. He even failed to eject and save himself. So what was he thinking about? Was his mind functioning properly? If his oxygen mask wasn't working adequately, his brain cells could've been dying from oxygen deprivation. He might've *thought* he saw almost anything, and he may've even fired his rockets at the creatures of his imagination."

The explanation sounded very convincing, Jenny thought. Very convincing, that is, to anyone who hadn't seen Thompson's corpse, consequently learning that up until a week ago he was very much alive and the crash about which Dr. Cameron was so exhaustively hypothesizing hadn't taken place at all. She wished she could say what she knew instead of fighting to keep it locked in. Probing deeper along the path she had almost unwillingly opened up, she said, "A few months ago, Dr. Norman Teague, who we could tactfully say was more than only a colleague to both of you, was legally declared dead. Now that seven years have passed since his disappearance, how would you evaluate his professional relationship to you and his contributions to science?"

"Do we have to get into this?" Martha snapped, her face reddening.

Sally stopped swinging her legs and sat stock-still on the sofa, arms straightened at her sides so stiffly that if her palms hadn't sunk into the soft furry-white cushions she'd have lifted herself into the air three inches. Her green eyes were keenly alert but her lips formed neither a smile nor a frown.

"Mother, I really don't see why you're taking the heat," said Jenny. "I'm approaching this as an assignment, I'm trying to ask the same kinds of questions any good reporter would ask, and I'm working hard to keep my personal feelings out of it."

"I understand, Jenny," said Gary Cameron. "So should you, Martha."

"As Jenny says," Martha intoned rather snidely, "I'm treating this like any other interview, Therefore I reserve the right not to answer any questions I don't deem pertinent. Or that I deem impertinent." She managed a mild chuckle, but her little joke did not succeed in lessening tension.

In a valiant attempt to skate over the rough spot—the way he probably smoothed over rough spots when he was hitting people up for grants—Dr. Gary Cameron cleared his throat and spoke with calm enthusiasm about Jenny's father. In some respects, his speech amounted to a eulogy. He said that Dr. Norman Teague was a brilliant astrophysicist who had made extremely important contributions to the American space effort and to the development of rocket propulsion Systems. "He was as demanding of himself as he was of others, and I believe that those who accused him of being egotistical didn't truly understand the depth of his commitment to scientific inquiry. Prior to his unfortunate disappearance, he had made some of his greatest discoveries. His genius seemed to be peaking, at its zenith, so to speak, and we can only wonder at the marvelous things he might've done, had he not been taken from us."

"Taken from us," Jenny repeated meaningfully. "Are you implying that you feel he was kidnapped—instead of willingly defecting to…to some foreign government?"

"The Norman Teague I knew was staunchly patriotic," Cameron declared. "The last thing he would do is turn traitor."

"I hate to say this," said Jenny, trying to calm her own quickening pulse, "but do you have any doubts that Dr. Norman Teague is dead?"

"Jenny!" Martha gasped. "I thought we agreed to leave that subject alone once and for all? Aren't you ever going to grow up and put it behind you?"

"Not till I see his dead body!" Jenny snapped. "And I don't see what it has to do with growing up, Mother?"

"As far as I'm concerned, this interview is over," Martha said, sitting back in a huff. "If you feel otherwise, Gary, then *you* may answer my daughter's question."

"I think that if the Soviets ever had him, they didn't keep him alive for long," Cameron said. "If he was a defector—which I don't believe for one minute—they would have boasted about it for the glory of communism. On the other hand, I would hardly be surprised to find out that the KGB was behind the disappearance of both Norman Teague and Abraham Vickers. The Soviets could've milked them for all the top-secret information they could provide before murdering them."

Once again, as in the case of Colonel Kevin Thompson, Gary Cameron was espousing a convincing-sounding hypothesis—and one that Jenny knew to be false in its most important particular. She was boiling inside. She couldn't stand it anymore. Keeping silent was like being a hypocrite, an accomplice to the cheats and liars behind whatever kind of hoax had been perpetrated. Her eyes flashing angrily, she whirled toward her mother, crying, "But what if my father is *not* dead? Then, if you go ahead and remarry, you'll be committing bigamy!"

"How dare you!" Martha cried. "Don't you think it's been hard enough for me to pick up the pieces of our lives? Aren't you mature enough to realize that I have to salvage some happiness for myself? And for you and Sally! How long do you expect us all to go on waiting for a man who isn't coming back anymore?"

"You don't *know* that he isn't coming back anymore!" Jenny shouted, tears streaming down her face.

Suddenly Sally screamed hideously. She jumped to

her feet and started spinning in circles, fluttering her arms through the air, crying and babbling incoherently.

"See what you've done!" Martha said, running to soothe Sally.

"I know my father is alive!" Jenny shouted above the din. "I have proof! I…" She made herself stop. She almost went over the deep end and blurted out all her experiences in Wheeling. But her eyes met Gary Cameron's, and what she saw there choked the words in her throat. He was gazing at her intently, weirdly.

"Did you see him, Jenny?" he asked her in a near whisper, and his words were like a scalpel opening her psyche.

"No," she heard herself answering, despite her wish to remain silent. "I almost did…I went to meet him but…he was gone…I don't know where…I…"

Again she stopped herself. She got shakily to her feet and ran out of Cameron's office. She was totally upset now and wished that the few words she had uttered wouldn't be believed.

Why had she blurted them? Out of a deep inner need to drive Gary Cameron away from her mother? Her childish impulse, her loss of self-control, may have put her—and her father—in more danger. The look in Cameron's eyes—she knew he wasn't to be trusted. Oh! If only he'd think that what she had said didn't really mean anything!

Irrationally, she thought of throwing a fit in the reception lounge so he might conclude she was as mentally unreliable as Sally. But instead she pushed a button for an elevator, waited frantically for one to arrive, then rode it down to the lobby and rushed out of the building. It was raining and she didn't have an umbrella, but she kept going, walking briskly among the

Manhattan throngs, stepping around puddles, letting the cleansing rainwater wash over her, soaking her hair and her clothes. A few blocks away, when she calmed down, it dawned on her that she had forgotten her camera and tape recorder.

Gary Cameron was lucky. Martha apparently hadn't picked up on Jenny's babbling there at the end because she was too busy with Sally, who was making plenty of noise. Gary lent a hand in calming the child down and making her swallow a double dose of the sedatives that Martha always carried with her, in her purse. Whimpering like some piteously maligned animal, curled up in a tight ball on the office sofa with her mother cooing to her and stroking her hair, Sally finally fell asleep. All this took about half an hour, and Gary and Martha were frazzled. He fixed two stiff scotches right there in the locked office, and they sipped, trying to unwind. "I hope I don't have to put her back in St. Francis," Martha said. "I'm disappointed in Jenny, too. Maybe we were arguing, but she still didn't need to just take off instead of trying to be helpful."

"She's been away from this sort of scene for a long time," Gary said. "She's not so used to coping with it anymore."

"Well, she caused it," Martha snapped.

"I agree," said Gary. "Obviously Jenny's still very troubled, more troubled than we may have realized." He was laying some groundwork in case it should become necessary to have Jenny "removed" from the family. He had already confiscated the interview tape and had it locked in his desk; he wanted to listen to the tail end again when he was alone.

Martha still looked beautiful to him, even though she was a nervous wreck. He loved her very much. He had always loved her and wanted to marry her. But there was much more at stake here than their personal happiness.

Running her fingers through her damp, disheveled hair, she said, "I don't understand it. I thought Jenny had accepted the fact that her father is dead. Now she gets herself off on another tangent. Do *you* have any doubts about it, Gary? Tell me the truth."

"None whatsoever. The drug made him and Vickers both act crazy. They were both talking about defecting, remember? For God's sake, they even tried to convince me to go along with them! In my opinion, they must have tried to act it out somehow, came off like mentally disturbed bunglers, and got themselves killed."

"But," said Martha, "you and I both took quantalibrium, too. Why didn't it affect *us* that way?"

"Maybe," said Gary, "our personalities are more stable. Maybe Abe's and Norman's brains were chemically more susceptible to the bad side effects of the drug."

"Like Sally," Martha whispered, gazing sadly down at the child sleeping on the couch. "Poor baby. I'll never stop blaming myself for what's wrong with her."

"I don't think you should allow yourself to think that way, honey," Gary consoled, putting his arms around her. "It must have been Norman who had the defective gene, or whatever, that caused Sally to respond the same way he did."

"But we'll never know for sure," said Martha, trembling and snuggling closer to Gary.

He kissed her on the forehead. He wished desperately that this present crisis would end satisfactorily. He didn't want to lose Martha, or Jenny for that matter, if he didn't have to. He couldn't believe that after seven patient, guilt-ridden years it was all threatening to blow up in his face. He was tired of carrying secrets but he knew he'd have to go on carrying them to his grave.

He knew, of course, that Dr. Norman Teague was on the loose, for Meade and Lieberman had told him. He also knew something else: neither he nor Martha had ever actually taken any quantalibrium, although Martha believed that they had. *All* the members of their think-tank group had received periodic injections, but thanks to Gary he and Martha were the "controls"—so their injections were harmless. Gary knew at the time that quantalibrium hadn't been sufficiently tested; it had been given to convict volunteers, with the desired results as far as enhancing mental abilities, but it hadn't been subjected to a long enough waiting period to see what the side effects might eventually turn out to be and how undesirable they might prove. So Gary hadn't wanted to risk himself or Martha in the experiment. He was already in love with her, although she did not seem to know it. And now he had to let her continue to think they had both taken the drug, like everybody else in the group, because if she found out how selfish his love had been she might turn against him.

The irony was that because Martha believed that she did take quantalibrium, rather than a placebo, she remained convinced that both she and Norman were responsible for their daughter Sally's mental defects. She thought that one of her genes or her husband's genes had been altered prior to conception, with a devastating biological effect upon the fetus.

Cameron was greatly relieved that he had found out that Jenny apparently had no idea of her father's present whereabouts and had not actually seen him in the flesh. Perhaps he could use this insight to prevent her from being rolled up by Meade and Dorsey. If she didn't actually know anything, if all that she imagined she knew could be kept in the realm of fantasy and speculation, maybe she wouldn't have to be disposed of in any of the harsher ways that the Agency was prone to employ. Cameron didn't want any more blood on his hands. He didn't want to bring any more suffering down upon Martha and her family.

He wished that he had not argued for having Teague and Vickers put in the sanitarium when they started to "go bad" seven years ago. He and Martha would be better off if they were really dead. Perhaps this time they *would* be killed before they could show their faces. It might be the only way to save Jenny.

18

B rian Meade and Wayne Dorsey met with Gary Cameron on Saturday morning in his office at the Foundation. They informed him that they were now concerned with only two of the three Blue Ridge escapees because Abraham Vickers had killed himself in a West Virginia forest. "That's too bad," Cameron said, only partially meaning it. Like the other two men, he felt guilty that due to impinging priorities he wasn't able to wholeheartedly empathize with the death of a fellow human being. Earlier this morning, Martha Teague had told Cameron on the telephone that she had to commit Sally to the psychiatric ward of St. Francis Hospital because the child was still acting strange when she came out of sedation. Martha was terribly distraught, and Gary was worried about her and anxious to see her this afternoon; they were scheduled to meet at a TV studio to tape a segment of a show they were producing for syndication and cassette distribution.

For the CIA men, Cameron played the tape on Jenny Teague's tape recorder. After he clicked it off, Dorsey said, "We have to roll her up. Grill her. Find out who her contacts were. Who told her the escape was going down? Whoever was behind it might know where Teague and Thompson are right now."

"And might not," said Meade in his slow, sonorous rumble. He leaned back, rubbing his drooping jowls.

"Who cares?" said Dorsey, growing more excited. "I'd like to get my hands on the bastards behind the break-out. At least then we'd be batting five hundred on this goddamn case instead of a big fat zero. Let's put some KGB guys outta business, for God's sake!"

"Rolling up Jenny isn't the answer," Meade rumbled soothingly, sounding so sleepy it slowed down the pace of everything around him. "In fact it's exactly the wrong thing to do. Once we question her, we can't let her go, we've got to make her disappear. No way to keep a thing like that from making national if not international head-lines—Famous Scientist's Daughter Copies Disappearing Act. If Teague's trying to get to Jenny, he'll know we've snatched away the prize. Then who knows what he'll do? Probably go bananas, come roaring into the limelight like a bull in a china shop—and that's precisely what we're supposed to prevent. Our job is to keep the wraps on this whole caper, right? Only way to have a ghost of a chance of doing it is to make all our moves behind the scene."

"Why do you think Teague and Thompson aren't coming forward?" Gary Cameron asked nervously.

Meade said, "For one thing, we don't really know they're both still alive. Another thing, they've only been on the loose for a week, and whoever broke them out has to be primarily concerned about not getting caught. They might've laid down a game plan for moving slowly and cautiously at first, covering their tracks and letting the heat cool down."

"But it seems as if whoever was helping them isn't helping them anymore," said Cameron. "Didn't you say that Teague and Vickers appeared to be on their own when they were spotted at the truck stop?"

"Could've been only a temporary split-up to help shake us off their trail." said Meade. "Or if they were trying to run from somebody they might not have gotten away clean. Besides, they're losing their minds, right?"

"Yeah," said Dorsey, "and if the KGB gets hold of them for real this time, they're gonna milk them good! They might not want to go public any more than we do. So when they finish with them they'll send them up to work with Vickers in the Great Laboratory in the Sky."

Dorsey chuckled, but nobody else did.

"What should I do with this tape?" Cameron asked, holding up the cassette from Jenny's recorder.

Meade said, "Let her keep it after you erase the tail end so she won't have any record of what she said or didn't say...but first make me a dub of the whole thing. It proves she doesn't really know much...in effect she's like somebody walking through a dream. If we play her right and get a few breaks, we won't have to hurt her, she'll end up not being able to tell what was real and what was unreal."

"Wishful thinking," said Dorsey. "In the end we're gonna have to roll her up."

"But there's no point doing it now," Meade insisted. "Use Jenny as bait to get her father...rope him in without her even knowing about it. Then make Teague lead us to Thompson and everybody else involved in this fiasco."

Jenny lay flat on her back staring up at her bedroom ceiling. It was eleven o'clock in the morning, and she had been up since five, trying to undo some of the damage she had caused, by helping her mother cope with Sally. In the end it had proven hopeless, and the ambulance had to come. It was horrible seeing a person subdued that way, given a shot and carried in an almost lifeless condition out of the apartment.

Jenny's mother had ridden with Sally to the hospital to get her checked in, and now she was back, trying to make herself look fresh enough to tape a television show. Through the wall that separated their bedrooms, Jenny could hear the hair drier being used. In her haggard condition, Martha was going to gulp down some food and some black coffee, then take a taxi across town to the TV studio.

Jenny hadn't eaten anything for breakfast and didn't feel like having lunch either. But Grandmother Dudley was making a *frittata*—a crustless Italian pie made of scrambled eggs filled with fried potatoes, mozzarella cheese, onions and green peppers. It smelled delicious, but Jenny didn't want to face her mother and grandmother at the table. She was too guilty and embarrassed over what she had done to Sally. She knew that her impulsive, self-serving behavior had provoked the blowup that sent her sister plummeting into another psychotic episode.

She was so miserable she couldn't help wishing she had Aaron Stasney to lean on. She even thought of phoning him at his Georgetown home—but she knew she wouldn't actually do it. When she needed him most was exactly the worst time to call. First she had to prove she *didn't* need him. She could do things right without him. She wouldn't always be a little girl looking for a father.

He *wasn't* right about her, she told herself defiantly. If she was so hung up on a "father image," why wouldn't she accept Gary Cameron? It would be the easy way out.

He was so perfect. So ideal. Millions of people thought so. But Jenny didn't. Beneath the facade of the handsome, charismatic intellectual, she sensed something creepy about him. Yesterday her fear had surfaced, making her realize that it had always been there, deep inside her, even though she couldn't say why.

She jumped when suddenly someone rapped on the bedroom door. Pulling herself together, she got up and opened it. First she had to unbolt it; she was obliged to continue using the bolt even though Sally wasn't here so the real reason for it wouldn't be absolutely apparent.

Martha was standing in the hall, looking tense but remarkably refreshed. Jenny had the thought that if only her father could see her mother now she'd look almost the way he remembered her. She was wearing a blue suit with a white ruffled blouse. Her makeup was delicately applied, not lathered on the way many people imagined it ought to be done for the TV cameras. "Jenny, please," she said timidly, "let's be friends. I'll forgive you for our argument if you'll forgive me. Let's try our best to make it nice around here for when Sally comes back."

"It...it was my fault," Jenny stammered. A tear rolled down her cheek.

She and her mother hugged, and then the phone started ringing. After three rings Grandmother Dudley picked it up in the kitchen. "Jenny! It's for you," she called out,

Martha kissed her daughter on the forehead, then disengaged from the embrace. "Go ahead, take your call, dear. We'll talk this out later. I have to run or I'll be late."

"You look nice, Mother," Jenny said. Then she closed her bedroom door and picked up the phone, sitting on the edge of the bed. "Hello?" she said, and heard the kitchen extension being hung up.

"Jenny? Hi!"

"Who is this?"

"Don't you remember? Harry Paulson. The University newspaper? The article we ran on Rolf Kollar?"

Jenny's heart skipped. There was no such article. Who was this Harry Paulson? What did his call mean?

"Would you have lunch with me today? A date, I guess you would call it. I'd like to see you again…I'd also like to discuss a follow-up article for next semester."

"Sure, Harry," Jenny heard herself saying. "Where can I meet you?"

———

IN KOLLAR'S STUDY, while Kollar was tending to the grim business of burying his dog in the back yard, Norman Teague sipped scotch and anxiously looked forward to seeing his daughter, again.

The master plan was in the works. It wouldn't be long now.

Yesterday, on Friday morning, Rolf Kollar had driven Teague to the branch of the Manhattan National Bank where Teague had his two safety deposit boxes. He got out the videotapes. He also took out five thousand dollars for pin money. He left the rest of the cash in the bank. Kollar agreed that Teague should keep all of it now that Chaney was too "indisposed" to enjoy being rich. Kollar wanted so badly to be instrumental in breaking the UFO story that money was no object.

Either that, or Kollar was trying to lull Teague's suspicions and sucker him into a trap. But Teague was no fool. He wasn't about to let his guard completely down. Anybody who tried to cross him would die regretting it.

He downed the dregs of his watery scotch, then

picked up the big .45, stuck it in his belt, and went to the kitchen window to make sure Kollar was still out in the yard burying his dog instead of trying to run away or pull some other kind of crazy trick.

———

BY NOON IT WAS RAINING, a light but constant drizzle. Wearing jeans, sneakers, and a red nylon boating jacket with a hood, Jenny hurried to a coffee shop two blocks from her home, where she waited for the young man who had phoned her. In a few minutes, he came in carrying a dripping umbrella, his eyes meeting hers immediately. He was about her age, slender, with a mass of unkempt curly brown hair that looked as if he never combed it, a long hooked nose, and a pair of thick, square-shaped eyeglasses with greasy smudges on the lenses. He wore blue jeans so faded they were almost white, a yellowish T-shirt that said Cape Canaveral, and a tan corduroy jacket with raindrops on the shoulders and the sleeves pushed up to his elbows. He joined Jenny in her booth, beaming at her as if they were lovers, while she did not recognize him at all. "Hi! Nice to see you again so soon, Jenny," he boomed in a surprisingly rich baritone, taking her hands in his and bending to kiss her on her cheek before he sat down. Trying not to look and sound as awkward as she felt, she picked up on his cue, smiling and acting cheerful and vivacious, as if she had known him for a long time rather intimately.

"How're things at the magazine, Harry?"

"Fine! Fine!"

It was of course a very weird lunch date. She didn't dare mention what was uppermost on her mind. They both made small talk about the weather and about the

Rolf Kollar article Jenny had never really written and about the fictitious follow-up article he had used as an excuse for this meeting. They ate grilled cheeses and coffee, but her stomach was churning so much she figured that even this light lunch would give her heartburn. Afterwards Harry said, "Let's go to my place so I can show you my notes. I should've brought them with me, I guess, but I wanted an excuse to be alone with you." He smiled and winked, carrying off his makebelieve flirting.

"Oh, sure! I'll come up and see your etchings!" Jenny kidded. She even managed a fake laugh, but the fact that he obviously thought this intrigue was absolutely necessary made her more scared than she had been before coming here.

She put on her rain jacket and he popped up his umbrella as he escorted her outside and hailed a taxi. He gave the cabbie an address in Greenwich Village. On the way, he whispered, "I belong to the American UFO Congress, I'm a friend of Rolf's. He didn't clue me in to everything, he just asked me to help him. If you do what I say, we can shake anybody who happens to be tailing us. Then I'll tell you what to do next, and you'll be on your own."

"Okay," Jenny said, wondering what she was getting herself into.

"I like the rain," Harry said. "What you're wearing is going to help us."

The two agents who were following Jenny in a silver Datsun pulled over when the taxi stopped in front of a Greenwich Village brownstone. They stayed about thirty yards back so as not to be obvious. They watched Jenny and Harry get out. He held his umbrella over her as they entered the brownstone. The taxi did not depart but remained with its meter obviously running. In a little while, Jenny and Harry came out of the building. Her jacket hood was up but he was still sheltering her with the umbrella since she was carrying an armload of books and file folders. They got back into the taxi and it pulled away from the curb.

The agents in the Datsun followed, their windshield wipers squeaking back and forth, but it was the kind of drizzle that materializes as fast as it can be wiped. The agents saw Jenny get out of the cab and go into her own building, Park West Apartments, carrying her armload of books and file folders, hunching over them to protect them from the rain. Harry stayed in the taxi, and it went away.

Jenny did not come out of the building, though the agents stayed and waited, radioing to their headquarters the address and description of the young man Jenny had met with, so he could be thoroughly checked out and put under tight surveillance if necessary.

Meantime, Jenny Teague was on her way to Rolf Kollar's home in Long Island. The young lady the agents thought was Jenny really wasn't, though they closely resembled each other.

They were almost exactly the same height, weight, and build.

Jenny had changed clothes with her at Harry Paulson's apartment. She had waited twenty minutes. Then, wearing the other young lady's clothes, she had come back out to the street and hailed another taxi.

The rain was coming down much harder now, pelting the windows with driving force, especially when the taxi picked up speed on the Long Island Parkway. She hoped the storm would wear itself out before she reached her destination because the girl she had swapped clothes with had not been wearing any kind of rain gear, just a pair of green cotton slacks, a lightweight brown turtle-neck and an old denim jacket—cheap stuff she didn't mind giving away; she had made out well on the trade. Even her shoe size must've been the same as Jenny's, though, because thank God her scuffed-up loafers and brown wool socks felt pretty comfortable even though they weren't much for looks. And wouldn't be very waterproof either.

Jenny's expectation was that Kollar probably wanted to see her to deliver some news. He didn't dare show his face around Park West or the Cameron Foundation, and of course he wouldn't phone because the lines were almost certainly tapped. Going through all the trouble of helping her shake her surveillance must mean that the news he had come up with was important. It struck her that her father *might* have made contact with Kollar, but she pushed the thought away so her hopes wouldn't climb too high. Along with her fears.

Harry Paulson—if that was his right name—had advised Jenny not to let the cabbie take her right up to Kollar's front door. So even though it was pouring she got out on the main drag of East Point, which was called Beach Avenue, a spiffy little shopping district reminis-cent in a small way of Ocean City or Wildwood. Jenny had never been here before, and she imagined it all looked better in the sunshine. There were chic restau-rants, shops and boutiques that probably thrived on throngs of people who rushed to the shore on hot summer evenings and weekends. But it was too cold yet for the influx, the ocean was probably still below sixty degrees in late May, and besides the storm was keeping everybody off the streets. After paying the cabbie, Jenny ran into a five-and-dime and bought a cheap plastic umbrella. Then she started walking toward Rolf Kollar's house, following the directions Harry Paulson had given her.

It was only a ten-minute walk, down to the end of Beach Avenue, which terminated at a rocky pier, then five blocks east. Along the way Jenny got soaked from the waist down and her loafers got waterlogged. She stood in the downpour, gusts of cold wind blowing sheets of water in under her umbrella, and stared at the old Victorian beach house as if it were a ghost mansion in a horror movie. There were lights behind the curtains. The gas lamps in the lawn and by the driveway were burning. But the place still seemed lifeless, foreboding. Jenny shuddered when she looked at Kollar's Volksbus because she associated it with her trip to the safe house which had turned out to be a house of death. However, she hadn't come this far to cut and run. Summoning her courage, she went up to the gate in the chain-link fence and found it locked.

Just when she was in a quandary, wondering what to do to get in, there was a sudden noise and Kollar charged out onto the gingerbreaded wraparound porch, leaned over the banister, his head in the rain, and shouted, "Jenny! Wait! I'll unlock it for you!"

19

K ollar came out without an umbrella or even a raincoat and got drenched fumbling with the padlock and chain. She hurried up the porch steps because he was behind her—as if some part of him might stay dry if she didn't poke. Once they were in the living room, he slammed and bolted the door and they both stood there dripping on the oriental carpet. She noticed all the furniture was Victorian, probably genuine antiques. "I'll get some towels," he said. "Take off your jacket, Jenny. Put your umbrella over there in the stand. My God, you're soaked to the bone and so am I. I don't know if I have any clothes that will fit you."

"Do you have an old bathrobe or something?" she asked. "And maybe a clothes drier for the things I'm wearing?" She was surprisingly glad to see Kollar. He was the nearest thing she had to an ally, a friend. At least with him she didn't have to keep everything in.

"I have a bathrobe, certainly," he said.

But before he could go for it, Jenny's father came into the living room.

Her mouth gaped open. Electricity shot through her like a bolt of *deja vu*. She had imagined this moment thousands of times and at last it had come to pass. It was a dream made real and yet it was as different as reality always is from dreams. They stared at each other. She couldn't meet his gaze for long, the emotions were too overpowering. Her eyes dropped to her still-dripping umbrella. Shakily she backed into the foyer and slid the cheap wet plastic thing into an ornate brass stand where there were other umbrellas, elegant ones of black cloth with handles carved to resemble angry lions and glinty-eyed falcons, like the handles of old English walking sticks.

Her father embraced her. "Jenny...Jenny..." he murmured as her tears and her wet hair and clothes made him wet. Rolf Kollar looked on, smiling as smugly as he had smiled on the way to the safe house. The gun butt sticking out of her father's belt, pressing her abdomen, was a reminder, if she needed one, that this was less than a perfectly serene reunion. Her father stepped back, still with his hands on her shoulders, and let his eyes feast upon her. Soaking wet, with her hair in frizzy ringlets, she tried not to feel as if she might not measure up to his expectations. She remembered that when she was a little girl he had hugged her every time she ran to him, even when she was sticky with jelly or smeary from finger paints. He kept on smiling at her, and she dared to hope that maybe when he got to know her at her best he would be pleased with the way she had matured into womanhood. But how could anything ever make up for the years he had lost of watching her—and Sally—grow?

"I'll get the bathrobe and towels," Kollar muttered, and he went away.

"Oh, Jenny, it's really you…it's been so long," her father said. "You'll never know how much I missed you. I thought about you and prayed for you every day."

"I did for you, too, Daddy. I always believed you'd come back."

She was glad she could truthfully tell him this, impressing him with her loyalty. She wanted him to love her. Somehow everything would turn out all right.

But—the gun.

Had he pulled the trigger on any of the men at the safe house?

He narrowed his eyes, his expression hardening as he read the fear and suspicion in her face. She trembled, not just from the chill of her damp clothes.

Kollar came in and handed her a fuzzy blue bathrobe and a thick white towel. "Use the powder room down the hall," he said.

Suddenly there was a loud clap and Jenny froze. Norman Teague had clapped his hands so loud that the noise reverberated in the living room. "Hah!" he exclaimed with sudden exuberance. 'Wow we'll see who's crazy! Behold, I have arisen, I'm *alive.* Jenny! They didn't want you to know. They locked me up in limbo, and now they want to treat Sally the same way. But they won't get away with it from now on—I'll outwit them at every turn!"

"Who…who did it?" Jenny asked haltingly.

Her voice sounded meek, overpowered by his boisterousness. He was pacing frantically, huffing from his outburst of energy. A couple of times his hand went to the butt of the pistol in his belt, but he didn't draw it out.

"Would you believe, your mother?" he sneered. "Your

mother the adulteress and her two-faced seducer Dr. Gary Cameron."

"No! Not Mom...I..."

"Your mind boggles at the idea?" Teague cut in, stopping his pacing momentarily to leer at her. "Nobody wishes more than I that my darling wife had been faithful, but it wasn't in her character. She and Gary told the CIA that Vickers and I were planning to go public with what we had seen in New Mexico. But we would never have done that. It was a preposterous lie, but it was believed. We thought the government ought to go public of its own volition, and we strongly urged that approach, but once we lost the argument we were willing to go along, as always, with the prevailing views of our colleagues and the decisions of our military and civilian bosses. We certainly wouldn't have defected to the Russians—they've had extraterrestrial encounters of their own and they don't let their people know, either. Going to them wouldn't have done us a damn bit of good. But we were painted as defectors and traitors once the CIA made us disappear."

Jenny still hadn't moved. Kollar took the bathrobe from her and laid it on the couch. "Try to dry yourself a little," he encouraged.

The mundane concern seemed bizarre under the circumstances. But she halfheartedly wiped her face and rubbed the towel through her hair and found that it was already fairly dry. She ought to get out of her shoes, socks and slacks, which were still soaking wet, but now wasn't the time. "Mom loved you!" she told her father vehemently. "After you were gone, I didn't think she was going to make it. She didn't start dating Gary Cameron till two years later. No matter what you think, she couldn't have been one of the ones who told on you—it just doesn't ring true!"

"Humph!" Teague snorted. "I'm happy to hear she's an accomplished actress, in addition to her other talents which I see have been making her somewhat of a media star—thanks to her publicity-hungry fiancé. It's perfectly clear they wanted me removed from their lives, and to deflect suspicion from their true motive they also made up lies about Vickers so we were both kidnapped at the same time."

"What about Thompson?" Kollar broke in. "Had they made up their minds from the beginning that they were going to say that he died in a plane crash?"

"No, they wouldn't have had to say he died," said Teague. "They could've said he ejected safely and parachuted down. But once they felt they had to roll up me and Vickers, they had to do the same to Thompson for fear he might talk. We were all such close friends."

Kollar raised his eyebrows, shooting a piercingly skeptical look at Teague. "But Thompson was reported dead several *days* before you and Vickers even disappeared. The way you're telling it now, it would've had to have been the other way around. What you're saying doesn't make perfect sense, Dr. Teague."

Teague's face reddened and his lips curled into an angry scowl. He yanked his .45 out of his belt and pointed it at Rolf Kollar.

"No!" Jenny shrieked. "Rolf isn't your enemy, Daddy. He spent a fortune and put his own life in tremendous danger to get you out of the sanitarium."

"Double agents…both of you," Teague muttered. He had a wild, frightened look in his eyes, like a man facing two coiled-up snakes, either of which might strike him if he didn't succeed in dispatching them both. He pointed the gun at Jenny, then back at Kollar.

"I know you're going to do it," Kollar said. "Well, go on and do it to me...it doesn't matter. I'll join my father...my mother...so many I helped into oblivion. I'm overdue by forty-five years."

"Go, then." Teague chuckled mirthlessly. Then he fired. With a roaring belch of flame, the slug slammed into Kollar's chest at close range, hurling him against a wall, streaking it with blood as he slid down and crumpled sideways, his eyes bulging, his mouth open wide.

Jenny screamed.

"Shut up!" Teague yelled. "Shut up, you bitch, or I'll kill you right now!" In a frenzy, he jammed the gun up under her throat, pushing her head back with the cold barrel, shoving her against the same wall Kollar's dead body had slid down. "No...please...Daddy...," she managed to choke out.

"How do we know *I'm* your father?" he jeered. "Maybe it's Gary Cameron! Maybe it was going on for years behind my back! You knew about it, didn't you?"

"No...Oh, no," she babbled. "No, Daddy...it's not true."

He rammed the muzzle into her throat, choking off her words and banging her head hard. She was sure he would pull the trigger. She tried to prepare herself to die and was even somewhat surprised that she didn't want to, as Kollar had wanted to, now that a seven-year dream had turned into a nightmare.

"Where's your mother?" Teague barked.

"I don't know."

"Liar! Tell me or you won't draw another breath!"

Should Jenny refuse to talk, sacrificing herself to protect her mother? She only had seconds to decide, the length of a few pounding heartbeats, a desperate gulp of air. Through her fear, it dawned on her that by telling the truth about her mother's whereabouts she might lure her father into a trap. There was a good chance that Martha already was protected, under surveillance. Same with Gary Cameron. Jenny only wished she hadn't shaken her own surveillance to come here and be sucked deeper into a world of madness and murder. She was sure her father was crazy now—though a part of her still ached to deny the awful realization. No sane person could kill with such ease, such demonic delight. She was nothing to him. Nothing but an enemy, someone to hate and destroy. The father that she remembered never would have put a gun to her throat.

His face was a red mask of rage, his jaw muscles bulging, his teeth tightly clenched. His breath smelled putrid—like Sally's when she was out of control. His knuckles were white, gripping the butt of the gun. "Say your prayers, dear," he hissed as his finger tightened on the trigger.

"Stop!" Jenny shrieked. "Mom's with Gary Cameron at a television studio today. They're taping a show called *Life in Outer Space*."

Teague laughed in her face. His laughter was tinny and hollow. Spittle drooled from his thin lips. His blood-shot eyes resembled the eyes of a rabid beast. "*Life in Outer Space*," he said, chortling. "A perfect theme! I'll have *so* much to add to the content of the program!"

"Are you…going to kill me?" Jenny quavered.

"No, not yet. You're coming with me, darling daughter…we're going to go see Mommy."

20

Terrified, Jenny drove Kollar's Volksbus through the rainy New York streets. Her clothes were still clingingly wet, even with the heater on. She was itchy and sweaty. The backs of her legs were damp against the vinyl seat. Her socks were sopping inside her borrowed loafers. At least her hair was dry, for she had worn a waterproof hooded jacket to run out to the Volksbus, a blue and red one that had belonged to Kollar. Every time she thought about how he had died, it shook her up so badly she thought she might lose control of the steering wheel.

Her father had a hooded jacket of his own, a gray one, but he wasn't wearing it at the moment. It was spread over his lap, concealing the gun he was pointing at her. She considered wrecking the Volksbus on purpose and trying to get away. But she knew it wouldn't work. He'd shoot her dead before she even got her door open.

Strangely enough, he no longer looked so demented, just intense, keyed-up. "You're going to be my hostage," he told her. "You'll get me into the TV studio. I'll settle some old business with sweet, sweet Martha." He chuckled wryly. "Mostly Martha," he corrected himself, winking slyly. "Do you remember that old-time song, 'Mostly Martha'? I used to sing it to her when we were dating. Mostly Martha…and sweet, sweet Gary, a helluva sweet guy. With pals like that, who needs enemies? But maybe if they'll tell the world I'm not dead, I can afford to let them live. Live and let live instead of dog eat dog. I'll take Sally out of St. Francis—she doesn't belong there any more than I do—and we'll hop a big bird down to Mexico and live happily ever after."

"I'm sure Mom didn't have a thing to do with what happened to you," Jenny ventured. "If she could have…"

"Don't you dare try to tell me that," Teague pounced. "I know the truth: I've paid for it in blood. The cuckold is always the last to know, but once his wise eyes are wide open you can't pull the wool over them ever again. Professional rivalry is what this is all about. Professional rivalry and jealousy! Cameron had the big name, but the great discoveries were all *mine.* So was the woman he coveted. He had to get rid of me, you see?"

Suddenly he started to hum the song "Mostly Martha" in a twangy, off-key voice. At first Jenny thought he was doing it badly on purpose, as a sarcasm. She remembered him as a good singer; in fact, he was the one who had taught her to sing when she was only about three. But now he couldn't carry a tune. Hearing him set Jenny's teeth on edge. It was every bit as unsettling as having him pointing a gun at her. His voice was as out of tune as his brain.

He stopped humming as suddenly as he had begun. "Vickers and I examined the alien corpses," he said. "And the wreckage of the saucer…we examined the wreckage. We couldn't reconstruct it and make it work again. There was too much we didn't know. The engineering was centuries beyond us. All the instrumentation was in an incomprehensible language—we'd have needed an intergalactic Rosetta Stone."

"How about the mathematics?" Jenny asked, wanting to keep him talking so he wouldn't be so dangerous. "Wouldn't the math have been decipherable? I thought music and mathematics were the universal languages."

"Music and math...the same thing, Jenny. All based on numbers and frequencies. Harmony. We tried it, but it didn't work. We couldn't figure the damn thing out. Maybe if one of the creatures had survived, it would've been a different story. They're gonna come back some-day, and we've gotta be ready to talk to them and convince them we didn't shoot them down."

Jenny felt an increased sense of foreboding the closer they got to the TV studio, Metro Teleproductions, which was on 46th Street, near Times Square. Right now they were hung up in heavy Manhattan traffic, the windshield wipers beating back and forth, everything moving slower because of the storm. Jenny wanted to get there and get it over with—whatever was going to happen. At the same time, she didn't want to get there because to finally arrive might be to hasten her own death.

Her father was talking about death, too—the death of the earth. "This planet is dying," he said. "Our natural resources are being used up—they'll only last a few more decades. We can barely breathe the air anymore it's so hideously polluted. We don't need to blow ourselves to hell, we're going to suffocate first. We need growing room. We need to become independent of the limitations of just this one planet. But when I saw that saucer, how *advanced* it was, I knew we'd never make it on our own. It would require *centuries* to develop anything that good, and we just haven't got that kind of time. We won't be around that long, at the rate we're going downhill. The only way would be to make friends with the people from that other world so we can learn from them. They're the only ones who can save us from ourselves, but we're building a Maginot Umbrella to kill them if they come back!"

His speech was so passionate, so imbued with righteous conviction, that it made Jenny wonder if his being mad meant that all of his story had to be untrue. Did he really see a flying saucer or not? Maybe something that had happened to him during the experience—or something that was done to him in the sanitarium—caused him to begin losing his sanity. But no matter how he got that way, he was now a mortal danger to everybody—and Jenny would bear part of the responsibility if anybody else died. She had to try to smooth-talk him. Win him over, make him put his gun away. His one vulnerable spot seemed to be his desire to be *believed*, his yearning for respect from the world and particularly from his colleagues.

She said, "So is Mom. If these videotapes we have with us are such dynamite evidence, Mom and Gary will believe your story if you give them half a chance. Show them the tapes. I'm sure they'll support you once they understand why the truth was suppressed and how much you've suffered. So will I. We'll help you any way we can. I *love* you, Daddy, even if you don't care about us anymore."

For a long time he didn't answer. Yet she thought, from the way his eyes had blinked while she was talking, that she might be getting through to him a little.

"I'm the innocent, wronged party in all of this," he said at last in a lachrymose, self-pitying tone. "I had to deal harshly with Chaney, Rawlings and Kollar because they were traitors. But I shouldn't be punished for trying to be free. Everything I did was self-defense. I shouldn't have been locked up when I can still serve my country better than any man alive. In fact, what I have to offer transcends national boundaries. I should be working on that spacecraft, finding out how we can rebuild it or make one of our own. Instead my illustrious colleagues have given up on it as if the advanced technology will always baffle their feeble intellects. They're letting it remain dismantled, in storage in a special hangar at Wright-Patterson, like old pieces of junk, no good to anybody."

"That's appalling!" Jenny said. He had tried to hang on her father's every word, suspending all disbelief, so her attempt at empathy would sound convincing. If he suspected her of insincerity, he might squeeze the trigger. She wished she hadn't been so apparently successful in shaking the CIA agents who must have been watching her before the elusive maneuver arranged by Harry Paulson. She hoped they'd somehow pick up on her trail again.

Or that new ones would spot her and her father at the TV studio.

"Look, Jenny, you've got to help me," he pleaded. "I don't want to have to hurt you, believe me it's the last thing I want. There's already been too much bloodshed, too much suffering, all because of the Big Lie the government wants to hang over everybody. It's like they're making us live in some brand-new version of the Dark Ages, and the only way we can save ourselves is to rip open the curtains and let the rays of sunshine stream through."

"I'll do it if you put your gun away," she said. "You

don't have to order me around with it. I'm not against you, Daddy, and neither are Mom and Gary. You don't have to be afraid of us."

"Okay," he said, taking a deep breath. "Will this make you feel more comfortable?"

He stuck the gun in his belt.

She nodded her head yes and breathed a bit easier.

He smiled inwardly. He was playing Jenny like a fish on a line, the way she was trying to play him. But the big fish was infinitely smarter than the little fish, he thought to himself. He had decided that he could use all three of the little fishies—Jenny, Martha and Gary—to get his story on the air and confirm his true identity. Then he would reveal publicly how they had betrayed him in the first place, exposing them to ridicule and causing them to be punished. If the world wasn't willing to mete out true justice at last, then he would do it himself. He'd kill all the traitors even if he had to sacrifice his own life.

They parked the Volksbus in a garage on 46th Street. He got out the suitcase with the videotapes. They both put their nylon hoods up, cinching them tight, so that their faces barely showed. When they walked into the building that housed Metro Teleproductions they were huddled arm-in-arm under Jenny's clear plastic umbrella and it was pulled down over their heads, obliging anybody to look through bleary raindrops in order to recognize them.

In the lobby, where there were only a couple people milling around, she closed the umbrella as he promptly hit the elevator button. They had to wait about thirty seconds, during which time she hoped frantically that they'd be stopped and he of course hoped they wouldn't. He got his wish. They rode the elevator without incident up to the ninth floor, all of which was occupied by the TV studio.

The blonde receptionist looked very pretty and very bored, probably an aspiring model who had taken a mundane job because it enabled her to rub shoulders with the real action. "We're here to see Dr. Cameron and Dr. Teague," Jenny told her. "We have some props they asked us to bring, from the Cameron Foundation."

"They're in Studio A," the receptionist mumbled, picking up a phone and punching an intercom button. "Are you rolling?" she purred into the mouthpiece, relishing the jargon. "Good...some props are here." She cradled the phone and turned back toward the visitors, once again bored. "They're on break. You can go on back." She absently pointed the way. "Through that steel door."

Even when your life is in danger, you have to deal with ungracious people, Jenny thought. Beyond the steel door, she and her father proceeded down a thickly carpeted, sound-proofed corridor. He let her go first. Presumably he would shoot her if she tried anything funny, but at this point she couldn't think of anything she wouldn't be scared to try. Over a thick wooden door there was a sign that said Studio A, and a red bulb that wasn't glowing, therefore they could go in without disrupting a sound take. But it didn't mean they weren't going to disrupt plenty else.

"You go in and get them," Teague commanded, reaching under his jacket to fondle the butt of his gun. "I'll follow close enough to keep an eye on you but not close enough to alarm them. Bring them to me. If anybody panics, I'll start shooting."

So it was on her. Now she was responsible for the safety of everybody in there. Timidly she opened the wide, thick studio door. Her father nudged her inside. The lights were bright. Technicians were scurrying around. A cameraman and his assistants were rehearsing a dolly move across a soundstage that was empty except for a beautiful backdrop of Saturn, the ringed planet. The darkened area surrounding the set was a jumble of cables, booms and light stands.

"They're over there," Teague whispered hoarsely. "To your right, behind the mockup."

Her eyes darting, she saw what he meant: a mockup of a lunar landing module that apparently was going to be used in an upcoming scene, for Gary and Martha were moving around it, conferring with a tall, bearded man writing on a clipboard.

"Don't stall," Teague whispered, prodding her forward. "Go get them. I'll have my eyes on you every second."

Jenny stepped gingerly around a tangle of electrical cables and went to tell her mother and her mother's fiancé that Daddy was home at last.

———

TEAGUE WASN'T SPOTTED ENTERING the building, but Jenny was. She was "made" by a lanky young man named Morton Foster who was bored silly with his job and lately found himself constantly daydreaming about quitting the Agency to become a private detective with a raft of dangerous, exciting cases and a bevy of beautiful, sexy clients. To Foster's chagrin, being in the CIA wasn't anything like being in a James Bond movie. Working this stake-out was one of the most stimulating things he had done in his year and a half with the Agency. For the first year he had done little but shuffle papers behind a gray steel desk and punch buttons beneath a green, glowing computer screen. He was twenty-four years old, not handsome, not brilliant, but with a soul that yearned for adventure.

That's why his heart skipped a beat when he caught a glimpse of Jenny Teague's face just before the elevator doors went shut. He was lighting a cigarette, closing his eyes to the stinging smoke, and almost missed her. There were only so many ways to kill time and try to act natural while you were staking out a lobby. Smoke cigarettes even if you hated the taste of them and feared lung cancer. Study the building directory as if it was loaded with spicy quotations you wanted to memorize. Scope out and build wild spy-chase scenarios involving yourself with the dynamite chicks who sometimes went up and down from the modeling agencies and the TV studio on the upper floors.

Agent Foster almost convinced himself that he didn't really see Jenny Teague but somebody else who happened to resemble her, because he wasn't *supposed* to see her. Last word he got, when he came on duty at three, was that she had gone home at about one o'clock and had not left Park West Apartments after that. If another agent bad tailed her from there, he would've beeped Foster on his beeper, letting Foster know she was being turned over to him soon as she entered the building. He checked his beeper, eyeing it suspiciously. It was still functioning. The batteries weren't dead or the little red light would've stopped glowing.

So there must've been a major screw-up. Jenny Teague was loose with no leash. It *was* her on the elevator, Foster thought. He had a keen eye for faces, even when the hair was bunched up under a rain hood. Something was up. Maybe something exciting for a change.

His heart beating a bit faster, he went to the pay phone across from the elevator and dialed headquarters.

"So you're in love, planning to be married," Teague said, smiling benignly at Martha Teague and Gary Cameron. They were in the office of the president of Metro Teleproductions; the director and crew of *Life in Outer Space* had been given a two-hour break that Cameron Productions was paying for. Jenny noticed that while her mother still looked stunned, Gary Cameron seemed to be bearing Norman Teague's sudden resurrection with remarkable equanimity.

Watching Cameron closely, Jenny had to wonder if he could have been prepared for something like this all along. When she first broke the news, whispering to him and her mother out by the soundstage, Cameron appeared shocked. But the shock evaporated too quickly, making her suspicious. Scared as she was, she harbored an intense, suspenseful curiosity over what would transpire and what sort of true colors would be revealed now that a seven-year lie had crumbled.

Teague was sitting in a comfortable swivel chair behind the studio president's glass-topped desk, sipping scotch from the office liquor cabinet. His .45 was on the desk blotter within easy reach. Even though Teague had magnanimously asked Jenny to fix whatever anybody wanted, nobody else was drinking anything.

"Norman," Gary Cameron said chummily, "I'm deeply sorry for what you've apparently been through. I guess I feel guilty that Martha and I fell in love while you were gone, but how were we to know?"

"Don't worry, I understand perfectly," Teague broke in as Cameron's question died on his lips. "I'm a very understanding fellow. I've had ample time for introspection, and it has mellowed me. Sometimes absence doesn't make the heart grow fonder, right. Martha? It didn't work that way for you...and not for me. This may surprise all of you, but I harbor no ill feelings."

This pleasant little speech set Jenny on edge instead of comforting her. What was her father up to? On his way here, he had spouted plenty of animosity. She knew it couldn't have evaporated so easily. It must be seething inside him, ready to erupt with his next mood swing.

"No hard feelings," Teague repeated, as if savoring the taste of the sweet, forgiving words. "Hell, a man can't expect his life to be in perfect order after he drops out for seven years, even if it's not his own fault. I feel like Rip Van Winkle. But we'll work it out...you wait and see...we'll work it out just fine."

"Are you saying you won't contest a divorce?" Martha blurted, eyeing him nervously.

"Mostly, Martha," he said, grinning at his pun. "Mostly, Martha, what I'm saying is that I wish to resume a normal life and let others go on living theirs with the least amount of disruption we can all manage."

Abruptly he hummed a few bars of "Mostly Martha" while the other people in the room stared at him, waiting for his next move. When he broke off humming, he said, "First I want to screen the videotape for you so we'll all have a grasp of the big picture, so to speak." He chuckled, then sipped his scotch. "Is the screening room set up? Do we know how to run the equipment?"

"The technician put the dub on the machine before he took his break," said Dr. Cameron. "All we have to do is punch the start button."

"Excellent!" said Teague, clapping his hands with an air of joviality. "Know where we can get some popcorn, Jenny?"

"I'm afraid I didn't bring my popper," she said, lamely trying to propitiate his relatively benign mood.

He laughed heartily, entirely too heartily. He grabbed for his gun and they all jumped. But he stuck it in his belt. "There," he said. "Now that we're beginning to understand each other, I don't need to point this thing at you constantly…but I will keep it handy, just in case."

"Don't worry, you can trust us," said Gary Cameron. "None of us ever meant you any harm."

"Well, of course not!" Teague boomed without any overt sarcasm. "All of us were innocent dupes!"

Cameron led the way into a tape-editing room replete with a vast console, a bank of television monitors, and plushly modern leather furniture for the comfort of the studio's wealthy corporate clients. "Sit, sit," said Teague. But he remained standing by the door while Cameron punched one of the buttons on the console and the bank of monitors displayed a cueing slate that said:

BLUE RIDGE DUB #3.

This was one of the dubs made by Jason Rawlings just before he was killed; it had the stories told by all three sanitarium escapees dubbed from the one-inch masters onto a single three-quarter inch tape, so that all the segments could be viewed consecutively without rethreading the playback machine.

Cameron sat down to watch, next to Martha and Jenny on a tan leather sofa. He was as frightened as Jenny, possibly more so. Unlike her, he had not seen Norman Teague kill anybody and he did not know for sure that Teague actually had blood on his hands. But he knew full well what quantalibrium could do to a man's mind.

He got a jolt seeing and hearing Thompson and Vickers on the monitors, their images repeated in quadruplicate on the glowing screens. Part of the shock was due to guilt over the fact that he had helped put them away, while he had survived by taking placebos. The other unnerving thing was that they made their crazy story sound so believable! So did Teague. They were possessed of an unwavering zeal, an irrefutable aura of sincerity. They did not present any hard evidence because of course none existed. But all three of the Blue Ridge escapees, formerly men whose credibility and integrity were respected in high places, corroborated and verified every detail of their farfetched "experiences". They sounded so flawlessly convincing that even Dr. Gary Cameron—who knew better—almost wanted to open his mind and give them the benefit of the doubt.

Clearly *they* believed every word they were saying. That was what made their tape so exceedingly dangerous. If it ever got a public airing, it would convert even some of the hard-nosed UFO skeptics, and the fears that it would engender might panic the general population.

Cameron reached over and squeezed Martha's hand, furtively, so Teague wouldn't catch him and go on a shooting spree. She pulled her hand away. He stole a glance at her face and saw how intently she was watching the screens. He feared that she might be turning against him. Did she suspect that he knew all along that these three men weren't dead?

Worse, did Norman Teague suspect? Did he actually know? No telling what he might have learned in the sanitarium. No telling what damning facts may have been spilled by some indiscreet doctor, orderly or guard under the illusion that it could never matter, none of the patients were ever going to be let out into the world to do any damage.

Cameron wasn't obtuse. He could tell that Teague was toying with him. What did the madman want? When would he tire of his cat-and-mouse game and let the bullets fly?

———

WHEN AGENT MORTON FOSTER phoned headquarters he spoke to Brian Meade, who was immediately upset that somehow there had been a gap in Jenny Teague's surveillance. "I very much doubt that she could've shaken our guys on her own," Meade said. "She must've had outside help. And that could mean that something critical is going down."

"Yes, sir," Agent Foster agreed, trying to sound like a seasoned, unflappable operative, but his heart was pounding and there was a tight edginess in his voice. Discerning this, Meade said, "We don't want to move in on a situation without being sure it's not going to blow up in our faces. So sit tight, Foster, unless you're forced into action. Dorsey and I are on our way. We'll handle this, understand? Let the other people on your stake-out know something's up, but tell them not to overreact."

"Yes, sir. Should I try to get in closer, sir?"

Meade considered this for several seconds. It was true that somebody would have to go in closer to see what the actual situation was. Meade and his men couldn't just barge right in. They didn't want to blow their cover at the wrong moment and come up empty-handed. That would be the ultimate disaster. The whole operation would be down the tubes.

"Can you pull it off?" he asked Foster. "Without getting yourself made?"

"Yes, sir, I believe so, sir. The logical assumption is that Jenny Teague went up to the ninth floor, Metro Teleproductions, where her mother is with Dr. Cameron. About ten minutes after I saw Jenny on the elevator, a bunch of people came down. They were the studio crew, all in high spirits because they suddenly got a two-hour paid break—I heard them chattering about it. Why did they stop work on the show they were taping right after Jenny went up there?"

"Good question," said Meade. He thought that Foster sounded smart and competent. Maybe he could be trusted to reconnoiter. "If you go up there, what would be your game plan?" Meade asked.

"I could talk to the receptionist," said Foster. "She's behind a desk in an open area, by herself usually. We know that from casing the place yesterday. I could pretend I have a message for one of the crew guys, so I just want to sit and wait for them to come back."

"Okay," said Meade, acquiescing. "Try to find out who's up there that we don't know about, if anybody. If you turn up a zero, that'll be important. It'll tell us to hang back and play it cool at this point instead of thundering in like a herd of bulls."

"Yes, sir," said Morton Foster. Although he had made every effort to sound levelheaded while talking to the team commander, his imagination was soaring when he got off the phone. He told himself he was now the point man of the whole operation, a scout going behind enemy lines. At last he was getting a taste of the sort of action that had caused him to want to be a spy.

He was even going to get to use a cover story to ingratiate himself with a beautiful young lady—the blonde receptionist who looked like a model. Maybe, Foster thought, he could get her to give him a tour of the TV studio by pretending he had never seen one before. Then he could scope out what was happening behind that steel door.

————

BY THE TIME the tape ended, Norman Teague was pacing back and forth in front of the console, punching his fist into his palm, elated to have himself vindicated in front of Gary, Martha and Jenny. "You see?" he crowed. "It's the truth—every word! All *three* of us can't be crazy. Why do you think they kept us bottled up all these years? Then when we escaped they tried to kill us—and they did get Chaney and Thompson and that fellow Rawlings. I think they must've got Vickers, too. Now you can understand the real reason behind the arms race and SDI. It all makes perfect sense—why the superpowers don't want to stop building bigger and better weapons— why they intend to militarize space. They're trying to arm themselves for an expected invasion by extraterrestrials who so far have behaved peacefully toward us even though they've obviously been coming here to study us."

Martha Teague's eyes scarcely left Norman's face as he paced back and forth. She was scared of him, frightened out of her wits by the big black gun in his belt. It amazed her that such an intelligent, rational man, a man she had once loved, was reduced to the sad, pathetic specimen that was parading before her, threatening her life. She didn't believe a word of his story. She knew that he was mentally unbalanced before he disappeared, and he seemed worse now. She could only wonder and be grateful that she and Gary Cameron had taken quantalibrium without losing their sanity. Yet. For who could be certain of the long-term effects? Maybe it was like certain slow-acting cancers that didn't show up in some people till they were well advanced in years.

Jenny was the only one of the three people sitting on the couch, held hostage, who entertained the notion that some parts of Norman Teague's story might be true. If he and Vickers and Thompson were mad, why would their madness, their delusions, all take the same shape? Was there really a UFO cover-up?

Gary Cameron knew he had to pretend to be convinced, as a matter of self-preservation. He said, "What do you want us to do, Norman? I admit this tape is strong stuff. If the CIA—or whoever—doesn't want your story to leak out, how can we try to break it without getting killed or locked up for our trouble?"

"We have to get it on national television," said Teague, smacking his fist. "The tape needs to be viewed by people in important, responsible positions. It also needs more corroboration."

"This studio isn't affiliated with a network," Cameron pointed out. "It can't broadcast. We only use it as a production facility."

"I know," said Teague, still pacing. "But what I have in mind is...putting you, Martha, and Jenny on the tape, as an addendum. I want you to confirm the circumstances under which the addendum was made. And I want you to swear to the true identities of me, Vickers, and Thompson. Then we can deliver copies by courier to all three networks, right under the noses of whoever might have us under surveillance."

Gary said, "Martha and I are personal friends of the president of the network that runs our science series. I can phone him from here and get our material on the air right away, before it can be confiscated."

"Great! Perfect!" Teague enthused.

But Jenny sensed the true meaning of his enthusiasm, the sly, gloating look in his eyes. "Daddy," she said haltingly, "if we make a tape for you, if we do what you want...you're going to kill us afterwards, aren't you? Tell us the truth, Daddy."

Teague stopped pacing. He tried to suppress a smirk, but his wife picked up on it and she knew Jenny was right. A chill shot through Martha. She had barely uttered a word during the past hour but now, out of desperation, she broke her silence. "Norman...please listen to me. We all took that drug, remember? When we were working together at Universal Dynamics?"

"What *drug!*" he sneered, drawing his gun, pointing it at her. "I never took any drug, Martha! What are you trying to *prove*? That I'm a dope addict? That I don't have control of my faculties?"

She knew she had to soothe him, calm him down. In a low, sad voice, she said, "You're not yourself now, Norman. I think you know what I'm talking about, if you only think back. You, Gary, Abe, Kevin and I...we took quantalibrium. Somehow it didn't affect me and Gary, either positively or negatively, but it drastically changed the rest of you...altered your personalities." She glanced at her daughter Jenny, apologetically, hoping for understanding, then went on. "Remember Dr. Melvin Lieberman and his Faustian pipedreams? He said there was virtually no limit to human intelligence, *he* was the modern alchemist who had discovered the true philosopher's stone, the key to human potential. His drug benefits certain people—it magnifies their intellectual powers—but it destroys as much as it creates. It produces hallucinations, Norman—fantasies that seem totally *real*. So these tapes aren't going to convince anybody of anything. You're still chasing rainbows, still under the influence of the drug. Let us get you into therapy...find professional support for you—and help you remain free."

Teague laughed, a wild, maniacal chortle. He cut it off abruptly. Then he hummed, mostly Martha, mostly Martha—two times. His lips curled into an angry, demented leer. "*You* gave me a drug, darling wife? You *admit* it? Then what did you do—have me declared mad? It's all that I wanted to hear—your confession. Now that I've heard it, I don't forgive you. I condemn you to hell!"

He thrust the gun toward her, ready to fire.

"Wait!" Gary Cameron cried, throwing himself across Martha's body, shielding her. "Wait: *I'm* the one you should kill!"

"Both of you," Teague said.

"No...no," Cameron babbled. "Martha is innocent. She never knew the truth. *I* did it. I let all of you take quantalibrium even though I knew it hadn't been sufficiently tested. It affected your mind, Norman. And your genes. It's responsible for what happened to Sally."

"Then why didn't it happen to you?" Teague shouted. His eyes brightened with a sudden rush of mental clarity. "You and Martha took the drug, too—you traitors!"

"We were the only two who never were given any actual doses," Cameron meekly admitted. "Your wife and I were the controls, injected with a placebo. You, Vickers, and Thompson were the only ones at Universal Dynamics who actually received injections of quantalibrium. You were the only ones to suffer the consequences."

Appalled by Gary's confession, Martha asked, "Why, Gary? Why were you, and I spared?"

"Because I loved you," he told her, his eyes meeting hers. "I wanted you and I dreamed of having you someday. But I didn't *plan* for anything to go wrong with the drug experiment. In fact, I was jealous when it seemed to be working so well, and Vickers and your husband were coming up with all those marvelous breakthroughs. I was going to start taking it myself—and would've done so if I hadn't become aware of the disastrous side effects just in time to preserve us from them, Martha."

"*Both* of you deserve to die," Teague screamed.

Jenny jumped up and ran at her father, yelling, "Daddy! No!"

BLAM! BLAM! Two loud rapid reports echoed in the console room. Martha Teague was shot in the chest, Gary Cameron in the stomach. His body was flung across hers on the leather couch.

Jenny clawed at the gun, pushing it aside, and her father grabbed her in a choke hold, twisting her, wrenching the gun free.

At that moment, Agent Morton Foster appeared in the doorway, his own pistol drawn. "Drop it!" he cried.

Choking Jenny, Teague held her body in front of his own, shielding himself. The young CIA agent hesitated, not wanting to shoot the girl, and Teague fired. Morton took a .45 slug in the heart and died instantly.

Teague dragged Jenny through the doorway, stepping through blood to get around the dead agent's body. The blonde receptionist, who had led Foster back here for a look at the studio soundstage, was running down the hall screaming. Teague fired at her twice, but both slugs missed, chipping puffs of hallway plaster, as she made it through the steel door.

Wayne Dorsey burst through that same door and caught a glimpse of Norman Teague dragging Jenny into the taping studio. Dorsey withheld his fire. Teague got inside, slammed the thick wooden door and bolted it shut. Then he pushed Jenny away from him, shoving her so hard she crashed to hands and knees. He took aim at her. She looked up, tears streaming down her face as she tried desperately to crawl away. He squeezed the trigger. Click. Click. Click. She was getting away. He couldn't believe the gun was empty. He stared at it, dumbfounded. Then it occurred to him to use it like a hammer. He jumped on Jenny, clubbing her skull. Crushed under his body weight, the wind knocked out of her, she barely managed to get her left arm up, warding off repeated blows. Her head was bleeding profusely. She was dizzy, on the verge of losing consciousness. The gun smashed twice into her arm—the pain was excruciating—and she thought she could hear bones breaking.

She groped for something to fight back with, and her free right hand touched a cold metal rod—a movie light stand. She grabbed it and pulled hard, and it toppled, grazing her father's head, making him duck. Momentarily startled, he stopped bashing at her with the gun butt. She had hold of the steel stand but it was too long and unwieldy for her to swing it at him unless she could get to her feet. She tried to use it to fend off his blows—and the gun smashed into it—clang! bang! Then he started beating her fingers, bludgeoning them loose.

She let loose an agonizing scream and the heavy steel stand dropped across her throat as she caught another glancing blow from the gun butt on her left temple. Somehow her aching, bleeding fingers found the switch to the thousand-watt studio light. She clicked it on and swiveled the powerful beam into his face, hoping to blind him temporarily. But the gun butt smashed into the high-wattage quartz filament with a loud sizzle and a shower of sparks.

Teague was jolted sideways by the initial surge of the powerful current, and Jenny used her last ounce of strength to roll away. She could hear him screaming, being electrocuted. "Daddy!" she cried in a whimpering little-girl voice—the part of her that still yearned for the fatherly love that had been absent from her life for the past seven years. His body jerked and kicked, then lay still, sparks still zapping from the light to the gun, filling the air with the stench of his burning, blistering fingers.

On the tape he had talked about inmates dying that way on an electrified fence. Jenny trembled, her eyes swimming with tears. She tried to get up but she was so weak and groggy that she fell back onto a tangle of studio cables that coiled under her like snakes. She heard the door being splintered, managed to raise her head one last time, and had a blurry impression of two men with guns barging through. Then she blacked out.

21

Brian Meade and Wayne Dorsey supervised the exhumation of three bodies—Thompson, Chaney and Raw lings—from the grave Rolf Kollar had dug behind the barn at the safe house. The remains, already burned beyond recognition, were put into body bags and driven to Blue Ridge Hospital to be cremated.

That same morning, Meade and Dorsey viewed one of the confiscated videotapes with Dr. Melvin Lieberman. On a nineteen-inch screen in Lieberman's office, they watched Thompson, Vickers and Teague telling the story of the UFO crash, the examination of the wreckage, and the autopsies performed on the extraterrestrials.

"Pretty convincing, aren't they?" Dr. Lieberman said when the tape ended.

Dorsey guffawed. "Darn tootin', Doc! Now I see why the rascals even passed polygraph tests, according to what you told us.

"True, true," Lieberman chuckled. "They were utterly convinced they were telling the truth. None of it ever registered as a *lie* because it wasn't a lie in their own minds."

"I've never seen a sincerer group of witnesses," Meade admitted.

"*Folie a trois,*" said Lieberman, smirking.

"What?" asked Dorsey, befuddled.

"Well, you see," said Lieberman, "there's a psychological condition known *as folie a deux,* which in French means 'madness for two.' Here we have a case of madness for three, or *folie a trois.* We've found that paranoid schizophrenic disorders can be communicated in families or in any closely knit group, not by bacterial or viral infection, but by mental infection, so to speak. The people around the sick person start to buy in to his sick thinking. One group member becomes psychotic and then gradually transfers the disorder to another person who begins believing in his delusion. *Folie a deux* was the name given to this phenomenon when it was first studied by two French psychiatrists back in 1877." Lieberman smiled. "I think it's one of the most fascinating manifestations of mental disease."

"About as fascinating as watching cancer grow," Dorsey said with a sick grimace.

Lieberman continued smiling. Stifling his dislike of the hairy little doctor, Meade asked, "How did this freaky little quirk happen to Thompson, Teague and Vickers?"

"Quantalibrium made them especially susceptible," Lieberman said, obviously relishing the power of the drug even though he tried to sound blandly objective. "They were brilliant men, an asset to our nation. But they had a hunger to be even more ingenious, to make even greater breakthroughs and more wonderful achievements. So they volunteered to take quantalibrium, and they signed the releases waiving the further testing of the drug that ought to have been done. There was reason to believe that it was almost certainly safe, since it had been tested on prison inmates with no ill effects, but it hadn't been followed up for a sufficient number of years, and that's why the waivers were necessary. Soon some of the prison inmates started to exhibit bizarre behavior—but at first we attributed it to the pressure of becoming more mentally potent while the potency was inhibited by living behind bars. Then Colonel Kevin Thompson went berserk and thought he was seeing flying saucers. He ejected himself from the cockpit of a 57-million-dollar airplane and let the plane crash into a mountain while he parachuted to safety. When he was picked up he was babbling, telling his debriefing officer this wild tale about how he was taken into a flying saucer, airplane and all."

"But you had the wreckage to prove otherwise," said Dorsey.

"Of course. But nuts like Rolf Kollar wanted to believe Thompson. Rumors got out about what he had said on his radio transmitter—the UFOs that were supposedly closing in on him."

"What about Teague and Vickers?" Meade asked.

"We had to put them away at Blue Ridge, along with Thompson. They were all three becoming paranoid schizophrenics. At least here at the sanitarium we could give them drugs to control their psychoses, to keep them reasonably calm instead of in straitjackets or padded cells. I kept them under close observation for a time, studying them and even letting them do some of their scientific work, in the wing I've come to call 'the sanity ward.' But eventually they started talking to one another, in the exercise yard, the cafeteria, and so on, and their delusions developed and fed on each other, blending into a coherent fabric of insanity."

"*Folie a trois,*" said Meade, rubbing his jowls.

"Exactly," said Lieberman. "Over a period of time, all three inmates became absolutely convinced that the UFO incident was a reality. In their own minds, Thompson had been captured by a flying saucer, and Teague and Vickers had been members of a commission that had examined the wreckage of that saucer and had seen the corpses of the extraterrestrials."

"Very spooky," said Dorsey.

"You told us," Meade interjected, "that quantalibrium is a derivative of angel dust. If you ask me, a better name for it would be devil dust, Doctor."

"Well," said Lieberman, "we still might be able to get the bugs out. Quantalibrium has such promise. It could turn out to be very beneficial, sometime in the near future. We're going to continue keeping an eye on Sally Teague, even if she improves enough to be released from St. Francis. She's the only subject we have at present whose DNA was affected by a parent who was taking quantalibrium when she was conceived. We may be able to learn how to improve our control medication by studying her and trying to help her behind the scenes."

"How so?" asked Meade, masking his skepticism.

"We didn't know," explained Lieberman, "that the quantalibrium Teague was taking was altering his genes. That's why Sally is now psychotic. But what if her psychosis had been anticipated and controlled? Perhaps she might have benefited intellectually from her father's ingestion of the drug. And perhaps she may still benefit, if we can develop a partial antidote that can take the edge off of her psychosis."

The doctor went on, becoming more and more enthusiastic, his beady eyes gleaming. "Think of it, gentlemen! Thanks to my work, it's within our reach to develop a world free of mental retardation! We can raise the level of brilliance in our society, not only for purposes of national defense, but for the preservation of mankind and the blossoming of human culture! With the increased brainpower that quantalibrium provides, we may someday reach the far planets that Teague, Thompson and Vickers could only fantasize about in their psychotic imaginations!"

Meade thought that Lieberman might be more psychotic than anyone else at Blue Ridge, but he refrained from voicing his opinion. "Let's go," he told Dorsey. "Gotta get back to New York. We still don't know how we're gonna resolve that one issue."

"Jenny Teague?" Dorsey said.

Meade nodded.

"Let me have her," said Lieberman.

"Frankly, Doctor, I'm hoping we won't have to," Meade said quite coldly.

Lieberman shrugged off the disappointment. After all, he had bigger fish to fry. After Meade and Dorsey left, he was still excited, still imbued with the fervor of what he had told them about his drive to unlock human potential. In his zealous mood, he felt compelled to visit the newest occupant of the sanity ward.

The sanity ward was close by, in the corridor directly adjacent to Lieberman's office. He went down to the third door on the right and peeped through inch-thick Plexiglas at Dr. Gary Cameron, who was hard at work behind a huge desk littered with books, star charts and other astronomical paraphernalia.

Dr. Lieberman was proud to play host to such a brilliantly famous guest, a scientist whose name was a household word. By a stroke of sheer good fortune, Cameron survived the stomach wound he received from

Teague's .45. But Teague's wife wasn't so lucky. Lieberman wondered how the CIA would have disposed of her if she had lived. He would have tried hard to get her here, but he doubted that he could have succeeded. After all, she hadn't willfully tampered with the experiment seven years ago.

But Cameron had. He had taken it upon himself to foul things up with placebos. Jealousy and infatuation had spoiled his objectivity. Passion had gotten the better of him, to the detriment of his career and his country. A man like that could not remain at large in a free society. Who could predict his behavior?

It was best to keep him at Blue Ridge. Inject him with quantalibrium so he could legitimately take part in the grand experiment he had tried to subvert. Poetic justice. It was poetic justice, Lieberman thought. He was constantly in need of new "lab animals." Here at the sanitarium, he got a fairly regular supply of them, but not as many as he would have liked. He had to keep battling for a large enough budget and enough human resources. Some of the bureaucrats were fond of pointing out that so far he hadn't been able to prevent any of his test subjects from gradually going insane. But it wasn't his fault. He was working hard to find the solution to the problem. And, all along the way, he was making great contributions to America. While they were able, all of his lab animals worked as hard as possible in their chosen professions, so the nation could benefit enormously from their quantalibrium-inspired insights and discoveries.

Cameron's suite in the sanity ward consisted of a bedroom, a bathroom and a study. The study was replete with all the research materials an astronomer could desire. Within the parameters of the mental institution, every effort was made to make the suite homey and comfortable. Dr. Lieberman even knocked politely before he let himself in with his key. "How's it going, Gary?" he asked cheerfully. He prided himself in his tactful-ness and sensitivity. He always behaved as colleague to colleague instead of doctor to patient.

With great zest and verve—the same qualities that had made him so successful on television—Dr. Gary Cameron expounded on a new theorem he was developing concerning the formation of black holes. The intricacies went over Dr. Lieberman's head, but this did not bother him. After all, he was a psychiatrist by training and temperament, not an astronomer. And his IQ, though exceedingly high, was not enhanced artificially. The important thing was to capture Cameron's ideas so they wouldn't be lost to posterity, so in case his brilliance faded...

No! It won't fade this time! Please, God, don't let it fade, Lieberman prayed silently, gritting his teeth.

"Get it all on paper for us," he told Cameron.

"I will. I certainly will," Gary promised.

Closing the self-locking door, Dr. Lieberman marveled at the power of quantalibrium. Now that Gary Cameron was on the drug, he seldom worried about his past life. He didn't even care that the world thought him dead. He seldom mentioned the Cameron Foundation or his former colleagues or interests. He seemed largely unconcerned about the fate of his fiancée, Dr. Martha Teague.

This was because the first stage of the drug reaction always produced a feeling of incredible well-being—total wonderment and delight in the marvelous mental capabilities that were engendered. The subject would stay awake for hours, just thinking and enjoying. When new worlds of adventure and discovery were ripe for exploration, the old everyday world paled by comparison, and all its worries and concerns and even its pleasures were easily forgotten. Men of science, like Cameron, were, even under normal conditions, so completely caught up in their life's work that sexual and love relationships had a tendency to erode by virtue of neglect as they relentlessly pursued ideas and knowledge. Quantalibrium greatly emphasized this personality trait, this predisposition.

Dr. Lieberman knew that Gary Cameron was having the best time of his life. And now was the time for the United States to reap the benefit of his great mental leaps, before his mind could begin to deteriorate.

It was Lieberman's hope that his latest version of quantalibrium, with the new control drugs, would delay the onset of mental problems even longer than the previous regimen. So he was carefully monitoring Cameron's progress. Each new patient was an exciting challenge, a citadel of the search for glory that had caused the sanity ward to be built. Maybe Dr. Cameron would be the first to retain his sanity, thus perfecting the bold and noble experiment.

Brian Meade was satisfied that this case had wrapped with fewer loose ends than many other cases he had worked on during his career with the Agency. Through a combination of luck and skill, the mess had been cleaned up, if not spotlessly, about as close to it as could have been hoped for under the circumstances.

Rolf Kollar's true involvement was suspected by a few UFO nuts, but they couldn't prove anything. Dorsey had come up with the idea of moving Kollar's body from his home to Metro Teleproductions so it looked like all the murders took place at one spot. The blonde receptionist was so goofy from fright she couldn't contradict anything. The official story was that the murders had been committed by James Haskell, a renegade CIA agent who had come into contact with Dr. Martha Teague and Dr. Gary Cameron when they worked at Universal Dynamics, Inc. The Haskell story was a variation of the scenario that had been told to Lt. Cargill of the West Virginia State Police, so it tied in pretty neatly in case anyone should ever care. On the morning after the murders, Haskell's body was claimed by a phony next-of-kin and promptly cremated. His ashes were put in the urn that was sent to the small, private funeral service for Dr. Gary Cameron, whose mourners thought he died of his gunshot wound.

Just about every eyewitness to any part of the Blue Ridge escape was now dead or in permanent captivity.

Except Jenny.

Meade's case officer wanted to use anectaline. It was a colorless, odorless, tasteless chemical that made a person stop breathing and left no evidence in the body. The victim could even be released for autopsy without any fear that the murder would be discovered.

Jenny's grandmother wouldn't be able to question anything after she claimed the body. She'd be the only family member still alive to claim it. Alive and mentally competent.

Presently Jenny was in St. Francis Hospital, in the same psychiatric department as her sister Sally, though in a different ward—one for adults, not children. When she was first taken there, her wounds were treated, then she was interrogated. The interrogation continued more intensively after she was given an injection of sodium pentothal—so-called "truth serum." That was how Meade learned the full extent of her involvement in the escape plot, including the fact that she was present when Kollar found the bodies at the safe house.

Meade didn't see how what she knew could hurt anybody now. All her "evidence" had been made to evaporate for good. Once again she was left with no hard proof that her father hadn't died seven years ago.

She had suffered enough, in fact too damn much, Meade figured. He found himself wanting to help her somehow. Maybe he wanted to atone for not being able to help his own daughter, dead at age three in that senseless automobile accident. It wasn't his fault, but still he had blamed himself irrationally, over and over, for not being there to make something different happen. As if fate could be altered. Well, maybe sometimes it could. Meade wanted to try.

The terrible things that had happened to Jenny were worse than senseless. They were almost *planned*—put into action by supposedly educated, intelligent people who were willing to sacrifice damn near anything, even the innocent ones close to them, in order to gain something God never intended them to possess.

In this frame of mind, Meade met with his case officer in a hotel room in New York, after the case officer had visited Jenny at the hospital.

"I think we should release her," Meade said. "Let her go home. She's lost too much already. With her grandmother maybe she can build a new life."

"She knows too much," the case officer said. He was Meade's age but he looked fifteen years younger—handsome, slender, an All-American face with a dimple in the chin. He looked like a hero in a Hollywood Western. How could he ever hurt anybody except maybe make-believe Indians circling a wagon train? Yet he was calmly advocating the covert murder of a helpless young woman in a hospital.

"What she knows she can't prove," Meade pointed

out, slowly, patiently, affecting his sonorous rumble. "Even if important ears listen to her someday, they'll think she's mentally disturbed, like her sister. Grief and trauma can do that to a person, right?"

Meade was remembering his own grief and trauma of sixteen years ago. Sarah and Jean. Both suddenly gone. Ripped away from him.

"Maybe you've got a point," said the case officer. "Let me think about it."

"I know how to clean up a mess," said Meade. "And this one is cleaned up just right. Laying off of the Teague girl is the perfect touch. It adds to the credibility of *our* story. Nobody's gonna think we'd have let her out to talk if what she was gonna say was anything but baseless."

"Yes, maybe you've got a point," the case officer repeated.

By his ninth week under Dr. Lieberman's care, Gary Cameron began exhibiting signs of a developing psychosis. Dismayed, the doctor tried various combinations and dosages of control medication, all to no avail.

Dr. Cameron started talking about all the old bugaboos—UFOs and extraterrestrials and CIA kidnappings and murders. Dr. Lieberman had the unhappy task of making note of these adverse signs as they worsened and worsened.

Despite all that the good doctor attempted, the beneficial quantalibrium effects faded away rapidly. Antipsychotic drugs had to be administered to prevent further deterioration of Gary Cameron's thought processes. Finally, he was moved out of his special suite in the sanity ward. He was allowed to mingle with the general inmate population.

In the exercise yard and cafeteria, Cameron started loafing with a patient named Chudko, who had been a chum of Teague, Vickers and Thompson just before their escape. Chudko was a former astrophysicist suffering from schizophrenia of an ordinary—not drug-induced— variety. After a few weeks of camaraderie, Cameron and Chudko both became convinced that the CIA had locked them up to prevent them from telling the world the real reason behind the international arms race. They believed adamantly that the leaders of the United States and the Soviet Union were preparing for an extraterrestrial invasion that they didn't want their citizens to know about until the final moment. The arms race was a way of trying to get the necessary "Star Wars" weapons funded and produced in time to thwart this imaginary Doomsday.

Sometimes Dr. Lieberman had to chuckle to himself despite the seriousness and the personal disappointment involved in the mental illness of Cameron and Chudko. There was something terribly amusing and at the same time touching about some of the weird manifestations of *folie a deux*.

———

IN SEPTEMBER, Jenny Teague didn't go back to Georgetown. Instead she transferred to Manhattan University so she could live with her grandmother, helping to take care of Sally as they all worked their way through their grief.

For half of the summer, after she was released from St. Francis, Jenny had remained in psychotherapy as an outpatient. But in the end she decided that the doctor was unable to help her. Instead of encouraging her to deal with the things that were bothering her the most, he kept telling her to forget the past and concentrate on the future. When she tried to touch upon her version of the events that had led up to her mother's death, he stared out the window as if all of it was at best irrelevant and at worst a figment of her neurotic imagination. He didn't relieve any of the guilt she was carrying. She kept on blaming herself for cooperating with Rolf Kollar and helping the tragedy unfold.

A few weeks after she quit the psychotherapist, she got a phone call from Harry Paulson. Tremors shot through her when she recognized his voice, and she almost hung up on him.

He said, "Remember the article you wrote? I'd like to talk with you about it."

Maybe she should say no. Here it was again. The old intrigue, the old danger. But she agreed to meet Harry Paulson again in that same coffee shop.

He showed up wearing the same faded jeans, the same Cape Canaveral T-shirt with the worn-out corduroy jacket. His hair looked as if a comb still hadn't touched it. But his clothes were dry. This time it wasn't raining.

They ate cheeseburgers and drank coffee, making small talk in case anybody was eavesdropping. Then they went for a walk in Central Park, where they could be reasonably sure that their conversation wouldn't be bugged.

"I'm an associate editor now," he told her, "for the *UFO Yearbook*. I get a lot of letters and stuff, mostly about sightings that turn out to be fakes once I investigate them. Every once in a while, though, somebody comes up with something genuinely intriguing. Like, the other day I was contacted by this guy who claims to be an ex-CIA agent. He laid some stuff on me that could be dynamite."

"Pertaining to my father?" Jenny asked, unsuccessfully trying to stifle her anxiety.

"Yes."

"If it's about him, I don't think I should listen. I already know too much, or *think* I know too much, that I can't prove."

"This guy claims to have irrefutable proof, documentation," Paulson said avidly. "He had the ring of authenticity, you know? Not like the usual fakes and shysters. We met in a dark bar. He wouldn't tell me his real name. But he said he worked with some other CIA guy named Blair Chaney seven years ago, and the two of them were involved with faking the death of Colonel Kevin Thompson. See, the colonel was going to defect to the Russians with plans for the A-11 spy plane, so he had to be taken out of circulation."

"Then why didn't they just kill him?" Jenny said sharply. "Why bother faking an accident?"

"I don't know," said Paulson, angry that he was being challenged. "Look," he added with the fervor of a conspiracy buff, "I certainly don't have all the answers yet, but this ex-CIA guy seems real. He says Thompson set up Vickers and your father to be kidnapped by the KGB. You ought to be glad to hear that, Jenny. They didn't defect, the KGB had them all the time. Thompson, too—after the plane crash was staged and his death was announced, he escaped somehow from the stockade at New Mexico Air Force Base. But when his usefulness was exhausted, the KGB turned him loose—with his old buddies, Vickers and Teague. All three were dosed with a drug called haloperidol that the Russkies use on their own dissidents so they can be certified insane and locked up in mental institutions. So they were like three crazy men set free to wreak havoc. The KGB must've thought of it as a macabre joke they were playing on us."

Jenny let out a despondent sigh. "I've heard so *many* stories," she said wearily. "I wonder if the truth really matters anymore. Or if it will ever be discernible."

"As serious journalists we can't allow ourselves to think that way," Paulson said staunchly.

"I know my father is dead now," Jenny said. "I've got to concern myself with picking up the pieces of my own life."

"But we definitely owe it to the memory of Rolf Kollar to get to the bottom of it all," Paulson persisted. "I want you and the ex-CIA man to get together, Jenny. Let me interview both of you. We'll keep digging and digging till the truth finally unravels."

"I think it's already hopelessly unraveled," Jenny said sadly. "Like a ball of yarn, all tangled up, that can't ever be rolled up again, perfectly round, without any loose ends."

Or without any pain, she thought. Without any human suffering.

"I'm terribly sorry you feel that way," said Paulson. "I hope you'll think about it carefully and change your mind. If you do, you can get in touch with me at my office."

He handed her a card that said: Harry W Paulson, Paranormal Investigations. Then he pivoted and walked briskly away, leaving her alone in the park.

She was standing by a rubbish barrel. She thought of tearing up his card and dropping it in. But she didn't. She put it in her purse.

A LOOK AT: DAY CARE

From the devious mind who co-created *Night of the Living Dead* comes a frightening cautionary tale about the lengths some parents will go to in order to make their children "special"...

Fairchild Academy, celebrated as one of the most prestigious and innovative schools in the country, hides a dark and disturbing secret. Their lauded methods of bringing out the "genius" in a child are, at best, terrifying, and at worst...barbaric.

Augie, one of Fairchild's success stories, has his sights set on far greater achievements than his parents–or the Academy's doctors–could have ever hoped for. He intends to use his skills to rule the world...or does he?

Felicia Patterson, current golden child of Fairchild Academy, finds herself in the sights of a maniacal predator with little hope for survival.

For Shana Berkshire, a very young Fairchild Academy hopeful, things are about to get horrifying in ways her young mind can't even conceive. Will she become yet another victim, or will her extraordinary abilities save her from a fate worse than death?

Sometimes, stimulating a child's mind can have terrifying results...

AVAILABLE NOW

ABOUT THE AUTHOR

With twenty books published internationally and nineteen feature movies in worldwide distribution, **John Russo** has been called a "living legend." He began by co-authoring the screenplay for NIGHT OF THE LIVING DEAD, which has become recognized as a "horror classic." His three books on the art and craft of movie making have become bibles of independent production, and one of them, SCARE TACTICS, won a national award for Superior Nonfiction. Quentin Tarantino and many other noted filmmakers have stated that Russo's books helped them launch their careers.

John Russo wants people to know he's "just a nice guy who likes to scare people" — and he's done it with novels and films such as RETURN OF THE LIVING DEAD, MIDNIGHT, THE MAJORETTES, THE AWAKENING and HEARTSTOPPER. He has had a long, rewarding career, and he shows no signs of slowing down. Recently his screenplay for ESCAPE OF THE LIVING DEAD was made into a five-part comic book released by Avatar to great acclaim; it made the Top Ten of Horror Comics nationally and spawned two graphic novels and ten sequels.

Russo's latest horror novel is THE HUNGRY DEAD, published by Kensington Books. And his new mainstream novel, DEALEY PLAZA, has already garnered 13 Five-Star reviews on Amazon. He is also slated to direct two movies: a remake of his cult hit, MIDNIGHT, and a brand new take on the "zombie phenomenon" entitled SPAWN OF THE DEAD.

His popularity among genre fans remains at a high pitch. He appears at many movie conventions each year as a featured guest, and he considers his appearance at the Orion Festival 2013, hosted by Kirk Hammett and METALLICA, one of the highlights of his career.

Made in the USA
Coppell, TX
21 June 2023

18358503R00166